"Remind[s] one of Iris Murdoch, or Muriel Spark, or E. M. Forster . . . unusual intelligence and personality are alive throughout the book."—*The New York Times Book Review*

"What a wonderfully hideous, gruesome, grueling horror-marathon of a book! A cross between a Henry James novel and the Texas chain saw massacre. I loved it."—Carolyn See

"Terrifying and disturbing. Will keep you turning the pages late into the night."—*Cosmopolitan*

"[A] master storyteller . . . [L'Heureux] is elegant, cunning, and wickedly funny . . . a shocking, shocking denouement."
—*The Washington Post*

"*A Woman Run Mad* had me in thrall all the way. L'Heureux has written a taut, terrible story and done it superbly, mixing intelligence and wit with a strong dose of the macabre."
—Maxine Kumin

"A wicked and wickedly good novel to read . . . It's about the wages of sin and everyone knows what those are. . . . L'Heureux is a wild man who takes narrative risks few writers dare even consider, and pulls them off."—*Milwaukee Journal*

"It is L'Heureux's literary skill that brings together these seemingly unrelated insights into horrifying conjunctions. . . . L'Heureux serves notice that, pagan or not, modern man ignores at his peril the truths about human nature that lie behind traditional Judeo-Christian values."—*Newsday*

"An intelligent, captivating suspense story that leads to a frightening ending full of passion and surprise."
—*San Jose Mercury News*

"More than merely a tale of good against evil, *A Woman Run Mad* is an intellectual thriller and a good book for a rainy evening."—*The State*

"Some books ought to include warning labels on them to alert readers that once they are sucked in by the good writing and the crisp plot, at least in this case, they're going to be walloped emotionally in the end. *A Woman Run Mad* is such a book."
—*Palo Alto Weekly*

"A stunning climax. We alternate between wanting to read faster to get to the end and wanting to read slower so that we won't."—*Atlanta Journal-Constitution*

"Needle-sharp . . . A wicked, witty novel that is both introspective and exhibitionistic. Seemingly quiet and controlled, the story slides surreptitiously along, compelling and shocking the reader all the way."
—*Topeka Capital-Journal*

"The damned thing is amazing. . . . Question: Is there any rule L'Heureux doesn't break? Answer: Probably one or two. But it doesn't matter since he gets away with everything. He ought to be shot. We like our geniuses dead."—David Bradley

A WOMAN
RUN MAD

JOHN L'HEUREUX

A WOMAN RUN MAD

GROVE PRESS
New York

First published in 1988 by Viking Penguin Inc.

Published simultaneously in Canada
Printed in the United States of America

FIRST GROVE PRESS EDITION

The background of this book is the real Boston I've known all my life, but the characters, events, and obsessions of *A Woman Run Mad* are purely fictional. Other than actual figures of general renown mentioned in the book, all the characters are entirely a creation of my own imagination. All names are fictional and none are intended to represent or suggest any actual person.

This book is not, in essence, about sex or murder but about the restlessness that drives us on to fabricate our lives and—willy nilly—to accomplish our fates.   —J. L'H.

Library of Congress Cataloging-in-Publication Data

L'Heureux, John.
   A woman run mad / John L'Heureux.
      p.   cm.
   ISBN 0-8021-3731-8
      1. Man-woman relationships—Fiction. 2. Boston (Mass.) —Fiction.
   3. Married people—Fiction. 4. Shoplifiting—Ficiton. I. Title.

PS3562.H4 W6 2000
813'.54—dc21

                                                                00-037669

Grove Press
841 Broadway
New York, NY 10003

00 01 02 03   10 9 8 7 6 5 4 3 2 1

for my wife
JOAN POLSTON L'HEUREUX

A Woman Run Mad
was written with the aid of a grant generously given
by the National Endowment for the Arts.

...furens quid femina possit...

Aeneid, V

A WOMAN
RUN MAD

All Quinn wanted was a little peace. And some money, a lot of money. And a job. And to write a novel that would make all those smug bastards at Williams choke with envy. Fame and money, that's what he wanted. But right *now* all he wanted was a little peace.

He and Claire had fought again last night and went to bed mad. When he got up this morning—late, because after their fight he'd had a few more drinks—he found a note from Claire on the hall table. "I love you," it said. That was all. So Claire was one up on him, and now he'd have to find that damned bag she wanted, and buy it.

Quinn was moping around Bonwit Teller looking for the handbag department or leather goods or whatever they called it. If he could just get that bag—brown, small, rectangular—and have it waiting for her when she got home at five, then they'd have peace again. It was a special brown, not reddish brown or cocoa brown or anything brown. It was chocolate brown—Godiva bittersweet—and the only store in Boston where you could find that brown was Bonwit Teller.

Quinn stood in the makeup section and looked around. Everywhere there were glass cases full of gold and crystal jars, tubes of lipstick, mascara, moisture creams, astringents, cologne. And everywhere the scent of expensive perfumes, mingling. This was a money store. The shoppers looked bored.

The clerks were overdressed, made up like mannequins. The mannequins looked sexless, anorexic, poisonous. Quinn took all this in and decided the plain brown handbag was going to cost him a bundle.

And then, two counters away, he saw an array of handbags and right in the middle of them he spotted a small rectangular bag, Godiva brown, the exact thing Claire wanted. But before he could get there, this woman placed her hand on it proprietarily. She bent before a mirror on the counter and examined her lipstick. She pursed her lips, tipped her head from side to side. It seemed to take forever and the whole time she kept her hand on the bag.

Quinn stood beside her, at a discreet distance, and watched.

She gave the bag her full attention. She opened the flap and looked inside; she removed the tissue paper and closed the bag, holding it at arm's length; she put it on the counter and caressed the leather.

She was going to buy it, Quinn decided, and looked around for another one in the same size and color. No such luck. And there were no clerks that he could ask for help. All the clerks were over in the makeup section, getting beautiful. Quinn glanced at the woman again.

She was trying the bag for size in her hand, weighing it. She tucked it beneath her arm. She opened it and put the tissue paper back inside. She tried it in the other hand. She was going to buy it, that was certain. But then she put it down and moved a foot or so away, interested now in something else.

Quinn edged along the counter a few inches closer to the handbag.

The woman bent over to look at a display of tiny beaded purses. She kept on looking. And looking.

Quinn decided to wait her out, the bitch.

But she never moved. She kept right on staring into the counter as if she were hypnotized by the gold and silver and purple beads.

To hell with her, Quinn thought, and moved in the other direction. He stepped behind a glove display where he could see without being seen. Of course. He knew the kind. Rich. Spoiled. Nothing to do but shop and meet for lunch and then shop again. She wore a tan linen dress, a little nothing Claire would say, that probably cost her hundreds. She was thin, emaciated almost, with long blond hair wound in a knot, and a horsey face that came from generation after generation of ancestors who married only the best stock. A Wasp face. No Catholic had a face like that. Quinn's stomach filled with acid as he thought again, always, of those Williams bastards denying him tenure. They had the same faces, the same money. It made him want to kill.

She moved back, as he watched her, and touched the brown bag lightly. She picked it up, absentmindedly, and returned to her study of the beaded bags, bending before the counter.

Well, this was ridiculous. He would ask her directly, straight out, was she going to buy the damned bag or not? Because if she wasn't going to buy it, he was, and he didn't have all day. He wanted to get the bag and get out of Bonwit and get on with his life. He wanted a little peace; was that too much to ask? He came around the glove display and moved toward her just as she stood erect. Up close, she was much younger than he had thought, and kind of pretty.

She looked at him blindly, as if she saw somebody but not really him, and she gave him a frozen half-smile. Surprised, Quinn raised his hand to cover the scar on his lip, and then he took his hand away, quickly. It was an old habit, automatic whenever he was caught off guard, and he had grown to hate the gesture, and hate himself for making it.

3

He could feel himself blushing. In Bonwit Teller. In mid-afternoon. He indicated the beaded purses and, clearing his throat, he bent to examine them. Like a damned fool.

When he stood up, he discovered she was gone. He looked on the counter for the handbag, and saw that it was gone too. So she had bought it after all. But she couldn't have. There was nobody at the counter to sell it to her. And anyhow, it took a good half hour to ring up a sale at Bonwit. Still, the bag was definitely gone. He looked around. Everything was just the same. There were some bored shoppers in cosmetics, a bunch of clerks becoming beautiful, a short man in a gray suit who seemed to be lost. But the Wasp had disappeared.

And then he caught a glimpse of her tan linen dress. She was three counters away, then four, five; she was moving toward the front entrance. She walked slowly, but with purpose, looking neither right nor left. She had the handbag beneath her arm.

For one second it occurred to him that she was stealing it, that she was a shoplifter. But of course that was impossible; she was beautifully dressed, her clothes were expensive, she was rich. The rich don't shoplift.

She was approaching the entrance; in another second the thief-proof tag attached to the handbag would set off the alarm. Quinn stood, waiting. But nothing happened. There was not a sound. The woman pushed open the door and descended the stairs, disappearing from view.

Quinn took off after her. He walked quickly to the front entrance and—on the run—pushed open the huge glass doors. He skittered down the long flight of stairs to the sidewalk. He saw her at once, She was crossing Newbury toward Commonwealth, going toward the river. He started to jog after her, but at the corner the light was against him and he had to stop. He shifted his weight from foot to foot, anxious, sweaty. It was a very hot day. June, in Boston, was not a beautiful thing.

He saw himself saying, "Excuse me," and then explaining about the handbag, and he saw her confusion and embarrassment, and he saw her smiling, grateful, saying how kind he was and how foolish she felt. And then? They would walk back to the store together to return the bag? Yes. And later have coffee. A drink. Why not. And they would get to know each other a little, and perhaps, sometimes, they would meet for lunch, a long lunch, with wine, a good white wine, and then perhaps they'd go back to her place and fool around a little bit.

Well, that's how a real man would do it, Quinn figured. But not a wimp like himself. Not somebody who couldn't even get tenure at Williams. Terminal Tweed Williams. He was a virgin, practically, if you didn't count screwing Claire.

The light changed and Quinn trotted across the intersection, reaching the far side of the street just in time to see her turn left, going up Commonwealth away from the Public Garden. He continued to follow her at a distance as she crossed the Commonwealth greensward and kept on going toward Marlborough. Suddenly she turned right, going back toward the Garden again. She was making a square. He had nearly caught up to her when she stopped, unsnapped the bag, and tucked the tags and labels inside it. She continued along the sidewalk.

Quinn slowed down when he saw her conceal the tags, and he stopped in his tracks when he realized what it meant. She had taken the handbag deliberately. She was a shoplifter. He flushed again, embarrassed, and raised his hand to his lip. A man in a gray suit passed him, looking at him quizzically. Quinn only stood there, blushing, confused. The man in the gray suit stepped in against a wrought-iron fence and lit a cigarette. Abruptly Quinn made a decision: keeping a little distance, he continued to follow her.

5

And, at a little distance, the man in the gray suit continued to follow Quinn.

The woman had crossed to the left side of Marlborough, Quinn's street, and he walked behind her, excited and a little confused. As he passed the old brownstone where they had their apartment—Claire had found it for them, Claire was paying for it—for just a moment Quinn saw himself as ridiculous, an idiot. Following a shoplifter. Snooping, really.

Claire had said once that when Quinn died, it would not be from natural causes; he would die because he'd got caught staring into somebody's windows, not out of malice or prurience, but just to see how the table was set and how many people there were and what they were having for dinner. Claire had scolded, but she had been pleased; his curiosity was just another proof he was a born novelist. Claire was wonderful in her way.

And Claire would love this. It would be a story to bring home to her tonight, better than the handbag really. An adventure; something they could share, and laugh about, and *talk* about without having another fight: the Criminal Wasp from Beacon Hill.

The woman had turned up Mount Vernon Street now, the richest part of the Hill, and obviously—it would make the story perfect—she lived in one of those tall, skinny, breathtaking houses in Louisburg Square.

Quinn slowed his pace as he climbed the steep hill behind her. She crossed to the left side of the street and turned into the Square.

As Quinn watched, the woman went up a flight of stairs, felt in her pocket for a key, and without looking either way disappeared through the tall black door. Quinn walked quickly to the foot of the stairs and stood there looking up. There was a brass number 17 in the center of the door and, beneath it, a mail slot. But there was no name that he could see. He thought of going up the stairs when, suddenly, he became aware of someone standing behind him, to the side. He turned. It was the man in the gray suit.

The man took a long pull on his cigarette and tossed it into the street. He stared at Quinn. Quinn, flustered and guilty, stared back, watching the smoke the man blew at him in a thin gray stream.

"You want a blowjob?" the man said.

Quinn only stared, raising his hand to his lip.

The man took off his tie and undid the top button of his shirt. A gold cross hung at his throat, half-concealed by the black hairs curling around it.

"Well?" he said. "The choice is yours."

Still Quinn said nothing.

"If you ever decide to come out, let me be the first to know," he said, flashing Quinn a hard white smile. He pointed to a brass plate at the side of the stairs; 17-A, it said, and a little arrow pointed to a narrow stairway, leading down. "My name is Angie. Angelo."

He continued to look at Quinn for another moment and then he turned and disappeared down the stairs.

Angelo closed the door and stood facing it, listening for footsteps on the stairs. A minute passed and nothing happened, so he took out a cigarette and leaned against the wall, waiting. He planned to give the guy as long as it would take to finish the cigarette, but after only a couple drags on it, Angelo shrugged, and went into the bedroom to get undressed. He stood close up to the full-length mirror and blew a slow stream of smoke at himself the way he had at that guy on the sidewalk, and then he said, "You want a blowjob?" He said it again, studying himself carefully. Well, it should have worked; it looked pretty good to him.

Angelo undressed quickly, not looking at himself; his face interested him, but not his body. He put on his pale green shorty robe, cotton, Cardin, not bothering to belt it. Then he dialed the number for Slade, Winthrop, and Slade, Investments.

By the time the switchboard operator gave him Porter's secretary, Angelo was sprawled on the bed, pillows at his back, ready for a nice chat.

"Mr. Slade's office," a woman said. Angelo did not recognize her voice.

"I'd like to speak to Porter, please?" he said, adding, "This is Angelo."

"And may I tell Mr. Slade what you wish to speak to him about, Mr. Angelo?"

"This is Angelo *Tallino*. I'm his *brother*-in-law. Just put me through, please."

There was a pause, and then the woman said, "I'll see if he's in, Mr. Tallino."

Almost immediately Porter was on the phone. "Angie," he said eagerly. "Angie, hello."

"What is this anyhow," Angelo said softly. "Since when do I have to give my I.D. to get through the secretary? This is a little bit more than embarrassing, Porter."

"Angie, I'm sorry," Porter said. "I'm really sorry about this. It's a new girl we've got." He lowered his voice. "Maria's idea." Maria was Angelo's sister, Porter's wife. Porter lowered his voice further. "Or maybe your father's. I don't know."

"Why? What was the matter with Helen or Ellen. Ellen, I guess."

"Well, you know." There was only silence on the other end of the line. "Ellen was too . . . young, maybe. You know Maria. She worries."

"You mean she thought you were fooling around? With the

8

secretary? That's rich, Porter. That's funny." Angelo laughed, and then laughed again. "You don't think it's funny? Come on, Porter."

"Angie."

There was silence on both ends of the line and then Angelo said, "You're busy? Okay. I'll be brief. I'm calling because there's a small problem with your sister again. A pocketbook. At Bonwit Teller."

"Oh, God. Oh, my God."

"Nobody caught her, don't worry; there was no alarm-tag on it. But you should know she's doing it again."

"Angie..."

"If you'd care to stop by after work, say five, five-thirty, we could talk about it with perhaps more privacy."

"You *know* I want to. But Maria expects me..."

"Maria will understand, Porter. Just tell her it was her baby brother you were seeing, not your secretary." Angelo smiled, waiting. "It's your choice, of course."

"I'll see you at five."

"Yes, indeed." Angelo hung up the phone and stretched, arching his back and pushing out with one leg and then the other. Good old Porter. Poor old Porter. He could never enjoy anything without feeling guilty about it.

Angelo yawned and, rolling to the far side of the big bed, he glanced through the mess of books on the floor where he kept his current reading. There was an old novel by Murdoch, a new one by David Lodge, Paul Bowles' *Collected Stories*, Camus' *The Plague*, which he was reading for the tenth time, and there were his old paperback Kierkegaards that he had decided to reread: *Either/Or, Fear and Trembling*, the diaries—his favorite reading when he was at college—*The Present Age, The Works of Love*, and *The Concept of Dread*. Beside these, in a neat pile, were his television magazines: *People, Newsweek, The New York Times Book Review, The National*

Enquirer. He picked up *Fear and Trembling* and opened it at random. He read what he had scribbled in the margin. When? Eight years ago? Nine? "Man is doomed to freedom." He'd been with O'Brien then. He flipped the page and read, "Man is doomed to the freedom of choice." Choice was underlined twice.

From upstairs Angelo could hear the sounds of Sarah's stereo, playing Schubert's *Winterreise.* So she would be all right now, in a while.

Poor Sarah. He loved her in his way, but that way did not include the physical. He did not desire her. He desired her brother, Porter. He closed his eyes and saw Porter by the side of the bed, taking off his tie, his shirt, turning away a little to take off his pants. Porter was nearly forty, but he worked out three times a week, and all that iron-pumping had paid off. Angelo liked big men with good bodies. Blonds. Porter was all this, and shy as well. Angelo sighed, pleased. He was getting horny again. He was getting hard.

He put *Fear and Trembling* back on the floor and lay there on the bed, listening to the distant sounds of Schubert, waiting for Porter. In Porter he had chosen very well indeed.

Sarah Slade, on returning from her day's shopping, had closed the door behind her and had gone immediately to the living room to stand in the bay window looking out over the Square. As she suspected, someone had followed her, but one glance told her that he was not Bonwit Security. Who was he then, this man at the foot of her stairs? He had his hand to his mouth so she couldn't really see his face. Medium height, medium weight. He was average. He was nobody. As she watched, she saw Angelo approach him from behind. The man turned to look at him. Angelo said something and after a moment he took off his tie. Sarah knew well enough where this was going. She dismissed Bonwit Teller from her mind.

She had turned from the window then, and gone back to the entry hall, testing the front door to make sure it was closed, and she had started up the stairs. But suddenly she was exhausted, unable to move another inch. She sat down where she was, on the carpeted stairs, and waited for her strength to return. She had plenty of time now; she was almost done. A man on the street—Quinn, for instance—who happened to see Sarah Slade at the moment would have thought her a wealthy woman of thirty or so; well-groomed, well-dressed; perhaps a little retiring; a normal, ordinary, everyday resident of Louisburg Square.

A doctor, or even a social worker or a clever teacher, might notice that she was in something like a fugue state: her eyes were glassy and fixed, her lips slightly parted, her hands crossed, palms up, in her lap. If you spoke to her, she might not hear you. She seemed lost.

Angelo would have noticed—but Angelo knew, of course —that the real Sarah was gone, that she was traveling back in time to what she had once been for a few hours, for a day, for two days, when the shoplifting had been the least of it. But that was safely over now, and could not occur again. Ever. This was only a momentary setback, this temporary fugue state, a reminder to be careful. In a moment she would pull herself together, ascend the stairs, and sleep. And in the morning she would wake, once again the real Sarah—healthy and sane and practical. Angelo had been through all this before.

With a great effort, Sarah pulled herself to her feet and went back down the stairs. She leaned against the stereo for a moment and then flipped on the switch. Schubert's *Winterreise* was already on the turntable and Sarah listened, expressionless, to the chaste opening bars. Then she went slowly up the stairs to her bedroom.

But on the landing she remembered about the handbag. She crossed the corridor to the spare bedroom, the one the nurse had occupied in the old days when Sarah had to have somebody with her all the time; it was her studio now, littered with paints and paintings and abandoned sketchbooks. She ignored the mess and went straight to the closet and pulled open the bottom drawer. Inside there were two other handbags, new, stolen; she let this one fall into the drawer with the others. She pushed the drawer closed with her foot.

She crossed the landing to her bedroom and, fully clothed, crawled onto the bed. She could hear the *Winterreise* playing in the room below. She fell asleep at once. She would sleep now all through the night, and when she woke, the memory of this day would still be there, but not the feelings or the compulsions. They would be gone—the way of shoplifting and shock treatments and things too horrible to remember.

Aunt Lily was standing at the side door waving good-bye as Claire backed the car out of the old lady's driveway. "Have a nice bath!" she called.

Claire braked the car and rolled down the window. She couldn't have heard right: have a nice bath?

"Quid?" Oh, dear. "What?"

"Haul it off!" Aunt Lily said, heading inside. "Get going or you'll hit all the traffic on Ninety-three." The screen door slammed behind her.

Claire pressed hard on the accelerator and the little Ford, spitting gravel, lurched crazily out into the street.

This had been their plan: Claire would spend weeknights at her great-aunt Lily's home outside Hanover and her weekends in Boston with Quinn. From Aunt Lily's, it was an easy drive back and forth to Dartmouth, where Claire was teaching for the summer. And living with her aunt would give Claire a chance to help the old lady with her shopping and cooking and cleaning. And ot course she would be living free. Best of all would be the long weekends with Quinn in Boston.

Claire's great-aunt Lily was a woman in her eighties, a little hard of hearing, but active as ever. She liked to do her own shopping, and she had never bothered with cooking, and she did not really see the point of cleaning. Moreover she didn't need company, and didn't much want any. Still, Claire was no trouble. And, as a matter of fact, not much company either: whenever she was home, she always seemed to be in the bath. But if Claire wanted to stay with her—free—on weeknights, that was okay with her.

Claire had been with her Aunt Lily for two weeks now, and on several nights when the old lady had gone to bed, Claire had taken a quick bath, popped her two No-Doz, and had driven down to Boston to spend the night with Quinn, getting up before dawn and driving back to Dartmouth in time to teach. The classes themselves were exhausting, direct-method Latin, taught as if it were a modern language that could be spoken. Her students were all high school teachers, ecstatic at the chance to study at Dartmouth and relentless in their demands on Claire's time. She kept up a pace that would have crippled anyone, and she seemed to do it with ease. She managed, moreover, to look terrific all the time: relaxed and even glamorous for Quinn; trim and efficient and perfectly groomed for Dartmouth. Claire was indestructible.

Indeed, Claire had reason to pride herself on being inde-structible.

As a fat, unlovely teenager, she had put herself through college, working half-time and caring for an invalid mother; her mother died a week before Claire's graduation, and for a while it seemed that Claire herself would collapse. She had no reason to go on, she said; she had no one to work for. But with the help of her parish priest, she pulled herself together and went on anyway. Learning, the priest told her, could be an end in itself, a kind of salvation. Claire was not sure she believed him, but she had seen the alternative to going on, and she was not ready for that.

And so Claire put herself through graduate school at Georgetown. For five years she lived in a D.C. ghetto, ate at McDonald's, dressed from Turnabout Shops, but at the end she got her Ph.D. in classics and landed more job interviews than anyone else in her class. When none of the jobs materialized, her adviser, a Jesuit who knew these things, leveled with her and told her she would never get a job, any job, as long as she was so fat. Claire recognized the sound of truth. She spent the next year working as home help for a dying old lady, meanwhile starving herself down to 135 pounds. That winter the old lady was still alive—indeed, she was flourishing under Claire's expert attentions—but Claire found a replacement and took herself off to the MLA convention; she got three job offers and accepted the one at Williams College.

Claire had come into her own. She had a job and she had some money and, if she did not actually have friends, she at least had colleagues. Ravenous with hunger, she nonetheless kept her weight down and her spirits up and she was dynamite in the classroom. She had her entire department to dinner, in shifts. She said and did the right things politically. She worked on her book, publishing the first two chapters as articles. Tenure was a sure thing.

In Claire's third year, J. J. Quinn joined the faculty. He was in the English Department and she was in Classics, but they met at the dean's annual reception for new teachers, and at once Claire fell in love with him. She had never been in love before and so it did not occur to her that he might love her back. She was content to be with him whenever he wanted, and when he did not want to be with her, that was fine, too. So long as he was happy. Quinn, unaware of her feelings, responded very well to this arrangement.

They were the only faculty members who worked in their offices on Saturday and Sunday, and they began taking their breaks at the same time: at eleven in the morning, at three in the afternoon. They talked literature. They talked Williams. Eventually she found Quinn confiding in her: he could not bear to be called anything but Quinn; J.J., or John Joseph, or even John made him furious. They were names that screamed of the Irish immigrant, of ghetto Catholicism. "Of paranoia, of xenophobia, of hydrophobia," Quinn said, his voice rising. Claire laughed, clenching her hands in delight, because she had never known anybody who could make fun of his own deepest seriousness. Quinn confided his plans to her: he was going to circumvent the scholarship requirement for tenure; he was writing a novel instead. And he told her, finally, how he felt about his lip.

The accident that scarred him happened on his fifth birthday. He was marching around the kitchen, blowing air across an empty Coke bottle to make a foghorn, and after a while his mother told him to go do that outside, go show your father. At the door there was only one step down, a cement step, and though it shouldn't have happened, and—logically—couldn't have happened, nonetheless it did. He tripped, the bottle shattered, and his upper lip was torn so badly he needed twenty stitches. The scar was hideous. At school the kids called him Bunny and Peter Rabbit and J. J. Quinn, the dog-faced boy. It was five years before he had the plastic surgery that repaired his lip. The scar was tiny now. "But apart from that, how was your birthday party, Mr. Quinn?" he said. She didn't laugh. He told her that even now he sometimes felt as he had then. That he looked like a rabbit. A fool. He still had nights when he awakened and got out of bed and looked in the mirror, terrified of what he might see.

"But it's beautiful," Claire said simply, and meant it.

They went to poetry readings. To concerts. To films. It was late winter by the time Quinn began to notice that there were very few single women on campus. Or men. Anybody not married was gay, or thinking about becoming gay. He was lucky, he thought, to have this intelligent woman for a friend. Not a girlfriend, of course, but somebody to be with, to confide in. Somebody who cared. She was attractive in her way. And the most attractive thing about her was that she found him attractive. Nobody ever had. As the year went on, Quinn began spending evenings at Claire's apartment, reading, then after a while having drinks, and—by spring—kissing and groping in a rather tentative way. This must be, he figured, how normal guys had spent their adolescence. Making out. Getting it on. Well, getting it on lay somewhere in the future, but for the first time he began to think it might be possible for him to interest some girl. Some nice girl. Gorgeous. Brilliant. Some day.

In summer Quinn left for London, ostensibly to research British attitudes toward American Catholicism of the late nineteenth century, but actually to work on his novel. He had decided to break it off with Claire. They were getting too serious too soon. Their relationship, whatever it was, had happened by chance; they didn't really know anybody else; Quinn wanted to play the field. So a summer separation would be good, he told her. He could meet other girls, and in the fall he and Claire could start out on a whole new footing.

But his summer was a disaster. It was sweltering in London and he didn't know anybody and suddenly the novel looked foolish. He went to plays, but going to plays by himself was a bore. He missed having somebody to talk to about the performance. He missed having somebody to meet for a drink. He missed Claire, he realized.

He left London a week early and returned to Williams College. Claire's summer, he discovered, had been a triumph. She had completed her book, *Enterprising Women: The Heroine in Euripides,* and she had found a publisher. Princeton.

Quinn proposed to her and they were married at Thanksgiving.

In her fifth year Claire was promoted to tenure, and for the next two years she taught her classes, worked on a new book, and spent—it seemed to outsiders—all of her time shoring up Quinn's notion of himself as a writer. He had abandoned the novel for the time being; he was going to do stories, he said. Claire typed them. She sent them out. She waited for the mail with hope, with despair. And when the stories were rejected, often with thoughtful cover letters, she complained with him, bitterly. The publishing world was a closed circuit, she said, a cabal. It was rotten. It was unfair. And when Quinn finally published a story—to everyone's astonishment—in *The New Yorker,* it was Claire who Xeroxed it and put copies in all the faculty boxes. She carried on for months; it was a publishing event.

Nor did she care that they had become something of a joke to the rest of the faculty, who referred to them out of their hearing as "Mr. and Mrs. Indignant."

Through all this, they had grown closer. And as *The New Yorker* rejected Quinn's next story, and his next, and his next, they grew closer still. They never fought. They never even disagreed. And Quinn, to his surprise, discovered that he loved her.

He depended on her for advice and approval. Her silence after reading one of his stories would send him into depression. Anything less than total enthusiasm convinced him he had failed. "You're all I have," Quinn said. "Without you, there'd be no point to any of this," and he gestured at the English Department, at Williams, at the world. "We have each other," Claire said. "We have everything."

In his fifth year at Williams, Quinn was told that he had been denied tenure. He was distraught. He had seen it coming; he had even tried to head it off by applying for an NEH research grant—for a study, yet again, of nineteenth-century American Catholicism. He got the grant, and Williams was duly impressed, but still they denied him tenure.

Claire was ready with a plan of attack. Quinn wanted out. Out of Williams College, out of academe. And she could see the point to that. She proposed that they rent an apartment in Boston for the coming year; Quinn could work on a novel; she would commute on weekends. There was enough money, or almost. Her salary, his grant. And she had been asked to teach at Dartmouth during the summer. That would mean extra cash. They would have plenty. Would he do it? For her? For both of them? In a single weekend, she found the apartment at 65 Marlborough Street and moved them there from Williams. The building was an old converted brownstone, one apartment to each floor, and she had fallen in love with the little lobby and the winding stairway and the carefully preserved woodwork throughout. The apartment itself was large and luxurious, a foretaste of how they would live later, when Quinn's book was done, when money . . .

But she knew that money was not the problem, not really. Something had happened to them, something she couldn't explain. They fought a lot. She could never please him. He seemed to blame her for everything. Even when she agreed with him, she was wrong.

Well, she loved him, and that was all that mattered. They had each other. They needed each other. It was Claire and Quinn, Quinn and Claire. There simply wasn't anything else.

She pressed harder on the accelerator as she hit Route 93.

Aunt Lily had been right; the traffic was impossible. But Claire weaved her way artfully from lane to lane, fast and—as always—careful. She would be with her husband soon, her lover, her other half, her very life.

It was 6:00 P.M. in Boston and everyone was in bed. Claire and Quinn had just made love in their perfunctory way and were lying side by side, recovering.

"Wow-*eee*," Claire said.

"Hello," Quinn said, in his special voice. He knotted his right hand in her left and they lay in silence for a long while. Claire's stomach grumbled and Quinn patted it with his free hand. "Poor tummy," he said.

"I'm not even hungry," Claire said. "How was your day? Did anything interesting happen? Did you work on your novel?" And then she bit her tongue.

This was just why they had fought last night: Claire had been insisting that Quinn should write his novel, that he had no obligation to the NEH people. Quinn had insisted that he couldn't work on his novel because he had taken NEH money for research. They went round and round like this, until finally Claire had said, "But you aren't doing *either;* do one or the other. Do *something*!" And by that time the fight was full-blown.

Now she had done it again.

The refrigerator clicked on, humming dimly in the kitchen, and a cat screamed somewhere outside. There was silence in the room.

"Yes," Quinn said. "I wrote the first page. A page and a half."

"Oh, sweetheart, sweet adorable thing, I'm so happy for you. Oh, I'm glad. Quinn, that's wonderful. That's just wonderful."

And so he had lied to her, for the first time, ever. He had not told her about going to Bonwit Teller, about the criminal Wasp, about following her home to Louisburg Square. He had not told her what Angelo said; he would *never* tell her that. He had told her a lie.

Claire was on top of him, teasing the tiny scar on his upper lip with the tip of her tongue. She looked into his eyes with trust, with love. "Can I read it?" she said. "Will you read it to me?"

"Soon," he said, "not now."

"I'll wait," she said. "I can't wait, but I will."

She got out of bed and took a shower while Quinn lay looking at the ceiling.

He had lied to her.

How easy it was.

In another world, distant from Quinn and Claire by no more than half a mile, the clock struck six in Louisburg Square. Porter, propped on his elbow, gazed at Angelo's perfect profile and said, "I am the luckiest man in Boston."

"In the world," Angelo said.

Porter ran a finger across Angelo's brow, and then down the length of his nose, and then across his lower lip. Angelo nibbled at his finger.

"Oh," Porter said. "Oh, Christ."

Angelo continued to nibble at the finger, then he licked it, and then he nibbled it again. Porter moaned. Angelo went on nibbling. "Ready?" he said.

"Please," Porter said, feeling the darkness close in on him, feeling Angelo's busy tongue tickle and thrust and manipulate him in ways that still astonished him. Finally he came, with a short deep cry, strangled almost, and then with a long series of gasps. Angelo was gasping, too, and afterward they lay in silence, Angelo's head on Porter's chest as he listened to the wild racing of his heart.

"What are you thinking?" Porter asked.

Angelo laughed quietly. He had been thinking of Kierkegaard's "Anguish of Abraham."

"What?" Porter said. "Tell me."

"I was thinking of what perfect shape you're in. I was thinking of your perfect body."

Porter leaned forward and kissed the top of Angelo's head. "We've got to get down to business," Porter said. "We've got to talk about Sarah."

Upstairs, two stories above them in the ancient house on Louisburg Square, Sarah lay on her bed, fully clothed, while the stereo turned and turned in silence, the *Winterreise* having played itself out. Sarah slept the sleep of the dead, or so she had once described it to her psychiatrist.

She was dreaming. And in her dream she ran, naked, through the rain. And the rain was blood.

2

Sarah Slade had been—for a brief time—a celebrity of sorts. For two weeks following her twenty-first birthday, her face had been on the front pages of newspapers all over the country. She had disappeared, and was wanted for murder. Love had been involved, and money, and important families. Boston Debutante Wanted for Murder. Case of the Disappearing Deb. Slade Family Mourns. There were sensational details, never mentioned in print. And then suddenly she reappeared, turned herself in to police, ready to be tried. Nothing happened.

The newspapers reported that she was sick, perhaps dying. She was being held in a prison hospital, they said, or a private hospital, or a rest home. She was unable at the time to stand trial.

Her parents had long since disappeared from the picture; her mother was remarried to a Polish count; her father had been killed in a fishy shooting accident at a casino in Nice. A sister, Cassandra, had died a year earlier; O.D., heroin. Of the family, there remained only her brother and her grandmother. Then shortly after the murder, the grandmother was hospitalized with a stroke. The brother, Porter Slade—vice president of Slade, Winthrop, and Slade—requested a news blackout. The family had suffered enough, he said.

Sarah's picture appeared less frequently in the newspapers

and soon even her name appeared scarcely at all. There was other news. There were other murders. When at last a hearing was held, and the press was barred from it, an attempt on the President's life buried the Slade murder deep inside the newspaper.

At her hearing—there was never a trial—Sarah's counsel argued that she had committed a crime of passion while temporarily deranged, that she was no threat to the community, that a public trial and a public sentencing would do irreparable damage to an unfortunate young woman, to her distinguished family, and to society at large.

Counsel's arguments were effective, and so were the large cash gifts disbursed by Sarah's grandmother to the judge's wife, to the Chief of Police, to select members of the District Attorney's office. Sarah was spared a trial; she was sentenced to a minimum of three years' psychiatric custody and ten years' psychiatric parole.

Grandmother Slade, having once more seen the unique power of a family fortune, decided—despite her loathing for anything mercenary—that the time had come to give money her closest attention. She had long known that the family finances were in disarray, but when she sat down with her lawyers and discovered the full extent of that disarray, she was stunned. There was nothing left, or nearly nothing. She was down to her last few hundred thousand.

Provisions must be made for Sarah, since nobody would marry her now. Sarah had a tiny income from her father's estate, and apart from that, nothing. And there were only three years left to arrange everything.

Grandmother Slade went into action. She sold the summer house in Pride's Crossing. She sold the family house in Back Bay where the Incident had taken place; there could be no question of Sarah's returning to live there. She cashed in all her securities.

23

The family business, Slade, Winthrop, and Slade, had long since been sold, share by share, to the Tallino family. And Porter, she reflected, had been sold to them, share by share, as well. At any rate, married as he was to the only Tallino daughter, he was well taken care of. She did not have to make provisions for him.

With her new supply of cash, she bought the house in Louisburg Square and moved into the top floor with Cora, her housekeeper. She reserved the first and second floors for Sarah. The basement was for Angelo, who would act officially as chauffeur, unofficially as watchdog.

The Tallino family had purchased Slade, Winthrop, and Slade to serve as a respectable Brahmin front for some of their less respectable North End operations, and they were relieved at this turn of events. Of all things on earth, the last thing they wanted was publicity. From their viewpoint, marriage to the Slades had been a business deal: Tallino money for the Slade family name. Porter Slade was handsome and blond and a good husband to their Maria; he was the father of her three small children. But Sarah Slade had brought them all a great deal of unwanted attention. As would their own Angelo, if he were not kept under control.

And so the Tallinos were pleased with the grandmother's plan. They were pleased and they wanted to help. Sarah had to be watched; Angelo had to be kept occupied; they could both be taken care of by taking care of each other. The Tallinos put Angelo on salary.

Sarah came home to the house in Louisburg Square where Angelo had been in residence for some time. Her brother, Porter, came as often as he could to see how she was doing. She was doing well. Once a week she taught art at Pine Hill Day School, which her grandmother had endowed; twice a week she saw her psychiatrist. Angelo looked after her and, more discreetly than before, continued to live his private life. There was no further scandal.

The grandmother died and left Sarah everything, though everything translated to no more than the house and a good monthly income.

Things went on as they had been. Porter continued to make his visits. Angelo continued to read and to cruise and to look after Sarah. But Sarah had once again begun to shoplift. She had taken three handbags from three different stores, and there was no telling where this might end.

3

Claire arrived late because of the heavy traffic outside Boston, and then she had a terrible time finding a parking place, and now as she stood outside the door to 65 Marlborough Street, she thought that she would give a very great deal just to sit down, to lie down, to make everything stop for ten full quiet minutes. She took a deep breath and exhaled slowly. *Quod non mutari potest, subeundum est.*

Claire turned the key in the lock and, leaning against the heavy oak door, dragged her overnight bag in after her. The door hissed and slammed shut. She steadied herself for a moment and then started up the long winding stairs. But at the first turning everything went black and she slid down the wall to sit on the carpeted stair. She closed her eyes and concentrated on the dark. Red arrows shot back and forth behind her eyelids and a sharp pain began in her chest. *Nil timendum,* she thought, and after a moment she drew in a long breath, exhaling slowly, like a runner, through pursed lips. The pain lessened somewhat and she started up the stairs again.

On the second-floor landing she could hear Birdie and Jim quarreling again. Birdie was about eighty and Jim was about a hundred, so Quinn said. Claire herself had never seen them. But she knew that Jim was almost completely deaf and beginning to lose his sense of time. He would turn on the stereo, sometimes at three in the morning, full blast, and a few minutes later Birdie's piercing voice would rise above the music, screaming, "Are you out of your mind? It's three o'clock in the morning," and then the fight would begin. They were going at it now.

"... the pot is ruined," Birdie was shouting. "You can't put the pot on the gas and then go take a nap."

"I didn't take a nap. I just fell asleep."

"You're losing your mind. If you don't watch it, I'm going to put you in a home."

"I can't hear you."

"I'm going to put you in a home."

"I can't hear you."

Claire could still hear them on the third floor. She put down her bag and took another deep breath, and then she laid her head against the doorframe. She had to get up for this. She had to look happy when she told Quinn her good news.

She was about to put her key in the lock when she became aware of someone staring at her. But there was no one on the landing. She stepped to the bannister and looked down the stairwell. Nobody. And there was nobody on the stairs that led up to the fourth floor either.

And then, exactly at eye level, she saw two small fat hands clutching the railings of the bannister. She leaned closer and was able to make out tiny eyes and a wisp of hair. A little boy was crouched on the stairs to the floor above. He stood up suddenly and rested his chin on the bannister. He had a round head and a flat white face that made his tiny eyes look even tinier, and he was nearly bald. He was a very ugly little boy.

"I saw you," he said. His voice was thin and sweet.

"Hello," Claire said. "And what's *your* name?"

"I saw you," he said.

"You did?" Claire said. "When did you see me? Hmmm? What did you see me doing?"

The little boy stared at her solemnly.

27

"What's your name? Can you tell me your name?"

He ducked beneath the bannister and continued to stare at her. But as she put the key in the lock and opened the door, he came down the stairs and stood in front of her. He was even smaller than she'd thought. He must be five or six, but he looked ancient.

"Leopold," he said.

"Leopold. What a nice name you have. And do you live upstairs, Leopold?"

"Do you know what?" he said.

"What?" she said. "Tell me."

"My grandma smells like custard pie."

He turned and ran up the stairs out of sight.

Claire watched him go and then stepped inside the apartment, anxious suddenly about Quinn. They had been apart for a full week, the longest ever. What if he had changed? And how would he take the news?

"Sweetheart," Quinn called from the study, "I'm in here. Come!" and then after he'd kissed her, "Look," he said. "Look what I've done." A sheet of paper half-filled with words stuck out of the typewriter and next to it was his notebook and a few typed sheets.

"Oh, that's wonderful," Claire said. "*You*'re wonderful."

"I love you, Claire," Quinn said suddenly. "I love only you," and he kissed her with such intensity that she was surprised. "I am the luckiest, fuckiest man in the world," he said. "Num, num, num."

"You and me," Claire said, responding. "Just us."

They made love even before she unpacked, and for the first time since they'd married, their perfunctory lovemaking took on real excitement.

The truth was that Quinn was beset by guilt. In the past week he had written almost nothing, and on his few forays to the library and his one visit to the Massachusetts Historical

Society, he had not even taken notes. He had watched people and he had daydreamed. In fact, during the past week he had done nothing but think of that woman.

Several times Quinn had strolled through Bonwit Teller hoping to run into her again. And on the odd chance that she made a career of shoplifting, he had checked Saks and Lord and Taylor as well. Then, on Thursday, he saw her. She came out of Shreve, Crump and Low carrying several little bags and she went next door to Brighams for a cup of coffee. Black. He followed her, sat on the stool next to her, watched her—his heart pounding—as she drank her coffee and looked off into space. He started to follow her when she left Brighams and headed across the Public Gardens, but suddenly he felt foolish. He went home and wrote two lines in his notebook: "Subject for a novel; shoplifter steals a handbag from Saks; store detective follows her and later falls in love." He drew a line through "handbag" and, above it, he wrote "necklace."

Quinn was so pleased with this, he decided to take a break and go for a walk by the river. But once in the street, he turned toward the Gardens and then toward Beacon Hill. At the foot of Mount Vernon Street he passed a man in jeans and T-shirt whom he recognized at once as Angelo. Quinn lowered his head and walked faster. Halfway up the block he turned and looked back; Angelo, too, had turned and was staring at him. At once Quinn headed right, toward the Gardens, and from there he went straight home.

The next morning Quinn worked at his desk. He scribbled in his notebook: descriptions of place, of weather, and finally a lengthy description of the store detective, who looked a lot like himself, and notes for a description of the woman. He couldn't quite get her, so he wrote words merely: "blond, thin, very thin, horsey set, rich." But he realized that he had described nobody. He wrote "vague, ethereal." And then:

"thief." He sat there thinking for more than an hour but nothing further came to him.

He decided to go out for a walk. At the door, he was once again startled by Leopold who, as usual, was crouching on the stairs and peering at him through the bannister. "How are you today?" Quinn said, as Leopold studied him with his tiny eyes. "Keeping track of the world?" Leopold was the strangest little creature; no matter how often you ran into him, you were always surprised—unpleasantly, too—to discover he was there.

Out in the street the word he had been looking for suddenly came to him. Possessed. She was possessed. He thought of going back to write it down, but it was too hot to climb those stairs, and he didn't want to see Leopold again, and besides he would never forget it anyway. Possessed. The *mot juste*. The key.

In Louisburg Square, Quinn stood at a distance from the house, staring up at the bay window. What had he expected to see? It was a beautiful house, a rich house; there was nothing mysterious or magical about it. He crossed to the opposite side of the small Square and walked the length of the street. He stood there, examining each of the houses opposite, hers in particular. He wanted to be able to describe this, he told himself.

And then Angelo appeared, coming up the stairs from the apartment below; a young man trailed behind him. They stood on the sidewalk in a tight embrace, until at last Angelo broke away, pushing him off. They laughed. The young man took a few steps and then returned, whispered something, and put his hand on Angelo's crotch. Again Angelo pushed him away, not laughing this time. The young man turned and left.

From the other side of the Square, Quinn watched, repelled and fascinated.

Angelo lit a cigarette and sat on the stairs to Number 17, smoking, gazing off into space. To Quinn, Angelo seemed to be gazing straight at him, and after a moment's panic, he began walking, slowly at first, but then quickening his pace. At the corner Angelo intercepted him.

"Hello again."

Quinn stopped, guilty.

"Well, are you ready?"

"Sorry," Quinn said, and walked away rapidly.

"Just say the word," Angelo said. "I'm ready when you are."

Quinn went home, shaken. And it did not help when, at the head of the stairs, Leopold, unseen and unexpected, suddenly said, "I saw you." Quinn went inside and lay down.

Angelo had unnerved him, that was the trouble. It wasn't spying on the woman that was dangerous; it was that queer. He had never in his life been approached by a queer. He had never been approached by anybody. Man or woman. Quinn ran his finger across his upper lip, feeling the smooth skin, the single small ridge. Hideous. He got up and looked at himself in the mirror. The scar was redder than usual. Bunny Quinn. He was disgusting. How lucky he was to have Claire.

He napped for a while and when he woke, he went straight to his typewriter. He wanted to have something to show Claire when she arrived this afternoon. He typed up his notes, expanding them as he went. But there was something he had forgotten; the *mot juste* for that woman. What was it? He was puzzling over this when he heard Claire at the door.

"Sweetheart," he had called out to her, grateful suddenly for her soft smile and the shape of her head and her unconditional love. "I am the luckiest, fuckiest man in the world," he said, and was surprised at the sudden access of passion. In no time they were in bed making love.

Afterward they lay side by side, holding hands, confident —each for a different reason—that they had begun the best part of their lives, together.

The evening started out fine. They showered and dressed, chatting away about Claire's students and Aunt Lily and the strange little Leopold.

"His voice is interesting," Claire said. "It's thin and sweet. You don't expect it, because he looks like a dwarf, does little Leopold. A very old dwarf."

"No. He's a piglet, in glasses."

"But he doesn't wear glasses."

"Well, maybe he should. It's a good picture, don't you think? A piglet, in glasses?"

And so it all started out fine. Claire insisted that this was her treat, that it was a special dinner, that she had wonderful news. Quinn was excited. He put aside the anxiety caused by his encounter with Angelo. And he put aside the guilt that came from not working and from something else, from lying to Claire maybe; he promised himself he would never do that again. He put aside anything, everything, that might interfere with a good meal and a wonderful evening and a perfect weekend, just him and Claire, Claire and him, the two of them. But no sooner was he in a terrific frame of mind than Claire announced they were going to La Cigale. Quinn panicked; La Cigale was practically next door to Louisburg Square, and Angelo.

"No. Out of the question," Quinn said. "It's much too expensive."

"*Noli perturbare,*" Claire said. "Aren't you glad you've got a rich wife?"

And she led him off, down Marlborough, across the Gardens, and, as Quinn grew increasingly nervous, up Mount

Vernon Street to La Cigale. He was certain they would run into Angelo. He was certain that Angelo would smile at him or wave to him, and he would be stuck trying to explain to Claire who Angelo was and how he knew him. They entered the restaurant and Quinn ordered a double Scotch even before they were seated.

Safe inside the restaurant, a drink in his hand, Quinn began to feel less panicky. More cross than nervous now, he finished his drink and ordered another. He looked around the small, elegant room. The decor was dull rose and gray, with stiff linen napery and old silver. Frescoes on the wall. The maître d' in a tux. A sommelier. It was ridiculous. It was too expensive. Claire's idea of how the middle class should improve themselves. What a waste. What utter nonsense.

The waiter brought his new drink and Quinn raised it to Claire, a sour look on his face now. Claire smiled, confused.

"Are you all right?" she said.

"Of course I'm all right. I'm fine. Why shouldn't I be all right?"

"It's the walk," Claire said. "It's too hot for that walk, especially up the hill."

"I said I'm all right." He picked up the menu. "I'm hungry, I guess. I'll be fine once I've had something to eat."

"I'm hungry, too," Claire said, looking at the list of entrées, the *sole meuniere* and the *magret de canard* and the rosemaried rack of lamb, knowing that—fight fat, think thin—she would make do with a green salad and plain broiled fish with lemon. Quinn, she knew, would have the rack of lamb.

They finished eating and Quinn leaned back in his chair and smiled at her. Good old reliable, loving, generous Claire. He was so mean to her. He was such a bastard. And he didn't want to be. It was just that he had no job and he was a flop, and oh, God, how lucky he was to have her.

33

"Hello, sweetie," he said, and leaned toward her, reaching across for her hand.

Claire had been waiting for this moment; it always came if she waited long enough. "Guess what!" she said. And then she told him her good news.

Quinn went white and sat back in his chair, stunned. "A baby?" he said. "Are you sure?"

"I tested positive," she said, and as she looked at him her eyes filled with tears. "I thought you'd be pleased," she said. "I thought . . ."

"I am," he said. "I am pleased. I'm just . . . well . . . surprised, that's all. The news—and it's wonderful news, Claire; honestly—well, it's a surprise." He smiled at her and took her hand again.

"Oh, good," she said. "Oh, good. I knew you'd be pleased, even though we didn't plan to have one just yet; I mean, we agreed to wait, and everything, but I knew you'd be happy just the same. Oh, Quinn. I'm so happy. For *us*. It's going to bring us even closer together, I think. Don't you, Quinn? Don't you think so? The baby?"

"It's us," he said. "It'll always be just us." He was smiling and smiling. "Well, this *is* news," he said.

They sat, holding hands. So he was to be a father. Oh, God, if only he had a job. Well, at least he had Claire.

She sat there now, smiling back at him. It was more a simper than a smile; a pleased, self-satisfied simper. The little mother. She was already putting on weight. Her face was naturally round, roundish, but pretty and sweet. He had fallen in love with her because of the sweetness and straightforwardness of that look. She was exactly what she appeared to be. And she loved him.

The simper and the new weight—how much could she

34

have put on in only a week?—made her look plumpish, though. Dowdy almost. With her little cap of black hair and her big teeth.

His smile began to hurt.

"You're not happy about it, are you," she said. It was a statement.

"Well, let me just...but how could this have happened? I thought the pill was foolproof."

"I forgot it, I guess. I must have."

"How could you have forgotten? Didn't you *think* what this would *mean*?"

"Oh, Quinn."

"I'm sorry. I don't mean to upset you. I just can't believe you could be so...so careless. Wantonly careless." His voice shifted from anger back to concern. "I'm sorry, Claire, of course I don't mean that the way it sounds. I don't. Truly I don't. I love you. And I'll love the baby. It's just that it's a surprise. Okay?"

"Okay."

Quinn reached for the wine and discovered the bottle was empty. "Waiter!" he said, a little louder than he had intended. "Could we have our coffee, *please.*" The waiter looked startled for a second and then went to get them coffee. "Considering the prices here, the service—as the children quaintly put it—the service sucks!"

"But, even apart from the surprise, you aren't happy about it, are you. Are you?"

"Claire, look." His voice was flat, and patient. "Sometimes I feel I don't even know you. Certainly I fail to understand you. What do you *want*? You tell me in the middle of this fucking restaurant that we're going to have a baby—by accident, I might point out—and you expect me...well, I don't know what you expect."

"Let's talk about it," she said. "Are you worried about money?"

"Ha!" he said, nodding to the waiter who had brought the coffee and the check, "why should I worry about money? Just because I have no job and no likelihood of one? Because I've just begun a novel that I've been hoping to write for as long as I've lived, and now I'll have to give it up? Just because we don't even have a place to live, except that rented apartment down the street that costs us more per month than the national debt?" He saw that her eyes were filled with tears, but he wanted to go on; he wanted to say it all. And he just gave up. "Shit, piss, fuck," he said. "I don't know, Claire. I don't know. I'm sorry. For you. For me. I don't know."

"It'll be all right," she said. "It'll be okay."

"Okay," he said. "I'm sorry, sweetheart; I really am." And then, "Let's get out of this place." He took from his wallet the fifty and the twenty that Claire had given him, glanced at the check and, shrugging, threw some ones on top. "What the hell," he said.

Outside on the sidewalk Quinn was suddenly overcome by guilt. He pulled her close, whispered "I love you," and kissed her lightly on the lips. Claire stood there, defeated, and tried to smile.

"Well, hello again!" someone said.

Quinn looked up and saw it was Angelo; standing beside him was the woman, the shoplifter.

"Twice in the same day," Angelo said. The way he stood there indicated a man ready for a chat.

"Oh," Quinn said. "Yes. Good to see you."

Angelo, waiting for an introduction, looked from Quinn to Claire and back to Quinn. He was obviously amused, enjoying this. Quinn made as if to go.

"How was dinner?" Angelo nodded at the restaurant.

36

"Oh, very good," Quinn said.

"Very nice," Claire said.

"We should keep in touch," Angelo said, putting his hand on Quinn's arm, looking into his eyes, nearly laughing. Quinn turned away. As if it were an afterthought, Angelo said, "And this is my sister-in-law, Sarah Slade. I believe you've met."

"No," Quinn said. "It's a pleasure." He put his hand to his lip. "My wife, Claire. Claire, we really *ought* to go."

"Babysitter?"

Quinn flushed and said, "Very nice to see you." He nodded at Sarah Slade and, taking Claire's arm, he turned, decisively, toward home.

After a moment Claire said, "He wanted to talk. Who is he? And who is she?"

"Nobody," Quinn said. "Angelo something." And then, inspired, "He's a guy I met at the library; I don't even remember his name. That's why I didn't introduce you."

"And who's she?"

"I haven't any idea. His sister-in-law, he said. I think."

"Sarah Slade. I know that name."

"I've never heard of it."

"I know it from somewhere. Where did you meet her?"

"I didn't. I haven't."

"Angelo said you'd met. He said 'I believe you've met.'"

"Well, I didn't. We haven't. Where in hell would we meet? Does she look like somebody who does research at the library? And I don't know who he is, either. Frankly, he looks like a faggot to me."

"Faggot? My, you *are* angry. He doesn't look gay to me. I think he's quite good-looking."

"Can we talk about something else? Please? I don't really care about those people."

"Neither do I," Claire said. She pressed against him and said, "Let's start the evening all over again? All right? We've got so much to be happy about?"

"We do," Quinn said, slipping his arm around her waist. "We have everything and we have each other."

That night, halfway between midnight and dawn, Claire woke Quinn and said, in a frightened voice, "Quinn? Sweet? We don't *have* to have the baby, if you really don't want it." There was silence. "Quinn?"

"I'm thinking," he said. "We should do whatever *you* want."

"Well, I want it," she said. "If you do."

"Well then we'll have it," he said. "And that's settled, once and for all."

And then he rolled over and pretended sleep. Claire lay beside him, listening to his breathing, waiting for it to change from pretended sleep to real sleep. She waited a long, long time.

4

On Sunday night Claire and Quinn had a nearly silent dinner, after which she lay down for a nap while he read the *Times Book Review*. He was having trouble concentrating.

It was a lazy June evening, warm but not too warm, the kind of evening when they used to stroll the campus at Williams, hand in hand, married but very much in love. How their love had annoyed people! Well, not real people; just the old farts who had been around Tweed Heaven for the last two hundred years or so. The ones who hated him and his fiction writing. And hated Claire's popularity. He had heard them: "Mr. and Mrs. Indignant"—and they laughed—"with his one pitiful story in *The New Yorker*." They'd laugh in a different way when he published his novel. He looked at the *Times Book Review*, limp in his hands. Nobody gave a damn about novels, that was the simple truth. He'd never be anything. He had no job. No future. And *she* was pregnant.

Almost as if he had summoned her, Claire appeared at the door, suitcase in hand.

"I'm going now," she said.

She never left for the trip to Hanover until nearly dawn, and here it was only about eight o'clock. What was this, some new way of fighting? The suitcase, the dead voice, the beaten expression. She looked like a bag lady.

"All right," he said.

She stood there in the doorway for a minute, silent, waiting for something more, and then she said, "I'll see you next week."

"All right."

The door closed behind her and still Quinn sat there, the *Times Book Review* crumpled in his lap. Finally he got up and went to the window. He pressed his face to the screen to get a good look, and after what seemed a very long time, he saw Claire appear on the sidewalk below. "To hell with her," he said. "I'm fed up."

Quinn watched as she crossed the street and got into her little Ford. She was going; she was actually leaving. But she only sat there behind the wheel, her head bent slightly. Was she crying? While he stood up here at the window, watching?

All at once something in his chest crumpled, and Quinn thought, my God, she's leaving, I drove her out, and she's the only thing I love.

He ran to the door and down the staircase, taking the steps three at a time. On the second landing, he fell against the door and gave his elbow a terrible crack. From inside he heard Birdie shout, "Who is it?," but he kept right on going. By the time he reached the street, Claire was gone.

He was sitting at his desk now, writing her a letter. He had been thoughtless, stupid, impossible, he said. How could she stand him? She was the only thing on earth he loved. She was his whole life to him.

He went on for some time in this way until he had filled an entire sheet. He turned the second sheet into the typewriter and then paused to read over what he had written. A lot of emotion, a lot of run-on sentences, but that was all right; he meant every word, and the long breathless lines only emphasized the urgency, the honesty, with which he wrote.

Seized by this feeling of honesty, he began the second page

with a confession. He had told her a lie. It was the first time he had lied to her. It would be the last, the only, time. And then he told her about seeing Sarah Slade steal the handbag, about following her home to Louisburg Square.

Quinn leaned over the typewriter and read what he had written thus far. Was this the best thing to do? Really?

He plunged on. Angelo had propositioned him, and of course he had fled, embarrassed, humiliated. Obviously Angelo had misread his interest in Sarah. And then, during this past week, he had gone back a couple times to Louisburg Square...

Quinn typed a line of x's through this sentence and started again.

He had gone back to Louisburg Square, once, just out of curiosity, and...

Quinn typed another line of x's through this.

He had *thought* of going back to...

Quinn yanked the paper from the typewriter and inserted another sheet. He wished he hadn't lied to her in the first place—that certainly was true—but no good could come of confessing it now; he would simply resolve never to lie again.

Back to the letter. He sent her all his love, he said. He wanted whatever she wanted, and if she wanted the baby, then he wanted it too. Truly. Honestly. He loved only her, always and forever.

Quinn proofread the letter, put in a comma, changed another comma to a semicolon, and slipped it into an envelope. She would get it by Tuesday, he figured. Wednesday at the latest.

He felt much better now, as if they had already made up. But at once he thought of the baby, the dread baby, and wondered how in hell he was going to cope.

He poured himself a drink and tried to go back to his *Times*

Book Review. He still couldn't concentrate. He decided to mail his letter to Claire and then take a walk. Down to the river perhaps, but not to Beacon Hill, not anywhere near it.

An hour later Quinn stood outside the house in Louisburg Square. The windows were dark. He sighed, relieved. There was nobody home, and so he had nothing to fear, nothing to confess.

5

The hour was half over and Sarah had still not told the shrink about stealing the handbag from Bonwit Teller. She had told her nothing, really; she had kept silent for most of the time.

Sarah turned to the shrink who sat there looking and not looking—the professional's attitude of attention—and took her in once again, quite frankly staring at her. She was absurd, ridiculous. She was unattractive, even for a shrink. With her light blue suit and low heels, she looked mannish. No, she looked—Sarah searched for the word—bulky. Yet her clothes were good, well-cut and expensive, and her short wiry hair was freshly done. She was smart. She could talk authoritatively on any subject. Why then did she strike Sarah as ridiculous?

At last the shrink noticed that Sarah was staring.

"Yes?"

This was why she was ridiculous, this business of saying, Yes? The shrink was from Brooklyn, Sarah knew, and yet she affected this Viennese intonation—Yes? No? I am right?—and sometimes even an accent. She was absurd. No?

"Yes? You would tell me something?"

"There's a man who follows me."

The shrink nodded imperceptibly and said nothing.

"He has a scar on his upper lip."

"A harelip."

43

"No, it's not a harelip. It's nothing like that. It's a slight line—right here—in the center of his upper lip, like a scar that's pulled the skin around it tight. It's not even noticeable until you notice it." She smiled. "I mean, when you do notice it, it's not at all unpleasant. It's attractive even."

"Attractive?"

"It sets him apart."

Neither of them spoke for a minute, and Sarah became aware of the echo of her voice, a light sound, very slow, as if she were searching for the words. "It sets him apart," she said again, not because it was important, but because she wanted to hear how she must sound to this absurd woman who always made her feel so bad. But whom she needed. Whom she could not live without.

"And this interests you? Pleases you, perhaps? That he is set apart, by a scar on his upper lip?"

"He stands outside my house sometimes. Last night he was on the other side of the Square, just standing and looking. The lights were out. I was in my bedroom, standing at the window, looking back. He didn't know I was there."

"No."

"We were looking at each other in the dark and he didn't know it."

"No."

"I don't know his name."

"No."

"I met his wife. Last week, on Friday, Angelo and I had supper and then we went for a walk by the river and on the way back we met them coming out of La Cigale. Angelo has been after him, you know, propositioning him the way he propositions everybody, and when we saw them coming out of the Cigale, Angelo said, 'Well, hello again,' pretending he knew them. And then he introduced me, and so the man who's been following me had to introduce his wife, but I never found out his name at all. Her name is Claire."

"Why do you suppose this man, with his scar and his wife, didn't say to Angelo, 'I'm afraid you're mistaken. I'm afraid we've never met.' Wouldn't that make more sense than introducing you to his wife?"

"Oh, he couldn't say that."

The shrink waited, but Sarah offered no further explanation.

"He couldn't say that?"

"Oh, no. He's guilty, you see. Angelo has seen him following me, and of course he knew that Angelo knew."

"And he didn't want his wife to know."

Sarah nodded, smiling a little. "Claire," she said, making the sound ugly.

"Let us go back. There is a man following you. He stands outside your window each night . . ."

"Not every night. Some nights only. And sometimes in the day."

"He stands outside your window. You've met his wife. What does he want, this man with the scar? Why is he following you?"

"He started following me nearly two weeks ago. I came out of Bonwit Teller and I thought someone was following me, so instead of coming straight home, I made a square. I went up to Dartmouth and then over past Commonwealth to Marlborough and then back down Marlborough to the Gardens. He followed me."

The shrink nodded.

"It was the day I took the handbag."

The shrink suddenly sat forward, all attention.

"From Bonwit Teller," Sarah added.

"Yes?"

"I stole it. Nothing happened. I made sure there was no alarm tag attached."

"Yes?"

"Besides, Angelo was watching."

"And how did you feel?"

"I didn't feel anything."

"Nothing?"

"That's why I took it."

"Tell me, when you feel you want to."

"There's nothing to tell."

"It was a fugue state?"

Immediately, Sarah wanted to run. The room was too close, there was no air, she was being smothered. But if she ran, they would say she needed closer watching. They would sedate her again. They would lock her up. This shrink, this ridiculous woman, was her only hope. And she had done nothing this time. Nothing. She had merely stolen the handbag.

"You were in a fugue state?"

"Yes."

"And how do you feel now?"

"I feel bad."

"Yes."

"I don't want to be sick again. I don't want to hurt anybody. I want to be like everybody else."

"Yes."

"I want . . . someone. I want to love someone."

"You want to be loved; that's what you want. It's normal to want to be loved. But you know about the stealing. You know . . ." And then she fell silent.

"I try. I try so hard."

The shrink shifted in her chair. Her job was to lead this poor girl, not to push her. Deliberately, she looked at her watch. But Sarah said nothing.

"Your period? You are having it now?"

"I've just had it."

"And there were no—correct me if I am wrong—*fixations*? About the blood?"

"No."

"About the smell?"

"No."

"There were no fixations about the—correct me—*language* of sex?"

"No. Nothing like that. It was normal. I just bled like everybody else."

"Ah." The shrink sat back, relieved. "Now let us return to this handbag. Yes?"

Sarah nodded, relieved, too.

"This handbag. What did you do with it?"

"It's in the drawer with the others. In my studio."

"And what else is in the drawer?"

"Nothing."

"And why is that? Why are these stolen handbags given a home of their own, as it were?"

"I don't know."

"Well, think about that, and we'll see each other in a week."

What was there to think about? That she kept her crazy life separate from her sane life? Didn't everybody? What did this woman mean? What did she want? Sarah sat up on the couch, dizzy suddenly, exhausted. She wanted to lie down again and go to sleep, right here in this awful woman's office, where she was safe and pretty.

"I won't see him," she said. "I won't have anything to do with him."

"Next week," the shrink said.

"There's no connection. I'm sure, I'm absolutely sure there's no connection between that man and the handbag. I'm sure of it."

"Next week."

Sarah took the elevator to the lobby. She was shaken, defeated once again. She wanted to talk to somebody, anybody. She wanted a drink, but she couldn't have a drink; that was out of the question. A cup of coffee, maybe. What she wanted, she knew, was to be twenty-one and in love with Raoul, before any of the trouble started, before she had become this crazy woman.

She went out into the street to signal a taxi, and then suddenly she changed her mind. She would go around the corner to Brighams for a cup of coffee.

It occurred to her for a second that she had seen him once in Brighams, he had followed her there, but she put the thought from her mind.

She would have that cup of coffee. She would sit and look at people and not think. For a few minutes she would be like everybody else: normal, ordinary, sane.

The past, she told herself firmly, was gone forever.

Quinn spent the afternoon in the Massachusetts Historical Society sitting before a pile of manila folders containing the intimate and tedious correspondence of the Ripley family. How oppressively good they were, and how niggardly with stationery.

He sat at the long oak table, leafing through the letters of Sophia Ripley. He had decided to start small, to know one person really well, and then expand his circle of interest—he found himself thinking "circle of malice"—to include the others. He was annoyed with Sophia. She was a convert to Catholicism, and like all converts she was humorless and holier than the Pope. Furthermore, she had this spidery handwriting and she used watery ink and tiny scraps of paper, the silly bitch. And when she had covered both sides, she simply turned the paper halfway around and wrote vertically across her own letter. He was getting a headache just looking at the stuff, let alone reading it.

Near him, at other tables, scholars read documents and scribbled learned notes, all the while snorting and farting and coughing as if it were a goddamn hospital instead of a research library. They disgusted him. He disgusted himself, come to think of it.

Quinn pitched folder number 43 to one side and, hope slowly rising in him, he opened his fiction notebook.

New character, he wrote; call him Q. Brother to shoplifter. Wants to be a novelist, but has no talent. Is disgusted by everyone he sees—symptom of his self-disgust. He's shortish, black hair, very dark eyes with a woman's lashes, good build. Maybe foreign-looking. He paused for a moment, summoning the image of Angelo. Faggot, he wrote, and then crossed the word out and wrote aesthete instead. That was no good either. He would have to settle for "scholar." He set it off in quotes.

He sat back and read what he had written and then added, he has a harelip. Good, he thought. He read through his earlier notes, the descriptions of place and weather—not very useful, no sharpness to them, no specific gravity—and then the notes on the shoplifter and the store detective. He named the woman S and the store detective A. That would help him keep his notes, and his thinking, tidy.

What fun it was writing a novel. It certainly beat the hell out of research on nineteenth-century New England Catholicism. He saw himself at a large cocktail party. Hello, he said, I'm J. J. Quinn. Not the novelist, she said; are you the novelist? Well, yes, he said modestly; I *have* written a novel; it's called Blank; you've heard of it? Oh, Mr. Quinn, she said, what a pleasure to meet you; I'm so thrilled; I really am; and to think I could have taken your course at Williams! New scene: lecture hall, Williams College. And we are honored to present the novelist and screenwriter J. J. Quinn—or just Quinn, as *we* used to call him when he was a colleague of ours here at Williams. Quinn has flown in from London to talk to us on "Novel into Film; Symbol into Myth." And then shuddering applause. New scene: Sarah Slade turning her head slowly toward him, eyebrows arched, lips compressed, saying . . . but what is she saying? What would she say?

How absurd he was. How ridiculous, to pretend to be writing a novel. He wasn't a novelist. He wasn't even a scholar. To be a scholar all you needed was a little perseverance, but to be a novelist you needed talent. He sighed, loudly, and was aware of heads turning to look at him. He was back in the Massachusetts Historical Society. The coughing and the snorting stopped. Silence.

Well, fuck them all, he would write it. He leaned protectively over his notebook and went to work.

A was shopping for a handbag for his wife, he wrote, when he saw a beautiful woman pick up a handbag and walk out.

He paused and read it over. Not exactly Proust. He crossed it out.

There was a smell of new leather, he wrote, mixing with the smell of perfume. A was shopping for a handbag for his wife; he wanted to make up after their quarrel and he knew that the handbag would satisfy her desire for . . . would do the trick, he wrote. But as he spotted the handbag he was looking for, a blond woman in a tan linen dress—her name was S— leaned against the counter and, looking in both directions, picked up the handbag and tucked it beneath her arm. A watched in fascination as she walked from the store. He decided to follow her.

Quinn was completely absorbed now as he wrote, from vivid memory, an account of A's pursuit of S as she crossed the Public Gardens and turned up Mount Vernon Street to her home in Louisburg Square. He left her as she disappeared through the door of Number 17.

He read over what he had written, changed tan to beige in the description of her dress, put in two commas, changed a period to a semicolon, and sat back, satisfied with his afternoon's work.

He handed over the manila folder to the woman at the desk —who, he noticed once again, had terrific boobs—and walked slowly downtown.

A summer day in Boston, with no humidity to speak of, a light breeze. Perfect walking weather. This wonderful city, full of writers and scholars and artists. Girls in their summer dresses. Love everywhere; or possibility, at least. Life was good.

Quinn paused outside Lord and Taylor but only for a moment; he would *not* go in; this playing detective had to stop. When he got to Bonwit Teller, he thought, well, why not, and took a brief tour through perfumes and handbags, and then he headed for Shreve, Crump and Low. But he stopped first at Brighams for a cup of coffee. He had followed her once from Shreve to Brighams, and who could tell, maybe he'd run into her again.

The counter at Brighams had three bays, making it hard to see who was sitting where, but Quinn stood just inside the door, and by shifting from right to left and back again, he could tell that Sarah was not there. He decided to have coffee anyway.

He sat at the counter next to two girls; the stool was at a good angle to the mirrored wall so that he had a clear view of the entrance. He could watch for her. Immediately somebody sat down next to him, a woman, but he paid no attention to her; he kept his eye on the door, eavesdropping meanwhile on the girls at his left. They had orange hair and smoked long cigarettes. They looked about fifteen. One of them had just finished telling a long story about her mother.

"My mother," she said, "honest to God, she's something else."

"She's too much, your mother."

The waitress brought two coffees, one for him, one for the woman next to him.

"Really," the girl said. "Is that ever really true. Did I tell you about the time she threw the eggs before?"

"No. Not the eggs. She threw the eggs?"

"Oh, yeah. She threw the whole plate of eggs right in his face before."

"My God, she's too much, your mother."

"No shit. No fucking shit."

"Oh, you're something else, Rinnie, you're too much."

"Listen, did I tell you about what I heard about Margo before? With Mark? What she did? I heard it in gym today, right? Like, after lunch."

She lowered her voice and leaned closer to her friend, but Quinn could still catch a phrase here and there: "such a square," "her old boyfriend, right, not the new one," "that genarf," "and Mark said, Mark, he said, like," but Quinn couldn't hear what Mark said. Whatever it was, it sent the two girls into fits of laughter. Then she told another long story about Margo and a boy called Roofer. "Penis," Quinn heard her say, "he calls his dick his penis." And then there was more laughter.

Quinn finished his coffee and turned a little on his stool to get a close look at the girls. The one called Rinnie had fluorescent blue fingernails, gnawed to the quick, and acne that showed beneath her makeup. And all that smart talk. He thought of himself at fifteen and his hand shot to his lip. He wanted out.

He tapped his fingers on the countertop, impatient now, waiting for his check. He sighed, loudly, and said "God" under his breath. He heard the girl say, "Oh, Rinnie, you're too much, honest to Christ," and he heard Rinnie giggle. And still he had no check.

The woman next to him had pushed her empty cup away; she sat wih her hands folded on the counter, as if she were praying. She too was waiting for her check. Quinn glanced at her hands, and then looked hard at them, fascinated. They were not like any hands he had ever seen. They were white, unnaturally so, and her fingers were long and bony. She wore no rings. Her unpolished nails were cut short, blunt. Her hands were like precision instruments. An artist of some kind?

Quinn raised his eyes from her hands to the mirror, and was startled to see Sarah Slade looking back, her pale gaze fixed on him as if it had been there from eternity. Quickly he turned and looked at her, seated next to him, and then he looked back at her reflection in the mirror. Her gaze had not shifted.

He smiled and she smiled back, vaguely.

"It's easier to get the coffee, I guess, than to get the check." His voice came out high and strained.

"Yes."

"I didn't see you," he said.

Sarah sat there, looking at him in the mirror. Quinn was beginning to sweat. He was grateful that the waitress chose this moment to slap down their checks in front of them. "Well," he said, and stood up to go pay the cashier. "Well."

He moved away from the counter, but at once he turned back and stooped to get his notebook, which he had placed at his feet, and when he tried to stand up again, he banged his head on the counter. Sarah was leaving a quarter next to her cup, and Quinn, realizing suddenly that he had not left a tip, began with a show of haste to search his pockets. He had only a nickel and some pennies. But Sarah had moved away in the direction of the cashier by this time, and so Quinn just shrugged and followed along behind her.

She paid and then he paid, and he was pleased to see she waited outside the door.

"Well," he said.

She smiled that vague smile of hers and moved a few steps toward Shreve's and then to the crosswalk. Confused as to what he should do, Quinn did nothing. Sarah turned, waiting, and looked at him. He moved forward quickly as if he had been summoned.

They crossed to the Arlington Street Church, and from there to the Public Gardens. Neither said anything. In the Gardens, Sarah slowed her pace.

They were strolling, Quinn said to himself; he and Sarah Slade were taking a stroll in the Boston Public Gardens. Anyone seeing them would think they were having an affair. He was amused, and pleased, at the idea. She was wearing that same tan dress and her hair was loose about her face. She carried a large straw hat. Quinn liked the picture they made. He supposed that people who had affairs did exactly this; they strolled. They couldn't spend *all* their time screwing.

He thought of Claire, and at once he made up his mind: when they hit Charles Street, at the other side of the Gardens, he would turn and go home.

"We can watch the swan boats," Sarah said.

"I really should get home," Quinn said. "I've got work I should be doing."

Sarah said nothing; she kept walking toward the patch of water where the swan boats slowly chugged the children about in long lazy ovals and circles and loops. The boats were filled today with solemn little boys and girls.

"It's one of those things parents are convinced children love," Quinn said, "when any fool could see they hate it."

"I loved the swan boats when I was a child."

"It's like clowns at the circus. I could never see what was supposed to be funny about clowns. And the noise and all the people and everyone pushing. I absolutely *detested* the circus. I still do, I think." Why was he talking this way? He was making a fool of himself, and he couldn't stop.

He went on. "But the clowns were the worst. I could never *understand* them. One would hit another one over the head with a baseball bat—it was rubber, I suppose—and everybody would laugh at it. I'd look at the people around me and they'd all be laughing and I couldn't *laugh*. I used to wonder what was wrong with me."

They were crossing the footbridge and Sarah stopped to watch the swan boats pass under them. Quinn kept on talking about the circus.

"It always scared me," he was saying. "But I guess everything scared me when I was little. Crowds, and noise of course, but the clowns particularly. Who knows why. I guess I always thought they looked . . . deformed."

He put his hand to his lip, self-conscious, but Sarah gave no sign she had heard him. A little boy in one of the swan boats waved at them. Sarah waved back, but Quinn paid no attention. He was mortified, sweating. He wanted out.

"I've never been to the circus," Sarah said.

"Oh," Quinn said, all irony, "did you have a deprived childhood?"

"Yes."

She said it simply, as a fact, and Quinn was touched suddenly by her defenselessness. But what could he say? She was a stranger, a thief. They stood in silence, side by side, looking down at the water.

"You saw me take that handbag." She turned and stared at him frankly. "Didn't you."

Quinn was not prepared for this. Her eyes, he noticed, were the palest shade of gray.

"Didn't you."

"Yes."

"And you followed me."

"Yes."

"You know why."

She spoke slowly, as if she were just coming out of sleep, and her eyes were unnaturally bright.

"You do, don't you."

Did he know why? Was he supposed to know why? Quinn blushed, his face going slowly red. He wanted to ask why the thief-proof thing hadn't triggered the alarm, but he couldn't get the words out, and so he just kept on meeting her look. She sighed then, as if she had been holding her breath, as if the worst part were over.

"Come on." She started toward the far side of the Gardens, toward Charles Street. But before they were off the foot-bridge, they were surrounded by a pack of giggling children, five-year-olds, each of them dressed like the children in advertisements.

"I saw you." It was the thin sweet voice of Leopold, who stood before them, beaming.

"Leopold!" Sarah said. "What a nice surprise! Are you having your outing?"

"I saw you," the little boy said.

"And Jennifer, and Jason, and Mark, and Kimberly . . ." She went through all the names, smiling at them, touching them. It wasn't until Sarah had greeted each of them and was saying something to their prefect that Quinn realized the change in her. She spoke more quickly now, in a clear, sharp voice; that somnambulist way of hers was gone. He had never seen anybody change like this, and he was fascinated.

"*He* came to my house," Leopold said.

"I *live* there," Quinn said. "It's *my* house, too."

Leopold screwed up his face as if he were about to cry.

"Come along, people," the prefect said, and began to herd the pack of children across the footbridge.

"That's a good boy," Sarah said, and knelt down to give Leopold a hug. "I'll see you tomorrow, now, won't I. Yes. And we'll draw a beautiful picture—of whatever you want."

"I'll draw you," Leopold said, any sign of tears gone. He pressed his fists against his fat cheeks in excitement. "I'll draw you and my grandma." And then he ran to join the others.

"I teach them drawing once a week," Sarah said, "at the Pine Hill School. Just off lower Chestnut Street." She pointed.

"What's the matter with that child?" Quinn said.

"The matter with him? I think he's adorable."

"Well, why does he always say that? 'I *saw* you. I *saw* you.' It's enough to make anybody crazy."

"He just means that he saw you before you saw him. All children like to be first in things. They like to be special."

"He always makes it sound like an accusation."

"I think he's sweet." She went on about Leopold and the children and the school. But again she began to speak more slowly, in that same dreamy way.

Quinn felt left out. What the hell was this somnambulist act anyhow? It was phoney and annoying and he'd had enough of it. Twenty more yards and bingo! Sayonara Sarah! Anyway, this whole pickup business was crazy. Who *was* this woman? He didn't even know her, and here he was going home to bed with her.

"What do you do?"

But Quinn was silent, still astonished by the thought that had suddenly struck him, from nowhere. This is what it was all about: going home to bed with her.

"Are you a writer?"

"Please?"

"Do you write?"

"Well, yes, as a matter of fact," Quinn said. "I *have* written a novel."

"A novel! So you're a writer! What is it called?"

"Actually, I didn't publish it. I didn't think it was good enough. I could have, I think, if I had wanted to—I've published before, stories, mostly in *The New Yorker*—but I just didn't think that that particular novel was ready. It wasn't a mature enough work."

"But you've published in *The New Yorker*. You must be awfully good."

"Well, my new novel will be good, I think. But every writer thinks his new work is going to be his best."

"The way painters do."

"Exactly. Do you feel that way? I take it you paint, if you teach painting."

"I don't *really* paint. I just do it as a kind of . . ."

"Therapy?"

"Hobby," she said, smiling and looking at him the way she had in Brighams. She took his arm as they crossed Charles Street.

She was almost beautiful, Quinn thought. Her skin glowed and her eyes were truly extraordinary, a pale gray, and she was enticingly thin. Big boobs were a *Playboy* fixation, and that told you something. He noticed them, of course—who could not?—but he didn't find them a turn-on. More than a handful is wasteful; who said that? Her hair was blond chopped straight at the line of her jaw, and it moved with her, the way hair did on television ads. She must have had it cut in

58

the past week. Her face was long, longish, but not really horsey. Well, a little bit horsey. It was the kind of face that spoke money and class.

Quinn resolved that when they reached Mount Vernon Street, he would leave her and return home. It was the right thing to do, the responsible thing, and he would do it. He *always* did the right thing, goddammit, and he would do it again. Mind you, he told himself, any other man would have an adventure, a little afternoon fling. What was wrong with it, after all? It didn't hurt anybody, and it put a little zing in your life, and Claire wouldn't have to know. It would give them some variety, some change, in their lives; they were both so stale. Constantly with each other. Claire and Quinn. Quinn and Claire. Mr. and Mrs. Indignant. How boring they were. How interesting—and sane—to fool around a little bit when you got the chance. But of course Claire would never understand that. Would never dream of fooling around herself. Would be shocked at the way he was thinking. Claire and Quinn, with their boring missionary sex. Claire and Quinn and the baby. The thought depressed him suddenly. God, he was trapped. He wanted to die. Did he? Yes, he wanted to die.

They stopped at the window of an antique shop. Sarah was still holding his arm and Quinn could see their image reflected dimly in the window. They really were a very good-looking couple. And obviously she liked him. She was attracted to him. She found him sexy, maybe. He shook his head, no. It was too good to be true.

"No?" she said.

"What?"

"You just shook your head, no."

"Oh, I was just amused at that tiny Victorian chair," he said, improvising. "It's obviously a child's chair, but what kind of child would ever sit in it? It's so . . . stuffy."

"That's a nursing chair," she said. "For a Victorian boudoir."

"'How all things do inform against me.'"

"You have a baby?"

"No, oh, no. I meant that I should have known it was a nursing chair. I meant I was displaying my ignorance."

She pressed his arm, laughing, and they continued down Charles Street.

He was wondering, would he bore her in bed? What if he couldn't perform properly? He had never discussed sex with anyone, not even Claire really, but he knew from reading modern novels that other people were getting a lot more out of sex than he was. And putting a lot more into it. All those sophisticated preliminaries. All that warming up for performance. Quinn hated the very idea of performance; it seemed to necessitate reviews. Last night at the Fine Arts, Mr. Quinn offered a rather disappointing performance in the role of the lover. He attacked his part with energy and intelligence, but he gave out completely before the end of the first act. He is, alas, an inexperienced actor with small range and limited sensibility. In future, he should assay less demanding roles.

At the foot of Mount Vernon, Quinn stopped, and said, without conviction, "Well, I think I should go back now."

"To work on your novel?"

"Well, yes," Quinn said. "No."

"You have to use every minute? It's such a beautiful afternoon."

"I'll walk you up Mount Vernon."

Was she wondering the same thing? Should they do it? Should they go to bed?

But Sarah was not wondering, not even thinking. She had made her decision in Brighams. She had let that special vagueness of mind—it made everything easier—descend upon her,

60

she had welcomed it, and now it was only a question of his deciding he wanted her. Or rather, a question of letting him think he was deciding. Because, she knew, the matter was settled.

They turned into Louisburg Square. The afternoon sun flamed the windows on the far side of the Square, blinding them for a moment. Quinn laughed nervously. " 'Sometimes too hot the eye of heaven shines,' " he said.

"Perhaps this is a mistake," she said.

Quinn froze.

In front of Number 17, Sarah stopped and faced him. She fixed him with her gray eyes, and said, "Can I give you a cup of tea?" She said it innocently, as if all she was offering was a cup of tea. She smiled at him.

"I should be getting home," he said.

They stood there, looking at each other. She said nothing.

"I'd *like* a cup of tea."

"It's your choice," she said.

"What do you think?"

"I think you should decide what you want to do," she said. She had learned this way of talking from Angelo and she knew how effective it was.

"Well," he said, trying not to think.

As they stood there, close together, absorbed in the moment, Angelo entered the Square from Mount Vernon Street. With him was a thin young man with glasses and red hair; he had a pink chiffon scarf tied around his waist like a sash. Angelo approached them and said, "Well, well, well."

They looked at him in silence.

The red-haired young man pursed his lips, trying to look bored; he was no more than sixteen and he was pleased, clearly, to be seen with Angelo. The silence lengthened.

"I'd introduce you," Angelo said, jerking his head toward his companion, "but we haven't met yet."

The boy gave a little shriek and followed Angelo down the stairs to 17-A.

"Good God," Quinn said.

"I know," Sarah said.

Quinn shook his head, wondering how to get the conversation back on track. But it was too late now, he could see that. Everything had changed. The adventure was cheapened. He shifted from foot to foot, wondering how to end this.

"I'll take a raincheck on that tea, I think."

"A raincheck," she said.

He had never said raincheck in his life. He felt like a fool. And why not; he *was* a fool. He had a good wife. He loved her. She loved him. They were expecting a baby. And here he was about to throw it all away for a twenty-minute roll in the sack with a Boston Brahmin who had a horsey face and was —into the bargain—a shoplifter. He must be losing it. He must be crazy. He must be out of his fucking mind.

"Gotta go," he said, and turned definitively away from her. And from Louisburg Square. And from a life of subterfuge and petty lies and cheap deception. He was done with it, forever.

6

It was the height of the cruising season and, along the Charles River from the concert shell to the Mass. Avenue bridge, dim figures waited tensely on docks and benches, trailed one another in and out of shadows, disappeared in twos and threes behind the concert shell or down the embankment or beneath low-hanging branches of trees.

The evening was dark, midsummer, and rainclouds hid the white sickle moon. On a bench by the riverbank Angelo was smoking a cigarette. He had just given some old guy a blow-job behind the concert shell, and he was resting now with a smoke or two before strolling home for a long pleasant evening with Kierkegaard's *Either/Or*. He wasn't in the mood for any more sex.

"Mind if I sit down?"

"It's your choice."

The man sat on the bench next to Angelo and looked out over the river.

"Nice night."

"Mmm."

"You, uh, interested in company?"

Angelo turned to look at him, taking in at a glance the raw silk jacket, the expensive shoes. He could smell the booze on the man's breath.

"Do I pass muster?"

But Angelo continued his inspection in silence. The man was forty, forty-five. Blond, jawline going slack, but still passable, a good chest, muscles. A former football player... from Lexington, or Winchester maybe. Married. And very nervous.

"I can pay."

Angelo smiled.

"Fifty? Is that enough?"

Doing it for money. Why not? It had been a long time since he'd done it for money.

"How about it? Sixty? I can't go any higher than sixty. That's all the cash I've got."

"You don't carry American Express?" Angelo asked him.

"Are you kidding? You take American Express?"

"Let's settle for fifty. Afterward, if you think I'm worth more than fifty, you can give me a tip."

"You know what I like about you?" the man said, slipping his hand into Angelo's crotch. "You look like a man, a real one."

Angelo removed the hand and thought for a moment. Was this one of those maniacs who proved his manliness by sucking off queers and then carving them up with a paring knife? He'd never run into one, but the law of averages said that eventually he would. He turned and stared at the man, taking in once more his glassy eyes, his boozey breath, his heavy good looks.

"Come on, come on," the man said. "I'm so hot I'm gonna come right here, just looking at you."

No, not a maniac. Just psychologically all fucked up. "What's your name?" Angelo said.

The man thought for a moment, and then said, "Jim?"

And so they went back to Angelo's apartment at 17-A Louisburg Square where they had a quick drink and then tumbled onto Angelo's bed, groping and writhing, breathless, until one came and then the other came, and then they lay on their backs, recovering.

Angelo stared at the ceiling and entertained his customary post-coital thoughts. What an interesting illness sex was. How unvarying: a fever in the blood, five minutes in the sack, and then complete recovery. Followed by boredom with the whole sexual enterprise, until once again—*ta-daa!*—the cock crowed. He wondered if heterosex was the same. He supposed it was. Imagine, though, if sex and love could somehow exist together; if you could do all that sucking and fucking with somebody you loved, somebody who loved you. That would be paradise, even for old Kierkegaard. Well, it was impossible, so you had to settle for the next best thing: loving one person, and sucking and fucking with another, usually a stranger. But whom did he love, really, when you got right down to it? Anybody? Himself?

The man lying next to him, Jim or whoever he was, got up now and began dressing. He put on his shorts, and his socks, and then, more quickly, he pulled up his pants, zipped them, tightened his belt. He looked very stern, almost angry. He had disappeared into himself.

Angelo lay on the bed watching him. He liked seeing a score get dressed, returning from the reality of sex to the pretense of daily life. It was a nice part of the ritual, to lie there naked and watch the transformation.

"Faggot," the man said in a mutter, fumbling with his shirt buttons. "Fucking goddamn faggot." He undid his pants, shoved his shirttails inside, and then zipped the pants again. He paused, his hands at his belt, as he looked over at the bed. He was tense, breathing fast. "Cocksucker!" he said. "Pussy!" He tightened his belt, yanking it hard, and then he stopped altogether and just stood there motionless, looking.

There was a long silence in the room.

He approached the bed, uncoiling the belt from his waist

and winding it slowly, neatly, around his hand, looping the belt so that the buckle faced out.

Angelo lay there, watching. And then, in a single quick motion, he brought his knees to his chest and jackknifed his body off the bed and into a standing position, his legs spread, his back to the wall, ready for the attack.

The man was surprised, but only for a second. With his knee he nudged the side of the bed, edging it closer and closer until Angelo was trapped between the bed and the wall, with no room to move. He gave the bed a final hard push and Angelo, trying to keep his footing, slipped on the Kierkegaards he kept piled on the floor, and fell sideways against the night table. He felt a hot liquid pain in his right side and for a second went black.

At once the man was over the bed and on top of Angelo. But he had no room to swing, and Angelo, beneath him, was striking out blindly, trying to push him off. As the man pulled away for swinging room, Angelo caught him in the neck with a hard right punch; he fell back on the bed, stunned. He lay there, trying to swallow, and Angelo stood above him, breathless with his own pain, still trapped between the bed and the wall.

Angelo recovered first. He put one knee on the bed and then the other; the man gasped but did not move. Angelo was propped on his fists, leaning over him; he couldn't get his breath; he couldn't see. He looked up at the man's face but even before he could focus on it, a terrific blow caught the side of his head and sent him backward, crashing against the wall. Everything went black and then red. He heard a strangled cry, "faggot," and then something hard and sharp creased his jaw. He felt another blow, and then another, to his face, to the side of his head, to his stomach, to his head again, and then he felt nothing. He was in a dark place where he waited for the beating to stop.

And so he was not aware that the man continued to punch him again and again, saying "faggot" and "cocksucker," and sobbing finally when he was too exhausted to speak. At the end, he lay next to Angelo's body, recovering, the belt still knotted around his hand.

Two stories above them, Sarah lay in her bath, thinking of Quinn and love. Why not? You had to choose, Angelo said, but then you had to face the consequences of your choice. She moved her hands gently across the surface of the water, letting them come to rest on her small, firm breasts. Quinn, she said to herself, yes, I choose *you*. From downstairs she heard a crash and then silence. She cocked her head, listening; it was probably Angelo's television. She went back to Quinn, and for a long time she imagined him running his hands slowly from her breasts down to her hips, circling the soft mound of her belly, and then back again to her breasts.

Gradually, through her mounting excitement, she became aware of more noise; a shout; a curse. And then suddenly, intuitively, she knew what it was. Angelo. Somebody was killing Angelo, some crazy pickup.

She stepped from the tub, splashing water on the floor and on the mirrored wall. Without wasting time on a towel, she yanked her gown from its hook and tried to pull it on. But she was wet, and the cotton clung to her arms. She pulled harder and the fabric ripped, but she didn't notice. She must not let this happen to Angelo, her only salvation.

With her gown flying open she ran down the stairs and through the living room out to the kitchen. She was barefoot, trembling. She opened the panel that held the spice rack and concealed the narrow stairwell to the apartment below.

"Angelo?" She called again, "Angelo?"

Downstairs there was silence.

She pulled her gown close to her and started down the stairs. She could hear her heart beating, or the blood in her ears, or the blood... She lost her thought, whatever it was, and leaned for a moment against the wall. She was faint. Her eyes glazed over and she tried to draw a deep breath, but she could not. She let out a small involuntary cry. And then, slowly, she continued down the stairs, terrified, in a trance. It could not happen. This could not be happening.

She pushed open the door to Angelo's kitchen just as someone, a man, disappeared down the hall. She moved slowly from the kitchen to the bedroom and stepped inside, not hearing the front door slam, not noticing the shoes he had left behind. Her eyes were on the naked body of Angelo, striped in blood, his head twisted at an impossible angle. So, it had happened to her again.

"I am to blame," she said softly, confessing. "The fault is all mine. I did it. I did it." Her voice rose higher and higher, until at last she was screaming, and she was back again with Raoul and the rain and the blood, and she knew she was mad.

7

"But you are not mad," the shrink said. "Why do you want to think this?"

Sarah, still in the icy calm that had followed her hysteria, listened to the shrink's annoying accent and said nothing.

"You do not want to think this. This is what the world wants you to think, and it is not true. It was true, for a while, but it is not true now."

"Yes?" Sarah said.

"The world likes to put us in categories. That makes it easy to dismiss us. This is a Jew. This is a Black. This is a woman. This is a mad woman."

"Yes."

"But this is not true now. It was true, for a while, but it is not true now."

"No."

The shrink nodded. How good it felt to analyze, and then —instead of waiting an eternity until the patient discovered the truth—to just cut through all this murk and say it straight out. To hell with Freud. She warmed to her task: sometimes an analyst had to teach. "I wear these glasses, do you see, because I have a weakness of vision. You do not wear glasses."

"No."

"No. Your mother has perhaps some weakness of the lungs; she gets colds often; she is prey to pneumonia. Yes?"

"I don't know."

"We don't know, but it is possible. There are people who have some weakness of the kidneys, of the heart, of the liver. When they are unwell, it shows there first of all: in the kidneys, in the heart, in the liver. Yes."

"Yes."

"You have such a weakness, like all of us, but yours is here." She touched the side of Sarah's head, gently, almost lovingly. "A weakness only. You are not mad. Yes?"

Sarah said nothing.

"Yes?"

"Yes."

"Good."

"The weakness is congenital perhaps, or biological, or chemical; who knows. The brain is just another organ, with strengths and weaknesses. You have a small weakness here. We learn to live with this."

"Yes."

"And how do we learn to live with this? You remember, yes? We acknowledge..."

Sarah nodded.

"Yes," the shrink said. "We acknowledge our feelings. We *work* at finding out what we feel. It is hard work."

Sarah nodded again.

"Now, how do you feel?"

"I feel that I'm mad again."

"No! You don't feel that you are mad again. You are aware something has happened to you, but you don't feel mad again."

"No."

"No. You were mad once, you were mad when you murdered Raoul, but you are not mad now."

70

"No."

"There is no connection between Raoul and what happened to Angelo."

"No."

"So. How do you feel?"

"I feel that something has happened that I am not responsible for."

"Good. That's very good. What else?"

"There is no connection between what happened to Raoul and what happened to Angelo. Angelo is not Raoul."

"What *happened* to Raoul? Or what you *did* to Raoul?"

"What I did to Raoul."

"Yes?"

Sarah closed her eyes and said it: "I murdered Raoul and I confessed. But I was not responsible for what happened to Angelo."

"Very good." The shrink leaned forward, pleased. "Finding your brother's body as you did . . ."

"Brother-in-law."

"Finding your brother-in-law's body as you did, unconscious and nude and covered with blood, you would of course flash back to that memory of Raoul. But it is only a memory." She paused, significantly. "You understand this. You know it."

"Yes."

"Do not think of it."

"No."

"So." She waited.

Sarah thought of those stolen purses in her drawer. She had stolen a purse then, too, before that thing happened to Raoul.

"You are thinking?"

After a moment, Sarah said, "I have a weakness, here. Other people have weaknesses, of the lungs or the heart or the liver, and they learn to live with them. I must learn to live with mine."

"This is very good."

"This is very good."

The shrink folded her hands on her desk. She had set things straight. She had tied it all up.

"And so we will see each other a week from now. But, as always...," and she drifted into her speech about emergencies and the answering service and availability.

"Yes."

"Any time," the shrink said, standing up.

Sarah stood too. She was thinking of that week before the murder, when she was obsessed with her periods, with the blood running from her, black and thick, the smell of it, the taste of it. At the end, she had smeared it on his face, his chest, his stomach. Or was it his own blood? She could not remember whose it was.

"Next week."

"Next week."

The shrink frowned a little as Sarah left. It had all been too easy, too quick, too much. She could see that. She had this weakness.

8

Claire stopped at the sunroom to say goodbye to Aunt Lily and give her a quick kiss. She would be back on Monday, she said, early. Aunt Lily nodded, but kept her eyes fixed on the television screen where a very interesting car chase was in progress.

At the front door, Claire paused, uncertain, as she felt the saliva begin. She swallowed quickly, but it continued, sharp and burning in her mouth, so she ran back to the bathroom. She knelt beside the toilet bowl and laid her forehead on the porcelain rim, waiting. The hot stuff gushed from her throat. Once. And then a second time. How was it possible? She had been throwing up almost constantly for the past week. Nothing was left. But again she retched, choking. After a while, her hot face began to cool, and she sat back on her heels, breathing normally. All this, for a baby.

Claire wanted to go lie down on her soft bed, with a light sheet over her, and never get up. But *faciendum est:* Quinn was waiting for her in Boston; it was the weekend of the Fourth; his letter had been so sweet. His letter, she felt, had saved her life, and the baby's life. This was the least she could do for him.

Claire was at the door once again when she thought of Aunt Lily, who must have heard the toilet flush and would worry who it was and what had happened; or maybe she wouldn't. You never knew with Aunt Lily. She was odd and getting odder, a touch of senility perhaps. Claire had not told her she was pregnant.

Dutifully, she returned to the sunroom. The car chase was over now and Aunt Lily gave Claire her full attention.

"Back, are you?" Aunt Lily said.

"It was just nausea," Claire said. "I've had an upset stomach all week."

"Was it a nice trip? How is that Quinn?"

Claire shook her head. "I'm leaving *now*," she said. "I'm just *about* to leave."

"Again? Well, that's nice," Aunt Lily said. "Young married people should be together all the time."

"Goodbye, Aunt Lily."

"Have a lovely bath," Aunt Lily said.

And so Claire was on the highway at last, a box of saltines at her side. They seemed to work. They were the only thing she could hold down. Food in the abstract was as enticing as ever. It was only in reality that it made her sick. But, as always with everything miserable, there was a nice payoff: she was going to look slim and glamorous for a little while longer. For Quinn. He cared so much about how she looked. She pushed the box of saltines out of easy reach.

Quinn. Quinny Quinn Quinn. How sweet his letter was. She had it in her handbag, though she had no need to carry it. She knew it by heart. "I have been thoughtless, stupid, impossible. How can you stand me? You are the only thing on earth I love." She recited the words, doing Quinn's voice. "You are my whole life to me."

A horn honked and Claire realized she was drifting out of her lane; the fender of her little Ford was inches from the car next to her. The driver shook his fist and shouted something she couldn't hear. "You are my whole life to me," she said aloud to him, smiling, and then she turned her eyes back to the road. She recited the rest of the letter, repeating the last paragraph twice.

"I send you all my love, my dearest. We are one person; we always have been, right from the beginning. Claire and Quinn. Quinn and Claire. You know how much I need you and want you and love you. I want whatever you want, and if you want the baby, I want it too. Truly. Honestly. I love only you, always and forever."

The letter had come yesterday, one of her worst days so far. She had spent the past week in despair over Quinn and the baby, trying not to think of alternatives, trying especially not to think of abortion. She had awakened sick, and after a long bath, she sipped a cup of coffee which she immediately threw up. Morning classes seemed endless, and twice during the afternoon she had left class to get sick in the women's room. By sheer effort of the will, she had dragged herself back to class and somehow got through the day. And then, *felix feliciter,* back at Aunt Lily's she found Quinn's letter waiting for her. She read it three times, and then lay down for a while, so she would be her best self when she talked to him on the phone.

When she called him, though, Quinn had sounded strange. He was remote, distracted; he seemed almost to have forgotten the letter. But Claire knew him and did not allow herself to be hurt. She went right on talking through his silences, and after a while he warmed up and seemed more his old self. He was writing, he explained; he was out of it. Finally he asked how she was feeling, and when she confessed she had been sick every day that week, he became the old, warm, loving Quinn she had married.

"You've got to take care of yourself," he said; "you've got to get some rest. You work too hard, you do too much . . . for your class, for Aunt Lily; you do too much for me."

He ended by persuading her to skip the drive to Boston, the

traffic, the hassle, and just spend the long weekend in bed. She needed the rest. And frankly, he explained, he was working constantly at the novel anyway, and he was distracted, he was not himself. And so it was agreed: she would rest and he would write. He would phone her every evening. He loved her. He loved only her.

She went to bed at once and, for the first time that week, slept through the entire night. In the morning, she was sick again. But she spent most of the afternoon in bed and by evening she felt nearly normal. And so she had decided to surprise him with a visit. She would not disturb him, she would let him write; but they would both be aware, every second, that as he sat at his typewriter she was lying on the bed in the next room, near him, loving him.

It was Friday, the evening of the Fourth, and the traffic was ferocious. The whole world was converging on Boston for the Pops concert down at the shell and for the fireworks at midnight. It would be impossible to park. But Claire didn't mind; she was going to spend the weekend with her Quinn, her husband, the other half of her soul.

Sarah said she was going to memorize his body, inch by inch, and Quinn lay back on her bed, waiting for whatever would happen next.

She was stark naked and he was still wearing his shorts, but she insisted. "No," she said. "Don't take them off." And when he slid them down to his knees, she pulled them up again, saying, "Later; later you'll see."

Sarah spread his legs on the bed, so that he looked like the Leonardo sketch, and then she sat between them, her back turned to him, and took his right foot in her hands. She stroked his instep, using one silky finger to draw a line from his big toe up to his shin, pausing a second, and then back

down and around to his ankle. His foot was cold, and it
twitched, and he kept expecting her to put her hand on his
crotch. He wished she would. He had never gone about sex in
this elaborate way.

She was beautiful, or at least she had a beautiful body. Her
skin was white, translucent, and as she inclined her head, her
blond hair fell forward exposing her long neck and one thin
perfect shoulder. In the dim lamplight her back was a perfect
curve of white flesh. He reached out.

"Not yet," she whispered. "Don't touch me yet. We have
all night. I want to memorize each vein, each little hair." She
kissed his ankle softly and then, very softly, the arch of his
foot.

"But I do, too," Quinn said. "I want to touch you."

"Shhh," she said. "After. After."

Quinn closed his eyes and tried to enjoy it. After all, this
must be what grown-ups did, real people. He raised his head
from the pillow and looked down. He was nice and stiff inside those damned boxer shorts, but he couldn't guarantee
how long it would last.

She traced a line from his arch to his ankle and straight up
to the soft skin at the back of his knee. His shorts jerked and,
involuntarily, he groaned.

He was a little drunk, Quinn told himself, but even as he
said it, he knew it wasn't true. Two drinks did nothing to
him. It was the hateful, guilt-loving Catholic still lodged inside him that wanted an excuse. For sin. But this wasn't sin; it
was an adventure. So live a little.

He reached down and touched himself. It was still up, still
hard; it was fantastic. "Look at this," he whispered to her.
"Take a look."

Sarah turned, not looking, and said, "Wait. I want you to
wait," and she ran her finger from his knee to his thigh, stopping at the hem of his shorts. She lay her palm flat against the

inside of his leg, pressing gently, smoothing the hairs with her thumb. She let it rest there for a long time.

Quinn lay back, deciding at last just to let it happen, whatever it was, and try to enjoy it for once.

Sarah was sitting by his side now, her hands on his right arm. She touched his wrist, his forearm, the inside of his elbow. She traced a vein, slowly, up beneath his arm, then kissed his armpit, tugging the soft hair lightly with her teeth. She kissed his chest.

Quinn opened his eyes and looked at her. He was not even embarrassed. This strange girl. This beautiful girl. Her breasts were small and hard and very white. The nipples were a child's. They were so pink, so perfect that they looked unreal. "I have to," he said, putting his tongue to her breast and raising his hand to the smooth skin of her belly.

"No!" she said, and pulled away.

"Oh, you bitch," he said, surprised at himself. Was he playing a part? "You fucking bitch." He smiled.

Her lips skimmed his forehead, she blew lightly into his hair, put her tongue in his ear. She kissed his eyelids. "You have beautiful eyes," she said, and traced his brow with her finger. "Your nose, your mouth. Beautiful."

"Not my mouth."

"Beautiful." She kissed his neck. "And now your left side," she said.

"Please."

"We have time," she said. "And time, and time, and time."

She did his arm, his hand, his chest, his leg, his foot, the inside of his thigh.

"And now," she said, hunching up between his legs.

"Let me take these off," he said.

"No."

"Let me get my cock out, at least."

"Don't use that word," she said. "Lie back."

He snorted once—don't use that word—and lay back.

"I'll trace the outline of your thing. I'll make it mine." She pushed the hard bulge up until it lay against his stomach and then, slowly, she ran her finger along one side and around the head and back down the other side. She did this again. And again. "You're circumcised," she said. "I like that." She pressed the head between her thumb and forefinger. A drop of moisture appeared through his shorts. "Good," she said, tracing still. With her other hand she cradled his testicles through the cotton cloth, kneading them gently, and still her fingers traced and traced. "You're circumcised," she said again. Her voice was dreamy, from some other place. "You're cut. That's nice."

"I'm going to come," he said.

"Yes," she said. "Yes," and she lay her full weight upon him, she clung to him, so that both their bodies were convulsed, together. He arched his hips, pressing up against her one last time, and then he lay still.

After a while, Quinn said, breathless, "Fantastic. That was fantastic."

Sarah said nothing.

He could feel her warm face against his chest and he could sense the rise and fall of her breathing. He was covered in sweat. He would get up and take a shower as soon as she moved. But she showed no signs of moving. He closed his eyes to rest for a minute.

When he opened them, some time had passed. He took in several things at once. His shorts were gone. He was erect again. Sarah was kneeling between his legs. He raised his head from the pillow, and as he did, Sarah stopped what she was doing and smiled up at him. Her eyes were glassy.

"My cock!"

She held it in one hand, firmly, while with the other she used a lipstick to color it blood-red. She had finished the head and was making red stripes the length of the shaft. "It's just a lipstick," she said, holding it up for him to see. "Summer Blush."

He had begun to go limp, but he came back strong as he watched her methodically drawing those red lines, pinching a little, making the lipstick pull the tender flesh taut. He lay back and tried not to think. He wanted to feel it all, to feel everything, for once in his life. He arched his hips up toward the pull of the lipstick, and he heard her say, "Ahh," heard her say, "You'll last longer this time," heard her say, "Do it," and then he felt her forcing herself on to him, felt her opening to him, felt their flesh rocking together, pulling and kneading. This went on and on. He succeeded finally in feeling it all.

Bostonians from ten suburbs had emptied into the city and they had parked their cars everywhere: in driveways, at hydrants, on the greenbelt and sidewalks, in tow-away zones. It was the Fourth of July, and everyone had come for the Pops concert by the river, and for the fireworks afterward. Traffic was terrible.

It should have been impossible to find a parking space, but Claire—feeling magic, feeling invincible—found one immediately, right in front of 65 Marlborough. It was going to be a perfect weekend.

She bounded up the stairs and greeted ugly little Leopold who was peering, as usual, through the spokes of the bannister. He said something, but Claire ignored him and concentrated on catching her breath. Then she threw open the door, calling, "Surprise! Surprise!" No one answered. And at once she realized Quinn was not there. She felt deflated, angry almost; she wanted to cry. Again she heard that ugly little child saying something.

"What?" she said, not very pleasantly.

"I saw Mister?"

"Yes? What about Mister?"

"I saw him."

"Where did you see him, Leopold? When?"

Leopold lowered his eyes, shy again.

"Did he go out? Did he go out a little while ago?"

Leopold looked up at her and then looked down.

"Oh, for God's sake," she said. "I must be out of my mind. Good-bye, Leopold," and she went inside and shut the door, hard.

"In the Public Gardens," he said. "With Miss Slade."

But nobody was there to hear him.

Claire had been waiting three hours now, and still there was no sign of Quinn. It was dark outside. She could hear people laughing in the street as they went to and from the concert at the river. And now and then, during the parts that were heavy on brass, she caught a few bars of music.

At first she was anxious about him. She unpacked her things and hung them in the closet, she freshened her makeup, she pulled a comb through her hair. And then she stood at the living room window looking down at the street. He'd be along in a minute, coming back from...where? Everything was closed. Was he out buying flags? Balloons? She kept on watching.

Another hour went by, and Claire's anxiety turned to annoyance. She had driven all this way just to see him. She was pregnant. She was sick. And he, where was he? Out somewhere, having a good time. But not at the concert, unless he'd gone just to stare at people. Quinn hated music.

He had not even left her a note. She checked the hall table for the hundredth time. Of course he wouldn't have left her a note. He didn't even know she was coming. But maybe he'd written it and simply forgotten to put it on the table. He was always absentminded when he was working on fiction. Once, at Williams, he had made a pot of tea, and instead of drinking it, he had put it in the refrigerator. Another time he had actually thrown his books in the trash and taken the garbage to school. So perhaps, after all, his note was still in the typewriter. Dear, fuzzy, distracted Quinn.

She went to his study and looked at his typing desk. Nothing. His notebook was there, and an opened letter, and the few sheets he'd written for his novel, but no note to her.

She looked around the room at the books, the filing cabinet, the typing table; at the pictures on the wall, his framed *New Yorker* cover; at the braided rug on the floor. Something was missing. Quinn's clutter. Quinn's crazy sense of fun. Quinn himself was missing.

But that was silly. Quinn was hers, the same as always; just think of his letter. Claire and Quinn. Quinn and Claire. He hadn't yet recovered from the tenure trauma, that was all. He had no job. He was worried about money. Poor Quinn; she wanted to hold him in her arms and comfort him.

She went to the living room and sat there in the dark; she would close her eyes and rest, and wait for him. But in a few moments she was in the kitchen making herself a drink. She shouldn't have alcohol, she supposed, *causa infantis,* but she was disappointed, she was worried. And it was a lot less caloric than a piece of chocolate cake.

With the drink in her hand, she walked from room to room, putting on lights, making the place homey. She leaned against the door to the living room, and smiled: the hostess. When Quinn wrote his novel and became famous—well, not famous, but well-known among book people—she would have small dinner parties for his new friends in the Boston literary world: other writers, critics, editors from the *Atlantic* and Little, Brown. She would wear black—it was slimming —and... *where* could he be?

"Quinn!" she shouted, "Qui-i-i-in!"

She felt foolish. *"Amens es, Clara;* you're losing it," she said, and then, answering herself, *"Nullum magnum ingenium sine dementia."* Nietzsche said that, or Kierkegaard. One of those.

She poured herself another drink, just a little one.

She went to the door of his study and stood there, trying to see Quinn at the typewriter, her Quinn looking up at her with his big smile, that tiny imperfection on his upper lip. Quinn.

"Hello," she said, "lover."

She walked to the typing desk and picked up the letter. The envelope had a Washington return address. Washington? She put it back on top of his notebook and stood looking at it for a moment. It was open already; there would be no harm. She picked it up again and turned it over in her hands. On the back, in Quinn's handwriting, she read: S = impetuous, unpredictable, a creature of appetites.

Between Quinn and Claire there was absolute trust. They had never discussed it; they simply knew it; it was a given. A lie, deception of any kind, was unthinkable for either of them. Quinn had said to Claire once—not bragging, just stating a fact—that he could not remember ever having told a lie, not once in his entire life. He would never dream of reading letters she received, would not even ask her about them.

But this was intriguing, this S from Washington, who was impetuous, unpredictable, a creature of appetites. Claire pulled the letter from its envelope and read it.

"Dear . . . ," and then *"Mr. Quine"* was typed in. "Have you thought about leaving your loved ones lately? Have you ever thought about Mrs. Quine as a widow? Well, think now, before it's too late." It was a computerized form letter selling five varieties of life insurance.

Claire was furious with herself. How could she do such a

83

terrible thing. Invade his privacy. Betray his trust. It was stupid of her. Unworthy. She put back the letter and left the room.

But why had Quinn kept it? For the note, of course. About S. S? Something for his novel. S.

Claire finished her drink and began to pace: from the living room in the front of the house to the bedroom in the back, with a glance in the study as she passed it either way. Oh, *why* had she looked at the letter? *How* could she have done something so petty, so stupid? She began to cry; it was this baby's fault; she had never been like this before, doubting her Quinn, spying on him.

"Well, *experiendo discimus,*" she said. She would learn from this; she would be as trusting and as trustworthy as Quinn himself. Life was too short to be anything less.

In the kitchen she poured herself another drink. She would leave it on the counter until Quinn came home, and then they'd have a nightcap together. She would tell him how worried she'd been that something had happened to him; an accident, a mugging; and then he'd hold her, and everything would be all right. *Had* something happened to him, she wondered? No. Not to Quinn. He was down by the river watching people. Or off making love with S, that creature of appetite.

Quinn? With a lover? She laughed suddenly. Quinn wouldn't know what to do with a lover. Wham, bam, thank you, ma'am. But where *was* he? And *who* was this S?

Grim with determination, with her teeth clenched so hard they hurt, Claire marched into Quinn's study and picked up his notebook from where it lay beside the typewriter and began to read.

Her eyes raced from line to line, barely seeing the words, hardly taking in their sense. She was looking for signs of betrayal, for mention of a lover. But she found only a jumble of impressions, a writer's scribbling as he attempted to generate his story: a shoplifter, a store detective, S and Q and A. S for shoplifter, of course.

Claire breathed a little easier; she was safe, still; there was no betrayal here, no lover.

Suddenly she realized she was very tired. She put the notebook back in the study and got her drink from the kitchen counter. She drank it in three gulps and then lay down on the living room couch, abandoning herself to sleep.

But sleep wouldn't come. She had betrayed his trust by looking at the letter and then at the notebook; there was no getting around that. Still, anybody could see she wasn't herself. She was half-crazy with worry. She was pregnant, after all. Besides, what harm had been done? If she didn't tell him, he would never know. So. She would say nothing. Let sleeping dogs lie. *Canis dormiens, quiescat.*

In a while she felt a little better.

So Quinn was working on a detective novel. How interesting. And how unlike him. Claire reflected on this.

Could it be a serious work? *The New Yorker* did not publish detective stories. But perhaps this was just a break from his really serious writing, the way the English did it: translate the *Commedia* and then write a mystery novel. Well, at least it wasn't about a professor losing tenure. Just a detective and a shoplifter and a scholar. As usual, Quinn had spread himself out among all the characters: the detective looked a lot like Quinn himself; the scholar had Quinn's job and Quinn's lip, exaggerated of course; and the woman had Quinn's air of mystery—impetuous, unpredictable, blah, blah, blah. Claire was disappointed the woman did not resemble her. In his *New Yorker* story the heroine was recognizably Claire—tall instead of short, and glamorized a little—but in every important way,

Claire. This new woman, this S, was blond and thin and aristocratic, more like that Sarah Slade they had met a week ago outside La Cigale. With a gay gigolo, or whatever he was.

And then it came to her in a rush: Sarah Slade, Angelo, Louisburg Square. S and Q and A. "I believe you've met," Angelo had said to Quinn, indicating Sarah Slade. Quinn had been uncomfortable with them, even rude. Why? Could it be? No, it couldn't be.

Claire got herself a drink and took it to the study. She went over his notebook slowly, methodically, doing research. Quinn's fascination with S told Claire everything she needed to know. She set out for 17 Louisburg Square.

Midnight struck, and fireworks illuminated the black sky with stars and flowers and fountains of color. Cheers went up, applause. The Boston Pops was playing "Stars and Stripes Forever." It was the Fourth of July. Independence Day. For a moment everything went silver, and then black, and then a large American flag unfolded in the sky above the Charles River. It shimmered there while thousands of people watched, and even Claire, standing beneath a tree in Louisburg Square, raised her eyes to marvel at this pyrotechnical feat. She pondered, bitterly, the many things that man was capable of.

At the sound of the fireworks, Sarah rolled over in bed but did not wake up. Quinn came in from her dressing room, looked at her for a minute, studying her naked sleeping form, and decided she was not going to wake up for some time. He had never seen anybody sleep like this; as if she were unconscious; dead, almost.

Quinn returned to the dressing room and his exploration of her closets. The dressing room was actually a wide passage leading to the bathroom; there were closets on either side. He poked through plastic bags containing long dresses and short

dresses and tailored suits. Coats were by themselves in a separate section. Skirts and blouses in another. Everything was
wool or cotton or silk. A chest of drawers of some pale wood
held her sweaters. Shoes were lined up on long racks elevated
a few inches above the floor. There were hatboxes and handbags on a high shelf that ran the length of the closet. What a
setup, Quinn thought. How Claire would love to have something like this. And he would get it for her, too, some day.

In the bathroom, he peed, and then stood looking at himself in the mirror. His cock was still red from the lipstick, so
he stood on tiptoe at the high sink, and washed his crotch
with soap and water. He dried himself and looked in the mirror again. Pretty good, for an old guy. And he certainly had
performed well. Sex was fun. He gave a couple of pelvic
thrusts in the mirror. Sex was wonderful.

Quinn walked through the dressing room to the bedroom
and stood looking out at the Square. The sky was lit by
streaks of red and silver, but the best view would be from the
back of the house. He crossed the landing to Sarah's studio,
peered in through the open door, and then walked—naked
still—to the double windows that looked down over the city,
stretching away to the riverbank.

An enormous American flag unfurled in the sky, and the
Pops played "Stars and Stripes Forever," and thousands of
voices cheered.

"Hooray for our side," Quinn said, and went back to check
on Sarah. Still asleep. He returned to her studio to watch the
last of the fireworks.

He was naked and felt good about it. He never walked
around naked at home, with Claire, but it felt natural here.
He felt more in touch with the real Quinn. He put his hand to
his crotch and scratched, nonchalantly, the way the guys had
done in high school during gym. He was one of them at last.

Quinn flicked on an overhead light, deciding to have a look

around, though there was not much to look at: a high stool, an empty easel, a work table covered with crude sketches. No other furniture. The place was littered with paints and little bottles of stuff and abandoned sketch pads; it was a mess.

On the floor at one side of the room, large canvases leaned against the wall, three and four deep, their painted sides turned away. Quinn tipped one toward him, surprised. And then another. And another. They were awful things: abstract expressionist, he supposed. Muted colors in huge blocks— land masses, or chunks of water, or sky—were piled on one another, as if all creation were jumbled together, and might slide, crumble, collapse at any minute. And the colors were ugly. Muddy things. All the light was mixed with dirt. They were landscapes for a nightmare. Quinn tipped them back against the wall. *"Sufficit,"* he said. "Sufficient for the day is the fucking thereof."

He went to take another look at Sarah. Out. Gone. Zonko.

In the studio closet there was painting gear, rolls of canvas, turpentine. Nothing interesting. He looked in the bathroom. Towels and soap, the medicine chest empty and not very clean either.

He took another look in the closet; on the left side were four built-in drawers. Quinn tugged on the top drawer until it opened: inside were some old brushes clotted with paint, a bottle of fixative, six broken crayons. Quinn touched each item as if he were counting them. The second drawer was empty, and so was the third. But the bottom drawer had something in it: three handbags of different sizes and colors. One of them was smallish, rectangular; a Godiva bittersweet chocolate brown.

Quinn knelt by the drawer and took up one of the hand- bags. He opened the flap. Bonwit Teller, the label said. The price tag was still attached.

For a second he was frightened and wished he had his

clothes on, but as he turned the bag over in his hands, slowly, he began to feel aroused. Sarah Slade really *was* a shoplifter, and he had just been screwing her. A thief. His heart speeded up. He was excited now. He stood, and dropped the purse into the open drawer. He pushed the drawer closed with his bare foot.

Never before had he felt excited in this way. Deep in his groin there was an ache, a kind of anger. He wanted to let it out, he wanted to fuck her, hard, again, right now. He allowed himself a tight little smile. At last, he was beginning to understand what sex was about, how it worked. "My big red cock," he said, weighing it in his hand. He flicked out the studio light and returned to the bedroom.

He was about to enter her while she was still asleep, but something made him wait; her defenselessness, perhaps, or her small breasts with their tiny perfect nipples. No, he would not take her this way. He would give her something instead. He kissed her awake, and she smiled dreamily, lifting her arms to him, clasping them lightly around his neck.

"My turn now," he said, and for a long time he did to her all the things she had done to him, though he did them less gently, less slowly. He learned her body, inch by inch, and then he mounted her, letting that ache in his groin and that long slow anger burn and burn and burn into the core of her, until he was done, and she was done, and still they ground their emptied flesh together, ashes and no more.

Claire's long night drive was nearly over at last. The histrionics were over too, she was sure of that; she would cry no more tears for herself and no more tears for Quinn. What mattered now was this: to decide what she wanted, and then to get it.

Claire had cried silently in the dark of Louisburg Square

and she had continued to cry on the short walk back to Marl-borough Street. Quinn was still not home, however, and she cried loudly now, and for a long time, waiting for him to return. She lay on their bed, and struck her belly with her fists, lightly, halfheartedly, and then she sobbed into her pillow. She wanted to murder this baby; it was his fault; his; she knew it was a boy; another man in the world to torment women and betray them. She wanted to murder Quinn. She gave herself up, for the first time in her life, to an uninter-rupted orgy of grief.

But then it struck her; if Quinn came home now, she would lose him forever. Her eyes were red, her face swollen. She was a mess. Men did not love hysterical women, or spying women, or women in tears. She had to get away.

She put back his notebook—next to the typewriter, and at a slight angle. She put back the envelope, on top, face up. She put away her glass. She fluffed the pillows and smoothed the bed. And then she walked from room to room, checking for evidence. All clean. Now if horrid little Leopold kept his mouth shut, she could make it back to Hanover and Quinn would never be the wiser.

He would not know she knew. That's where her power lay.

But hours later, as she drove her little Ford through the streets of Hanover, the entire night began to seem unreal. Quinn having an affair? With a complete stranger? And all this hysteria, the tears, the baby. Truly, she must be losing her mind.

What she wanted was Quinn. And she had him. And he had her. All the rest was simply baby-fever.

She parked the car in Aunt Lily's driveway. She would get some sleep, she would have some breakfast, and tomorrow she would phone him, her Quinn. He would tell her he had been at the concert by the river. She would tell him how crazy she had been, that she actually thought he was having an affair. They would laugh, and they would love each other, and all of this would be a bad dream.

9

"Hello," Quinn said, more an accusation than a greeting. He had been in bed for only an hour, and he was in a deep trough of sleep. He had no wish to rejoin the real world, not even briefly, not even via telephone. And then he noticed he was erect again, ready for it; overnight he had become a sex machine. "Hello," he said, nearly awake this time.

"Sweetheart? It's me. Claire. I'm sorry I woke you."

"Oh," he said, pushing himself up in the bed. "What time is it?"

"It's nine. It's almost nine. Quinn?"

"Nine. Oh, Christ, I've been in bed only... How are you, honeybun? I couldn't sleep worth a damn last night. The fireworks and the crowds and everything."

There was a pause on the line. And then Claire said, "Oh, Quinn, I've been so silly. When you weren't there last night, I got absolutely frantic. I was half-crazy..."

"It's all right," Quinn said, beginning to talk over her words. "I had the phone unplugged. I was trying to work on my novel..."

Claire interrupted him: "But there was nobody home, and I waited..."

"I was home; I just had the phone unplugged and..."

"You weren't *there* and I waited and waited..."

"Claire?" he said. "Listen, Claire..."

"I'm not talking about the phone; I'm talking about being there..."

"I'm trying to tell you. I *was* here. I was writing. I had the phone unplugged and that's why you weren't able to get me." Claire stopped interrupting and Quinn rushed ahead. "I'd been getting these phone calls all afternoon, wrong numbers, and it was driving me crazy because I had just gotten on a roll with the novel, and I was afraid the interruptions would make me lose it, you know, and so I unplugged the phone."

"Oh, Quinn," she said, aching.

"All right, maybe I shouldn't have. But I called you before I unplugged it, because I promised I would. Right?"

She was silent.

"I called you twice, in fact. But there was no answer. Claire?"

"There was no answer," Claire said.

"No. There wasn't. Well, I didn't let it ring very long, because I figured you were out at the library or something, or if not that, then you were lying down, and I didn't want to wake you."

More silence.

"Claire? What's the matter with you?"

"I'll call back later." Her voice was dead. "I can't talk now."

"Oh, Christ."

"I'm sorry. I just find this awfully hard to take right now. I'll call you this afternoon."

"Claire? Claire! Listen to me. Now don't pull this stuff on me. You're always pulling this stuff. I don't exactly need this shit. You called, and we'll talk, and we'll talk now."

Again she was silent.

"What the hell do you expect of me? What the fuck do you *want*?" He listened to the silence on the other end of the line. "I've been fired from my job, I've got no future and no money, I'm married for Christ's sake to a woman who's *preg-*

93

nant, with a *baby,* and for once my writing starts to go well, and *you* get mad. That's terrific. That's really terrific. It makes me feel really special. You know?"

"I just want to know one thing. I just want to hear you say one thing."

"Christ."

"All right?"

"I'm sorry I didn't call," he said, exhausted.

"I'm not talking about that. That's not what I care. I want to know one thing. Are you having an affair with somebody?"

"Are you crazy? Are you going around the bend, Claire? Where do you get such ideas? What in hell could possibly make you think such a thing? Hah? Would you tell me that?"

"Are you having an affair? Or aren't you?"

"That's insulting, Claire. That's beneath you."

"The answer is yes. Or no."

He heaved a sigh, pure exasperation. "No," he said, "I am not having an affair." His voice sounded tentative even to him, so he pretended he was in the witness box. "I am not having an affair with anybody. I have never had an affair with anybody. I never will have an affair with anybody. Is that clear enough? Are you satisfied now?"

"I want to believe you," she said.

"Oh, Claire. We can't fight like this. This is terrible. This is . . . absurd. We're not like this. It must be the pregnancy that's getting to you. Why are you acting this way?"

"I just feel so lost, Quinn. I just feel . . ." Her voice rose: "If you left me, Quinn, I think I'd kill myself."

"Oh, Claire. This is so . . . bad."

"Yes."

There was a long silence on the line. Either of them could have spoken. Neither did.

So, it's begun, Claire thought; the end of all this has begun.

"I can't talk anymore; I have to hang up," she said.

Quinn held the dead phone in his hand, looking into it, as if he might see there just how much she knew, how much she suspected, how much she could figure out. After a while he smiled, putting the receiver back on the cradle. He had two women—two—who were crazy for him.

10

Angelo was propped up in bed, pillows at his back, books scattered at his side, Vivaldi playing softly on the stereo. He smiled a little, and then winced in pain.

His jaw was swollen and a large patch of greenish purple had begun to appear around his right eye. A small cut marred his upper lip. Beneath the sheet, his body was covered with scrapes and bruises. Remarkably, despite the thoroughness of the beating, he had no broken bones.

He was drinking a cup of tea Porter had made for him. "This is the life," Angelo said. "Kierkegaard, a cup of tea, and thou."

"Does it hurt to talk?"

"No. It hurts to inhale, and it hurts to exhale, but apart from that, it doesn't hurt at all."

Porter smiled.

"It's called the human condition. Fear and trembling. Sickness unto death."

Porter was lying across the end of the bed, propped up on one elbow; he squeezed Angelo's foot beneath the sheet.

"Thank you for the tea. It's good." Angelo reached down and touched Porter's blond head, gently, as if he were conferring a blessing. They remained silent for some time.

"Why don't you stop all this?" Porter said finally. "It's so dangerous, Angelo. It's so unnecessary."

"*C'est moi,*" Angelo said.

"But you don't know whom you're picking up. He could be a lunatic, a murderer. He could have AIDS, for all you know."

"So could I, for all you know."

"Don't."

"So could you, for all you know."

"Don't talk like that. Please."

"Fear and trembling, Porter. That's the name of this game."

"But it doesn't have to be, Angie. We've worked out something good, something that matters. I love you, and you love me, and that's all we should care about."

Angelo looked at him and said nothing.

"I know. There are sacrifices, real ones, in the way we live. Naturally. Times we'd like to be together when I have to be with Maria and the kids instead; the holidays, Christmas. And I can't be with you as often as I want to anyhow, holidays or not. We can't go out like a couple, like two people in love. But those are the compromises we have to make. Isn't that right? Not to mention the duplicity. That's just how it is. And it's not too hard. It's not too much to give up."

Angelo said nothing.

"When you love two people, you have to give up something. You can't have it all. Not all the time, anyway. We knew that at the beginning."

Silence.

"We love each other." Porter was pleading now. "That's all that matters. I love you."

Angelo took Porter's hand and squeezed it. He shook his head.

"Don't say it, Angie. Don't."

"I have never loved anybody," Angelo said. "I don't know what love is."

"That's not true. You love me. We have incredible sex together. I think of you constantly. You couldn't act the way you do with me, if you didn't love me. Who do you talk to the way you talk to me? Nobody. There isn't anybody. And it isn't just sex; it's a hundred other things. There's my sister; you love her too—poor crazy Sarah—or you wouldn't... you couldn't do..." He gave up for a minute and then he started fresh. "The thing is this: you've got some crazy idea —out of Kierkegaard or Sartre or Heidegger or I don't know who—that love has to be this supernatural feeling or something, some dark night of the soul, where everything else be- comes unreal and the only thing on earth that exists is you and the person you love, and—I don't know—you automatically *combust* or something. You *explode*. And then you don't have to bother with all the compromises that come from just being alive." He was making his point; he was getting to Angelo. "But there's no way, *no* way, that kind of love can exist in the real world. When the chips are down, it doesn't matter how you feel, whether it makes you happy or miserable or what- ever. When the chips are down, love is what you *do."* He paused for a moment and then repeated, "It's what you do."

"That's very good," Angelo said. "Good speech."

"Well, it's true."

"Gosh, Porter, you must have gone to Haw-vid."

"I learned it from you. You can make fun of me if you want, but I learned it from you, and it's true. And you know it."

Angelo took his hand away and touched his swollen jaw. He closed his eyes for a moment, and when he opened them, he said, "How handsome you are, Porter, with that frown and those age lines." He traced the lines on either side of Porter's mouth. And then he said, sadly, "You can believe what you want to or what you have to. But I've never lied to you, Porter. The truth is that I've never loved anyone. I don't know what it feels like. I don't know what it means."

Porter lay back on the bed and put one hand over his eyes. "I love you," he said softly. "You love me."

Angelo waited awhile and then he said, "I'll read to you, Porter. I'll get your mind off irrelevancies. Listen to this: 'Conventional religions are dream stuff. I have no religion except my own task of being.' I reversed the sentences, actually, for dramatic effect, but never mind. Who do you think wrote that?"

"Barbra Streisand."

"No. It's Murdoch. Big Iris. Or rather a character in Iris." He picked up another book. "Now, listen to this. 'My whole life is an epigram calculated to make people aware.' Guess who?"

"*That's* Barbra Streisand."

"Close. It's Kierkegaard."

"Angelo, do you have to do this? Doesn't your jaw hurt?"

"This is very good for you. It'll give you something to think about besides sex. Listen, now. Kierkegaard's talking about love, okay? You always want to talk about love. Listen: 'An ideal husband is not one who is such just once in his life, but one who is such every day.' Ahem, ahem. And, listen to this, Porter; this one's by me; in green ink, no less; it's written at the bottom of the page; what *earnest* handwriting I had; anyhow, listen: 'Thus, at the decisive moment in a man's life, he discovers he's already made that major decision by the thousand minor decisions that preceded it.' I wonder if I wrote that or if I'm quoting somebody. I wonder what it means. Or what I thought it meant."

"Have you ever thought of going back to school, Angelo? Getting a degree or something? You're not too old. You could get a Ph.D. maybe and teach somewhere."

"Listen now; here's what I'm looking for. He's talking about us, you and me. He says that what a man *is* is determined by what he loves. Got that? There are three kinds of men, he says."

Porter groaned. "Please," he said. "Stop."

"'We may speak of the self as passing through three main stages or spheres of existence: the aesthetic, the ethical, and the religious.'"

"If you don't stop, I'm going home."

"Well, I'll translate it for you. What he's saying is that there are really only three kinds of people. There's the aesthetic type—like me—who lives on his emotions and his senses and who only cares about the search for pleasure. That's me, don't you think? I think so. I'll blow anybody if I feel in the mood. Or if he feels in the mood. Or if there's just a loose cock lying around and there's nothing else to do."

"You're obscene."

"And then there's the ethical type; that's you. The ethical type is a lot like the aesthetic type, except he's not out just for sense gratification; he's big on the idea of duty and moral obligation."

"That's me, all right."

"That's you. You don't suck just anybody's cock; you only suck mine. And then you rush home, dutifully, to be a husband and father."

"Bastard."

"Then there's the religious type. The religious type is Kierkegaard's idea of the fully achieved human being. The religious type stands alone before God. That's it: just man and God. Except that God, being an ironical son of a bitch, puts you in the perfect bind; he always commands the one thing that will practically annihilate you; if you're the religious type, that is. For example, he orders Abraham to kill his son. Or, with the Greeks, he orders Orestes to kill his mother. Always, of course, in the interest of some higher good. For Abraham, it's to prove his obedience to God. For Orestes, it's to avenge the murder of Agamemnon. But the thing is, you're alone: just you and God. You do it or you don't. But either way, you lose, sweetheart. Nice?"'

"Just you and God; that's the religious type."

"Right, Porter. Well done."

Porter thought for a minute. "And who does he get to suck?"

Angelo laughed, and then winced at the pain.

"That's supposed to be some kind of love?"

"The highest type," Angelo said. "The religious type."

"And who *is* the religious type? Not me. Not you."

Angelo thought a minute.

"Well?"

"Sarah," he said.

Porter sat up suddenly. "You bastard," he said. "You lousy son of a bitch, making fun of my sister." Tears sprang to his eyes. "Take that back." He brought his fist up to Angelo's face.

"But I'm serious," Angelo said. "It's what you were saying yourself: when the chips are down, love is what you *do*. Who fits that description better than Sarah?" He took Porter's fist in his hands and held it. "Who do you know who's ever *done* anything for love?"

"But *kill* someone?" Porter said. "That's not love. That's madness."

Angelo shrugged. "The gods are not always kind," he said.

Angelo was lying with his head in Sarah's lap, listening to Act IV of *Les Troyens*. He should probably have been in bed, but he was tired of bed, and had sprawled full length on her living room couch to listen to a little music, and he had laid his head in her lap. Her own head was thrown back and her hair looked nearly white against the blue silk of the couch; her pale hand rested lightly on his brow. They often listened to music in this way; the picture of married bliss.

"Is this the Berlioz or the Purcell?"

"Shhh."

He lowered his voice to a whisper. "Which one is it? I came in late."

"Berlioz. Purcell's was written a hundred and fifty years earlier."

"What's the difference?"

"Purcell is silly."

For the rest of the act, Angelo said nothing. They listened, each in a separate world.

"Do you know what Kierkegaard says about music?"

"I don't want to know what Kierkegaard says about anything."

"He says: 'The most abstract idea conceivable is sensuous genius. But in what medium is this idea expressible? Solely in music.'"

"Shhh," Sarah said.

They listened then, silently, for more than an hour, while Dido's tragic fate as Queen of Carthage and lover of Aeneas was sung in aria and recitative and duet, in quintet and septet.

To Angelo, the music was engrossing; the purity of the voices, the effortless high and low notes, the melodic line absorbed him completely. It was an art form, beautiful, with no meaning. He didn't care what the opera was about.

To Sarah, the music was engrossing in a different way. From her earliest childhood she had attended the Boston Symphony children's concerts at Jordan Hall. She had listened carefully to explanations of how music works, what it does, the miracles of sound. She knew musical forms: sonata, fugue, étude, oratorio, opera. She knew all the instruments, from hearing them and from trying them out. And she knew voice—what was easy to sing and what was hard and what was nearly impossible.

"Je vais mourir," Dido sang, and Sarah—in her mind—sang along with her.

Sarah was utterly lost in the sound. It did not occur to her that Dido was a woman betrayed in love. A woman, abandoned, who refused to go on living. A woman with murder in her heart. Caught up in Dido's song, Sarah whispered along with the music *"en l'éternelle nuit,"* as Dido watched her soul sink to eternal night. It was only an opera; love, betrayal, the dark descent. Sarah heard no more than exquisite sound exquisitely orchestrated, and she was ravished by it.

Angelo, his head in Sarah's lap, had no idea what the words were saying; nonetheless, the meaning beneath the music moved him, and he was caught up in Dido's terrible fate.

Unthinking, Sarah took her hand from Angelo's brow and traced the line of his mouth, feeling him wince as she touched the cut on his upper lip. It was a tiny cut; there would be no scar.

She raised her hand to her hair, her eyes, her breast, touching herself where Quinn had touched her, and she smiled. She was happy. She was in love.

The music, instead of soothing him, left Angelo restless and upset. He said good night, turned off the stereo, kissed Sarah on the cheek like a brother, and went downstairs to sleep. But he could not sleep.

The music had depressed him, and being unable to follow its meaning, he had given his conscious thoughts over to Porter and Kierkegaard and the bland sublimity of death. "The bland sublimity of death," he said aloud, but it did nothing for him this time. Perhaps he had had enough of Kierkegaard.

It was simplistic, of course, to imagine you were one or the other: the aesthetic man, or the ethical, or the religious. You were a little bit of each; *mostly* one, but partly the others.

He himself was mostly aesthetic, that was certain. And partly ethical, maybe, because he *did* feel a duty toward Sarah. But religious? Man and God, face to face, alone?

Alone, yes. He had always been alone. Who wasn't. But alone with God? No thanks, not Angelo. Not Miss Piggy.

Anyhow, you had to be something more than an ex-hooker for God to choose you as his opponent in some mystical boxing ring. You had to be Abraham or Orestes or Joan of Arc, maybe, or even Kierkegaard... presuming, of course, that there *is* a God.

Is there a God? Was there? It would be nice if there were. He believed in God, he supposed; he'd never thought very much about it. Religion was not that big a deal in his life.

He had been raised Catholic; that is, he had made his First Communion and had gone to Confession a few times, and had even attended Boston College for a year... until he tried to make it with his young philosophy professor, the Reverend Francis Xavier O'Brien, S.J., and got thrown out.

That's when it all began, really. O'Brien, newly ordained and desperate for experience, pulled out of the Jesuits and announced to Angelo that he'd given up God for man, and that Angelo was the man in question, and so he wanted to move in with him. Angelo was terrified by the permanent sound of "giving up God for man" but he felt responsible for ruining O'Brien's Jesuit career, and so he said, "Sure, move in, why not, but let's not announce a wedding." They settled down together, the odd couple gone gay, for a lifetime of physical and intellectual bliss. O'Brien got a half-time job teaching philosophy at U. Mass. Boston; Angelo, with family money, stayed home and read Kierkegaard and Sartre and Camus. It was perfect, fulfilling, except that Angelo was becoming rather a bore, the former Father O'Brien thought, and certainly not what he'd bargained for when he left the Jesuits. After a couple months of domestic ennui—*sturm und dreck,* O'Brien called it—they began to hit the gay bars. Almost at once Angelo was seen by someone who knew someone who told someone to tell the boss's lawyer that Angelo was seen in funny company in a funny bar. At once the Tallino name and money and power descended on them. O'Brien was paid off and sent to California, Angelo was sent to a shrink, and peace was restored for a while. There was good news, too: the boy wasn't queer after all, the shrink reported; he was merely depressed.

Then, when everything again seemed normal, or at least under control, Angelo came out of his closet—with, quite literally, a vengeance. The depressed boy, as he referred to himself, seemed determined to squander his life haunting the gay bars and the riverside hangouts and the public toilets. He was defying his family and they discovered they could do nothing. They threatened. They begged. They cut off his money, but he didn't care. He slept wherever he could, with whoever wanted him that night or with whoever could pay; his clothes were borrowed or thank-you gifts; nobody knew when or what he ate. He had become a male prostitute and he seemed perfectly happy.

The truth was that he planned to commit suicide, and didn't care how he lived while waiting to do it. Life seemed to him pointless and cruel; sex made life funny, but not for long; drugs made life worse. He had the feeling that inside his skin he was absolutely alone, and he was waiting for one thing only: to touch bottom, and then to do it.

He read; he thought; he was not a fool. He did not see himself as the romantic Existentialist hero, Sartre refusing the

Nobel Prize, Camus in a fast car. He saw himself as a rich young man who was so fucked up that prostitution was the bright spot in his days. But it was prostitution, in a way, that saved him: it gave him something useful to do with his time; it let him feel needed and less alone; it made him put his suicide plans on hold. And then, when Sarah's sister, Cassandra, died from a drug overdose, Angelo went on a drink-and-drug spree that lasted over a week until, as he expected, he touched bottom, but instead of killing himself, he chose to go on living.

What had happened was this: he decided suddenly that he was a minor character in life, with no tragic fate awaiting him—indeed, with no fate at all—and so he might just as well live. He drifted. He waited. He read his books. And he continued to wander from the bars to the baths to the bushes.

And then Sarah went insane, committed murder, fled the country; her picture was in every newspaper—Boston Deb Murders Lover—along with a detailed account of the crime, though of course the goriest details never reached the newspapers. Here was no minor character, Angelo thought; here was somebody with a fate.

Sarah was, moreover, his own sister-in-law. She had a brother, Porter. Porter was married to Maria. Maria was Angelo's sister. He was linked to fate by marriage, so to speak.

Indeed, very much like one of the Fates of mythology, Sarah's grandmother plucked Angelo from his gay hangouts and set him down in Louisburg Square, with money and a home and somebody to take care of.

So here he was. A minor character in life, with no fate of his own behind him or ahead of him. Without worries. Without love.

He had a friend, Sarah.

He had a lover, Porter.

He had everything he needed or wanted.

Why, then, did he feel hopelessly alone?

Angelo woke to the ringing of the doorbell. But it was not his own doorbell; it was the one upstairs. He put on the light and looked at the clock: 1:00 A.M. There were voices. Laughter. The soft noise of lovers.

The idiot Quinn had come again for the night.

11

In the five days since she had seen the shrink—the five days following her discovery of Angelo's beaten body, and her hysteria, and her crazed confession that she had done it—in those five days, Sarah had made the return to reality by a slow, circuitous route.

She had lived once again through the first bright weeks of her affair with Raoul. She had lived through their first year as lovers, learning the new and frightening things he taught her in bed. She had lived through most of their second year. By now she was well into the best part of their affair: those long summer months when she was sure that no two people had ever loved like this, that the frightening sex acts binding them together would somehow save her in the end, that they would marry and love forever. She had been given a second chance, and this time she would not let it end, this time he would not leave her.

And so she went about her life as if it were real, eating and sleeping and listening to music. But she knew in her heart what was real and what was not real, and she did not intend to discuss it with the shrink.

"So at last you are convinced," the shrink said. "You are not mad. You are not as you were."

"No," Sarah said, "I'm certainly not mad."

"This is good, yes?"

"Yes."

"Good," the shrink said, thinking. They had covered all the emotional ground, and covered it twice, but still something was missing. Something was very wrong. "And so you have completely recovered, in five days, five and a half days, and nothing remains of that bad time when you thought you were once again a murderer." The words seemed to have no effect. She would try another way. "So. You have taught your drawing class with the children, you have listened to an evening of music with Angelo, you have even had lunch at this restaurant. La Cigale? Yes, I think so." She paused. Well, she would have to do it: "And what of this man, the one that follows you?"

Sarah turned her pale gray eyes full on the shrink and said nothing.

"He had an attractive scar. On his lip? On his upper lip. You have seen him again?"

"No," Sarah said, snappish. "I have not even thought of him. I was upset by what happened to Angelo, by my reaction to it. I haven't had time to think of things like that."

The shrink looked at her, puzzled. Sarah had never before lied to her, not even at the worst times. She had held things back, but she had never lied.

There was a long pause and then the shrink leaned back in her chair, waiting for Sarah to speak. Silence filled the room. So. She would have to be directive. Very directive.

"And Claire?" the shrink said, making the name sound ugly. "No Claire either?"

"No."

"This man saw you steal the handbag, he followed you home, you saw him nights—not every night, but some nights, and sometimes in the day—you saw him standing in the Square outside your windows."

Sarah nodded.

"You met his wife, Claire." Again she used that tone.

Again Sarah nodded.

"You insisted—I believe these are your words—'there is no connection, I'm sure, I'm absolutely sure there's no connection between the man and the handbag.'"

Silence.

"The theft. The fugue state."

More silence.

"You found him attractive. You found the scar on his lip attractive. You said—correct me if I misquote you—'It's not at all unpleasant; it's attractive even.'"

"That's right," Sarah said, and returned her stare.

Suddenly the shrink smiled.

Sarah fixed the woman with her pale gray eyes, but said nothing. The shrink continued to smile.

"And you have not seen him?" she said finally. Still Sarah said nothing.

"Why, then, do you think he has abandoned you?"

Sarah went white, just for a second, and then she folded her hands quietly, one over the other.

"He has not abandoned me."

"He hasn't? It would seem to me he has."

"He won't. Not this time."

She is absurd, Sarah told herself over and over. She is fat and ridiculous.

She left the shrink's office with a feeling of relief. She had told her nothing. She was completely safe.

Her heels clicked on the brick sidewalk. Absurd. Ridiculous. A wonderful sound. Real. Reassuring. She entered La Cigale, and Quinn was there, of course, handsome, waiting for her.

"Quinn," she said, a little out of breath, as if she had run to meet him, as if she could not wait. Her gray eyes glittered. She touched his wrist lightly, a promise.

12

Claire was driving home from class—Friday, the last *colloquium Latinum* for this week, *Deo gratias*—and she was trying to think about her baby: a baby was a wonderful thing. It was a woman's natural fulfillment. Or a natural woman's fulfillment. *Quid melior? Mater et infans. Mater potens. Mater purissima. Mater castissima.* She ran through the Mother Litanies of the Blessed Virgin, surprised that she remembered so many of those old hypnotic invocations, and she felt a moment of nostalgia, of longing.

She had given up her Catholicism for Quinn. They had been married by a justice of the peace in an awful little ceremony in the Town Hall. Her religion at first seemed too great a thing to sacrifice, but Quinn had insisted he would not marry in the Catholic Church, and so she did it. She gave up her priest friends, the sacraments, even her prayers. From here on, she would have to rely not on prayer but on luck. It seemed a fair trade at the time. *Ave* Quinn; *Vale Deus.* Hail and farewell. Farewell. Farewell. How ironic words sounded when you said them slowly enough.

Her stomach rumbled. She was hungry, as always, but the thought of food was not the same as eating it. Eating meant throwing up. She wanted never to throw up again so long as she lived, a thought which brought her back again to the baby.

The baby. If only Quinn had been pleased when she told him. If only he had seen it as a happy accident, rather than a disaster. *Felix culpa, non calamitas.* But from the first, his reaction had been disappointment, anger. Accusation, even: "But how could this have happened? How could you have forgotten? Didn't you *think* what this would *mean*?"

Quinn didn't want the baby; it was that simple. And she did want it. She had always wanted a baby. That discovery had surprised her at first, but now it made her feel good about herself, as a woman and as a human being. A little thing, warm, alive, someone to feed and clean and raise, a person that was part of her and part of Quinn. What could be more wonderful? What could make a perfect marriage more perfect still?

"Oh, Quinn," she said aloud, "why are you doing this? Why?" And she beat the steering wheel with the side of her fist.

It was exactly a week since the horrors of the Fourth of July: reading his journal, standing like a crazy person outside *her* house in Louisburg Square, the long drive back to Hanover. And then his lies. He was having an affair with Sarah Slade—where had she heard that name?—and he was lying about it. And they had never, ever, *ever* before lied to each other.

It was now six whole days since she had spoken to Quinn and twelve days since she had seen him. The ache in her heart, and in her brain, was killing her. Sometimes she felt that she was losing her mind.

How had this happened? She had become a joke, a spy, she was chasing madly after a man who didn't want her. He would leave her now, for this other woman.

Somehow she had always known—somewhere beneath the love and the dependence and the business of Claire and Quinn, Quinn and Claire—she had known, deep down, that it would end. He would find someone pretty, interesting, thin, and he would go away with her.

That's what men did. Any man. Every man. They always had. They always would. And the woman—abandoned, pregnant, *fat*—always killed herself. Except in Euripides, whose women—enterprising right to the end—always killed somebody else, even their children.

They were crazy, of course, those enterprising women in Euripides, and she was rock-bottom sane. She was good old Claire, sensible Claire, *mulier fortis*.

Well, she'd had enough of that *stercora*, thanks all the same. She wanted him back. She'd *get* him back, the son of a bitch, because he was hers and because she was not going to lose him to his middle-aged craziness or his tenure blues. *Or* to some Boston Brahmin with a face like a horse and a body like a mink. She would do anything to keep him.

Anything? At once she thought of her baby. Anything but that.

Still, old Claire had weathered too much to let him go without putting up a fight. The secret of holding a man, she knew, was the secret of the relaxed grasp.

It was Friday. She would phone him and say she needed to rest and so she wouldn't be coming down to Boston this weekend.

No pressures on him. No restraints.

She would wait him out. Give him room. Not press or push. She would let him come back in his own time, on his knees preferably, and then she would simply break his legs—break his balls, she almost said—and he would not wander again.

He would confess. She would forgive him. And then, with that relaxed grasp, she would continue to hold him, forever, or for as long as she wanted.

Quinn sat at his typewriter, composing. This was not easy,
but it was fun. He was rewriting chapter three of his novel;
actually, he was rewriting it for the fifth time. He had taken a
lot of notes for it, very detailed stuff that would give it specific gravity, and now he was trying to translate it into a scene
in the most economical, most *stunning* way possible.

This was the big breakthrough for him: this novel, this
chapter.

During the past week he had realized why *The New Yorker*
had bought "Masque" and rejected everything he'd sent them
afterward. In "Masque" he had forced himself to write so
close to the bone that he still couldn't think of what the story
really meant without covering his face in shame. He had disguised the lip as a terrible stutter and he had redeemed his
character with the love of a good woman, but it was the hard
truth beneath the fictional lie that made the story work.

He was going to do it again, only this time he would anato-
mize a sterile soul redeemed not by love, but by sex. The
ambiguities were dazzling. The challenge here was to deal
straightforwardly with sex; no masks, no fictional lies, just
the wonderful revivifying naked truth about himself. And he
would do it, too.

He had never written a sex scene before, let alone an ex-
plicit one, and he was having a lot of trouble getting it right.
There were so many little technical problems: did you call it a
penis or a cock or what? Did you say fuck or make love? And
did you ever, *could* you ever, say cunt? Just how basic could
you get without crossing that line between sexy art and sexy
trash?

There was a further problem: everybody *knew* ahead of
time what you were talking about; Can You Top This? So

wasn't writing about sex a lot like trying to re-create the first time anybody ate a baloney sandwich? "He lifts it in his hands, he feels the texture of the bread, soft, yielding, he bites into it, he chews, yummy yummy, he swallows." But of course it wasn't the same. Sex was unique. Unique and special and, in this book, it would be salvific. But as soon as he wrote the scene, it turned silly. Or boring. Or just dirty. Let's face it, Quinn thought, sex is almost always a disappointment in fiction. Still, he was determined to pull it off successfully.

So he sat at his typewriter doing yet another version of that first night with Sarah. He was working from journal notes he had made on July the fifth, the afternoon following The Event itself, their first time in bed together. The notes had been scribbled in haste, but they were detailed and precise; emotion recollected in tranquillity.

—she said she wanted to memorize my body—
—she ran her fingers (tense, exploring) from the arch of my foot to the inside of my thigh/crotch/groin, teasing, teasing, but not touching my cock which had actually begun to ache. Describe the ache—
—her tongue on my eyelids, the flash of (green?) light, the catch in the throat, the tug in the groin—
—afterward, waking up and seeing my cock blood-red, feeling the pull of the lipstick, surrendering—

The notes went on like this for two handwritten pages. And then there was another page detailing all the things he had done to her.

—arching my back, up and away from her, so that she rose to me, the head of my cock just touching her, just graz-

ing her clit, so that she wanted it inside her, thick and hard
and hot; no, that's a cliché; she was half-crazy—
—our slick bodies; an acid smell, and perfume—
—her lapse into a trance once she'd finally come, the deep
   sleep, as if she were the living dead—
—my feelings: triumph, vengeance, a soaring sense of freedom (something frightening, something kinky?); *com-
   petence,* yes. A lover at last: implications of this? sex as
   salvation? spiritual completion? the true, real, and secret
   discovery of my "self"—

The notes had an immediacy he couldn't translate into fiction.
He had been trying every day for the past week, but no matter how much he wrote and rewrote, the finished scene
always read like some kind of catalogue: A Boy's Guide to
Erotic Encounters.

But he would get it right this time, and if not this time,
then the next: a sex scene that was pure art.

Sarah stood before her canvas, dreaming.

She was painting again, better than she ever had. She had
always wanted to paint, and even as a child she had painted
surprisingly well; it was only when she grew up that other
people taught her what she was doing right and wrong, and
so managed to take all the joy out of it for her. But the joy
was back now. She had found herself once again.

Study had been her great mistake. Study and teachers. She
had studied art for a year at Emerson, and then for another
year in France with some crackpot in a beret, and finally for a
few months at Pratt. At Pratt they told her to forget about
painting, to go into art theory or art history or cataloguing,
because—quite simply—she had no talent. And so she gave

up studying art and returned to Boston, where eventually she met Raoul. In psychiatric detention, after what happened with Raoul, her doctors prescribed painting as therapy. Later, Grandmother Slade got her the job at Pine Hill. And so she had continued to paint, for therapy, and for her job, but mostly because she liked to do it. She loved what she was doing now. She was painting a picture of Quinn.

In the foreground there was heat. Slabs of yellow and slabs of white mixed and blurred and were transformed, one thing becoming another, like light in water. The background was a silver blue—solid, flat. No other color, no sign of life disturbed the canvas. Only warmth and calm and solidity were there.

It was a portrait, of a kind.

This was her new life. She painted each morning in the early light. Lunch with Quinn at La Cigale. And then home to the Square, together, for an afternoon of love. Afterward, they would lie in bed talking and talking. He was gentle, he was tender, he was not like Raoul.

And then Quinn went home to work some more. He was writing a novel. He was happy at last. Every morning he worked three hours; in the afternoon he revised the morning's work. He was dedicated, he was an artist, he was not like Raoul.

And then at night—she never knew when she could expect him—he would ring the bell and she would open the door to him and they would make love like animals, in a slick of sweat. At night he was always the dominant one. She liked that. It was new. He was not at all like Raoul.

There was no connection between Quinn and Raoul. Raoul had been a scientist. He had no soul. He had no feelings. And there was no connection between the handbag and Quinn. Besides, she had put the handbags out of her life forever—at the bottom of a hamper beneath a pile of towels—and they would never be seen again. Not by her. Not by Quinn.

Especially not by Quinn, who had feelings and soul, who would love her and leave his wife, who would save her in the end. She knew it all. It was only a matter of time.

13

"I like this restaurant," Quinn said. They were at La Cigale again, for lunch, another whopper on his American Express card. "I used to worry about how expensive it is, but I don't worry about that anymore. I don't worry about anything anymore."

He smiled at her in that way she liked—with his mouth sexy, a little crooked. Sarah smiled back and raised her left eyebrow just a fraction.

"Snacks?" Quinn said. "Yummies?"

"Not unless you finish your vegetables," Sarah said.

He tried to leer.

For one awful second, Quinn felt like a fool. Quite deliberately, he suppressed the feeling and put his hand to his crotch, touching home base. He was not going to allow guilt to spoil his fun with Sarah; this was a summer fling; a romp, pure and simple, and he intended to enjoy it. He should have done this when he was eighteen; when he was fifteen, for God's sake. It wasn't as if he were taking advantage of her. She knew he was married. She knew there was no future in it. They were adults; they were two mature people allowing their sexual natures a little self-expression, that's all.

He laughed, softly.

"What?" she said.

"Let's go," he said.

"No. Tell me."

"I was thinking of the lipstick. Where did you ever learn a trick like that?"

She looked at him.

"I mean, how did you ever think of it?"

"You don't like it?"

"I love it. It's sexy as hell. Just thinking of it gets me up, up, and away." He looked down into his lap.

"It was a lover I had. He taught me."

"A lover."

"Well, yes."

"Of course," he said. But his voice had changed. He was thinking. "He taught you about the lipstick. This lover did."

"About everything."

The waiter came and took away their plates. Quinn had fallen silent, and used the waiter's presence to continue the silence. But finally they had coffee before them, and no waiter around, and they had to speak again.

"Sorry," Quinn said.

"What's the matter? You can tell me."

"It's nothing, I guess. I guess I'm just immature."

"You can tell me. Or you can ask me anything and I'll tell you. I always tell the truth, even to my shrink. Except lately."

"No. It's silly. But, I mean, I'm just sort of surprised by your having a lover. Before me, I mean. You seem—I don't know—*above* that."

She looked at him.

"Were you lovers for long?"

"Yes."

"Very long?"

"For two years."

"You left him? Or he left you."

"He had a wife in Buenos Aires. He neglected to tell me that minor fact until the end."

"Oh." Quinn fiddled with his coffee spoon, trying to balance it on the rim of his cup. Finally, he put it down and said, "Were there many? Lovers? I mean, have there been?"

"One. Just that one."

"And he's back with the wife, I guess. In Buenos Aires."

"He's dead."

They drank their coffee, and Quinn tried to look at her in the sexy way he had before, but it didn't work any longer.

"I'm sorry," he said.

"I understand."

"I think maybe this afternoon isn't such a great idea after all. I think maybe I should go home and work."

"Whatever you want." She opened her handbag and placed a key on the table midway between them. "So you won't have to ring. The bell wakes Angelo."

"I don't think I should," he said, a vague resolution forming.

Sarah waited.

In his mind, far back in his mind, Quinn could hear himself saying: Frankly, Sarah, I think this has been one of those mistakes people make. I'm happily married; my wife is pregnant; I'm supposed to be writing a book on ninteenth-century Catholicism in America. So it's all over. It was fun, and it's good that nobody got hurt, but it's all over.

Quinn said nothing, however. Instead, he reached out and took the key, which felt cool against his fingertips, but warmed as he held it lightly, uncertainly, in his palm.

Outside on the street, they kissed goodbye. Sarah turned up the hill toward Louisburg Square and Quinn, watching her go, wished he had refused the key. Still, what else could he have done?

He would throw it away. He would toss it from the little bridge in the Public Gardens. As a symbol of his new resolution. For good luck. To be rid of the damned thing.

Feeling better already, Quinn pocketed the key—for now—and started down the hill toward Charles Street. The sun had disappeared behind a dark cloud and for a moment the day seemed unnaturally dull. "'How all nature doth inform against me,'" he said to nobody, and smiled because his mood was really quite sunny and good.

It was the end of the romance. Well, at least he had had one, finally. Moreover, he had acquitted himself well in bed, and *that* was a nice surprise. And he had picked up all the lunch bills, so there was no way she could feel used by him. And the breakup itself had gone smoothly, with nobody the worse for it—not Sarah, not himself, not Claire. He had acted pretty maturely, now that he thought of it.

He would make a new start with Claire, and the baby. He would put all this behind him.

Anyway, who wanted an affair with a woman who was so experienced? And not just experienced but...used. She'd done those sex things with other men. Another man, actually; only one. Still, he had taught her all those tricks, whoever he was, the Don Juan of Buenos Aires. The lipstick. And all the rest of it. Maybe everybody did things like that in Buenos Aires. Well, they didn't do them in Boston, that was certain.

Imagine Claire doing something like that. Imagine even telling her about it. He felt his face go red at the thought.

Good old Claire. Good old wonderful inexperienced Claire. He'd telephone her as soon as he got home. What a bastard he'd been these past two weeks. He'd call and make up with her right away. He was lucky to have her.

Quinn blushed again at the things he had actually *done* with Sarah. If that was his real self, then he wanted nothing further to do with it.

As he crossed the Public Gardens, he debated with himself about throwing the key from the footbridge. It was mid-afternoon; somebody would see him, surely, but did it matter? They were only tourists, Japanese mostly, and the usual bunch of semi-derelicts that hung out there. They'd probably think it was a coin. And then the tourists would all begin tossing coins, hundreds of nickels and pennies and quarters. And the derelicts would dive for them, like those cliff divers in Mexico. He'd start a new industry in Boston. Except the dive here would be about three feet, maybe four.

As Quinn approached the bridge, he felt nervous, self-conscious, and as he stood on it, looking down into the water, he began to feel like an idiot. Somebody would see him, and point, and laugh. Maybe somebody who knew him. Or, worst of all, that damned little Leopold would appear out of the bushes, with his fat face and his little piggy eyes, and say, "I saw you."

Quinn looked up from the water and the first thing he saw was Leopold. He was standing down by the water beside some woman, a teacher no doubt, and another little boy; they were eating ice cream cones. Leopold was staring up at him.

Furious, embarrassed, Quinn abandoned any idea of throwing the key from the bridge, and not knowing what else to do, he waved at the little boy. At once Leopold went shy, and buried his head in the teacher's stomach. Then, recovering, he turned back to Quinn and waved solemnly, with his ice cream hand, and of course in the very next second the ice cream plopped onto the pavement. The woman with Leopold shot Quinn a nasty accusing look before she stooped down to hug the little boy.

Quinn walked away fast, guilty, eager to get back home and telephone Claire.

A Star Market truck was double-parked outside the door, and in the foyer several grocery bags stood against the wall, each one marked 65 Marl–4 in purple crayon. Number 4 was Leopold's place: Quinn snooped. Froot Loops, Oreos, Twinkies, cinnamon doughnuts; all that sugar, no wonder Leopold was such a mess. Underneath were paper towels and oranges and some kind of vegetables and cans of fruit juice and a lot of frozen stuff; nothing interesting. But what had he expected? Eye of newt?

Suddenly the grocery boy came gallumphing down the stairs. He was tall and black, very skinny, with a big behind and a pick for his Afro sticking out of his back pocket. He was singing something with a hard beat. "Hello, there," Quinn said, but the boy ignored him and just kept rapping: "Nine bags of groceries up all those stairs. Nine bags of groceries and nobody cares. Muh-fuggah, muh-fuggah, muh-muh-muh-fuggah."

Quinn took the stairs two at a time. The whole world was crazy; all he wanted now was a little peace, a little normality, and his good simple honest sexless wife Claire.

Incredibly, Claire met him at the door. She was standing back in the foyer, timid, as if she had done something stupid by appearing unannounced in Boston and now she expected him to be annoyed with her.

"Claire, sweetheart," he said. He gave her a quick kiss and then, frightened by the look of fear in her eyes, he held her in a long embrace. After a moment he could feel the tension go from her. He held her closer. "I'm sorry," he whispered, "I've been so stupid. I've been so mean to you."

"No, no," she said. "It's not you at all. It's me. I should know better by now, I should trust..."

"Sit down," he said, "come on, sit down. We'll just sit here on the couch like two old married people who are still in love. Okay? Okay."

They sat on the couch. Claire leaned back and Quinn sat on the edge of the seat holding both her hands in his, looking at her. Her head was thrown back, and if her hair were longer, it would fan out across the cushion the way Sarah's did. But Claire had short hair and it was black. And, Quinn noticed, she had gained weight. The baby. He tried to feel glad.

"How are you feeling, sweetheart? Are you still having morning sickness or has it let up?"

"It stopped," she said, gazing up at the ceiling. "It just stopped all by itself. That often happens, the doctor says, near the end of the first trimester." She had looked frantic only moments ago and now she sounded absolutely content.

"Oh," he said. "Good." And not knowing what to do next, he put his hand lightly on her stomach. "Our baby," he said.

Claire sank deeper into the couch and spread her legs slightly. The movement made her belly puff up and he could see what she would look like—only worse, he thought—for the next six months. He looked at her face; her eyes were shut and she was content as a cow.

"Mmm," she said, reaching out to touch him. "Let's make love," she said.

He was shocked. It seemed, somehow, indecent.

"Lover," she said, moving her hand on his thigh. She had never called him that before; not once. Maybe pregnancy did things to your mind as well as your body.

"Now?" he said.

She got up from the couch, dreamily, almost as if she were imitating Sarah, and walked slowly to the bedroom, unzipping her dress as she went.

"Come on, lover," she said.

Quinn followed her, dutifully, to the bedroom.

At first he found he couldn't make love. Claire's body, without clothes, was the same as always, a little fatter maybe, but he was used to Sarah now and to the long ritual of their lovemaking. Sarah's initiative, her clever hands, her exploration of his body. And then his takeover, that sudden crazy

126

moment when he was completely in charge, and plunged into her, half-angry, half-punishing, and they ground their bodies together in a rush of sweat and semen and hard pulsing blood. This is what he wanted, needed. But with Claire?

He tried and tried.

"That's all right," she said, after quite a while. "We don't have to. I'm beginning to show a little, I guess. The baby."

He wanted to say he was sorry, it wasn't her fault, but no words came. He gritted his teeth and pulled at himself, desperate to get hard, but nothing happened. And then he closed his eyes and deliberately thought of Sarah, touched himself the way she touched him, and finally it began to work. "Here we go," he said nervously, "here we go. Quick. Quick." And at last they had their brief, perfunctory sex.

Afterward, they lay side by side, Quinn with his hand over his eyes.

It had been worse than usual. But the fact that he made love so clumsily, as if he were getting some unpleasant duty out of the way, proved nothing. They were still in love. It was still Quinn and Claire, Claire and Quinn. They had just never been interested in sex, either of them.

Was that true? Quinn thought it was. He would start over at the beginning. He would confess. He would love her.

"I have to tell you something."

"Yes," she said, patient, tentative, as if she expected the worst. And there was something else in her voice.

It crossed Quinn's mind that perhaps she had read his notebook, his novel. No. Impossible. Not Claire. Honesty was the breath of life to her. She was incapable of deceit. He saw suddenly how far he himself had traveled on the road of sex and duplicity and he wondered if he could break it off with Sarah after all. He wondered if he wanted to.

"Well?" Claire said.

"On the Fourth of July? When you called? I *wasn't* here," Quinn said.

"I know."

"I lied to you. I'm sorry."

She waited, hoping.

"I was people-watching at the concert. For my book."

14

Angelo stood before the mirror assessing the damage. Not bad. He was healing well. However, there was a moral to be learned from this: don't fuck around with married queers from Lexington and Winchester.

Before the beating he'd had a face like the Hermes of Praxiteles, but the day afterward it was like something from a film on fag bashing. His eyes had swollen half shut. The left side of his jaw was turning purple. His split upper lip might eventually scar.

But two weeks had passed now and he looked pretty good. Most of the cuts had healed and the bruises were fading. They barely showed beneath the skin bronzer; thank God for Pierre Cardin. Only the little cut on his upper lip still hurt. So he had survived the beating intact, more or less. He'd been lucky.

He gave himself a knowing smile, seductive, and his cut lip stung. Was he going to end up looking like Quinn? On Quinn that little scar was sexy as hell, but Angelo preferred his own face to be flawless. He turned to the left to study his profile. His nose was still perfect.

What a wonderful face he had! He marveled yet again at how truly beautiful it was; not beautiful like a movie star's face, but beautiful in a ravaged sort of way. Used-looking. He stared, trying to get behind his eyes. Who was he, inside there? *What* was he? He looked into the mirror, wondering.

And as he looked, and wondered, he heard Quinn approaching on the sidewalk, his quick feet scuffing on the stairs, and then the heavy door shutting behind him. So, Sarah must have given him a key. Silence followed. A short laugh. A cry of surprise, delight. In a few minutes they'd be whomping away, he supposed. Well, why not.

Because this could not end well: Quinn and Sarah. She had killed a man, for love. Angelo sang a few bars of "What I Did for Love," but his voice was flat and he was too depressed to amuse himself this way and so he went back to contemplating his face.

How could she have killed Raoul? But then how could anybody *ever* kill anybody else? He'd rather be beaten to death, as he almost had been. Yet he himself had a gun in his nightstand right now, a cutie actually, a Walther PPK, automatic, and only about five inches long. It was the gun of choice of the Family this year, a get-well gift from his father's lawyer's gofer. With the Tallinos, killing was a job for somebody who worked for somebody who worked for the family lawyer; besides, the way they looked at it, it was just business. With Sarah, the killing had been madness. Literally, madness. It was the end of her life.

Well, he'd watch for the danger signs. He knew them. He could at least keep it from ending badly, *very* badly. In the meanwhile, why begrudge her a little sex?

Poor Sarah.

Suddenly his eyes filled with tears; poor everybody. Poor Sarah. Poor Porter. Poor Quinn. Poor whatshername... Claire. And poor Angelo too. Why begrudge any of them a little sex? That's how they'd all *gotten* this way: fucking and sucking and squeezing a little juice and a little pleasure out of each other's bodies and what, *what,* was the point of it all?

Who was to blame for all the misery, the loneliness, the endless collision of bodies. This hopeless wreckage. This desperate mess. None of them was to blame.

God was to blame.

Angelo turned away from the mirror and dismissed the thought at once, not because it was blasphemous but because it might be true. Then, like Kierkegaard, he'd be having a quarrel with God. And he had enough sense to know who won and who lost a quarrel with God. Besides, *he* simply wasn't that important; he was just your ordinary, garden-variety queer trying to read Kierkegaard and get laid. A quarrel with God?

"None today, thank you," Angelo said, beating back his momentary panic. He turned again to the mirror, smiled engagingly, and whispered, "Get fucked, sonny."

What he needed was some good old-fashioned slimy sex. He wasn't up to cruising; he'd have to hit the baths and get it quick and dirty.

He put on his hustling jeans—they actually smelled of semen—and his Miss Piggy T-shirt.

He hadn't been out of the apartment since the beating. He'd spent almost two weeks now just reading Kierkegaard and Iris Murdoch. No wonder he was getting wiggy. He hadn't even celebrated the Fourth of July, a major holiday in the gay calendar. He'd make up for it now. He'd find a Syrian or an Iranian or any good-looking terrorist and he'd fuck the hell out of him for the good old U.S. of A. It would be patriotic, sort of.

He smiled. And that should be the end of any quarrel with God.

15

Claire leaned forward, making her point. "You sleep with anybody, Quinn says. You have some kind of commitment to her brother, but you sleep with anybody."

"I have *sex* with anybody. I sleep with *him.*"

"With Porter, his name is."

"With Porter."

"And you have a gun, he says."

Angelo thought about that for a while.

"So he says. Or writes, rather. Do you? Or is that fiction? It's from his notebook, not from the novel, so I presume it's fact rather than fiction. But with Quinn, you can't always tell."

"Not even Porter knows that."

"It's a small handgun, a bluish-silver color. You keep it in a nightstand next to your bed. Ever since the beating."

"Not even Sarah knows that."

"Well, obviously she does. Since it's she who told him."

Silence.

"The back staircase?"

Angelo shook his head, not in disbelief, but dazed by how very much this woman knew.

"She always uses the back stairs. In the kitchen. Behind the panel that holds the spice rack. Maybe she comes down here and snoops around while you're out."

More silence.

"I would imagine that it was originally the servant's staircase, wouldn't you suppose? In a house this old?"

"I'm trying to think how I feel about this."

"You're surprised, of course. People who don't write are always surprised. But that's just how writers are. They use everything. Or everyone. It's all the same to them."

"But does he write fiction *at all*? From what you say, it sounds as if he just transcribes what Sarah tells him."

"Oh, he'll transform it into fiction, not to worry. Quinn's the real thing. Sometimes he transforms it as he goes along, right in the notebook; that's why you can't ever be sure what's what. He gives *you* a harelip, for instance." She smiled, pleased. "In the end, the raw material doesn't count. It could have been anything."

"But in this case, it's me. It's us."

"It just happens to be. You can't take any of this personally."

They sat looking at each other in silence. Suddenly Claire laughed, a little choking sound, a remnant of her earlier hysteria. "You know, you look something like Quinn, with your lip like that. Do you suppose..." she said, gasping "...do you suppose I could have another little drink? Angelo?"

Claire had arrived an hour earlier, pale and hollow-eyed and soaked from the sudden downpour. She stood at his door, speechless, and as Angelo repeated, "Yes? Can I help you?" for the second time, she began to tremble and whimper and finally she burst into a torrent of speech, babbling a confused story about driving from Dartmouth and not being able to find a parking place and Quinn and Sarah and a restaurant and being fat, and then she bit at her knuckles and began to cry, and at once her hysteria became the real thing. Angelo had no choice but to let her come in.

He sat her on the living room couch and gave her a good

133

strong drink and told her just to rest for a while. He went to his bedroom and put on some clothes—as usual he had been wearing nothing but his shorty robe—and then he came back and asked her to say it all over again, slowly this time. Eventually he pieced together what had happened.

Claire had driven down from Dartmouth to spend the weekend with Quinn. As she had expected, he wasn't there. But his notebook confirmed what she already knew, and so she had driven to Louisburg Square and waited in her car for Quinn to come out of Number 17. She was going to accost him; she was going to accuse. But when he came out, it was with his arm around Sarah, and Claire had found herself speechless, unable even to get out of the car, as they had sauntered—"leaning together like lovers, like teenagers," she said, "it was disgusting"—down the hill to La Cigale. She had followed them on foot, had stood outside the restaurant, peeking in the window, until the maître d' came out and asked if he could help her. No, she told him, nobody could help her, it was all hopeless now, she wanted to die. The maître d' shrugged and turned back into the restaurant. She had run then, half-crazy with anger and shame, eager just to get away, to hide. But the hill was steep and she had on those damned high heels. At once she tripped on a loose brick in the sidewalk. She pitched forward, breaking her fall with the palms of her hands—she held them out to Angelo; they were scratched and dirty—but, worse than that, she had turned her ankle and torn her hose. The pain was awful, white hot, molten, and she was nauseous again. She realized suddenly that she *did* want to die. She sat down on the curb. That was when the skies had opened and the rain poured down. And so here she was, calm now, more or less, and halfway drunk, telling Angelo all the secrets of his life.

As he made her another drink—good God, her fourth—Angelo tried to get a grasp on how he felt about this. It had

happened so suddenly. He had been reading *The Black Prince*
for the past two hours, hoping to finish it before bed, when
he heard somebody come scrabbling down his stairs and stand
sort of whimpering outside his door. He looked through the
peephole and got a bubbled, swollen picture of whatshername—Claire. She was just standing there, scrunched up, as
if she were trying to disappear inside herself. So he had
opened the door and let her in. The whole situation was preposterous, crazy, like something out of Murdoch.

Angelo was not at all sure how he felt about it. Betrayed?
Yes, a little bit, by Sarah. And invaded, certainly, by that idiot
Quinn, who was not only idiotic but dangerous, too, since
evidently he kept a notebook recounting everybody's secrets.
And intrigued—was that the word?—by Quinn's moon-faced
little wife, Claire.

He returned from the kitchen with Claire's drink, well watered this time since she'd already had too much. But in the
doorway he stopped and stared at her. She had fallen asleep:
her head was thrown back, her mouth open, her legs spread
in a parody of sex.

Angelo turned away, repelled, but almost at once he turned
back to her, surprised at what he felt. The instant of repulsion
had given way to a sudden desire to stroke her hair. It was
black and silky and cut very short, making her look like a
child. One hand rested in her lap, palm up, with little streaks
of blackened blood; the other hung limp at her side. She
whimpered in her sleep, softly. Angelo dimmed the lights and
sat, for a long time, looking at her.

Claire was sleeping and Angelo was on his second drink,
when Quinn and Sarah returned from La Cigale. The rain was
still coming down heavily and so they must be soaked
through, but Angelo could hear Quinn laughing as he fum-
bled with the key; Sarah was laughing, too, that tinny laugh.
Had she had a drink? They were having a rip-roaring good

time for themselves, lovers in the rain and all that. Angelo was annoyed; they were going to wake poor Claire. He shot her an anxious look, but she slept on, oblivious.

He returned to *The Black Prince*. He hated it, he decided, and he hated Murdoch; he would never read her again. He had been sucked into it in the first place by a nifty little paragraph in the prologue. Indeed, he had tried to commit the paragraph to memory as he stood in the bookstore; but he couldn't retain it, and so he'd bought the damned book.

> I have no religion except my own task of being. Conventional religions are dream stuff. Always a world of fear and horror lies but a millimetre away. Any man, even the greatest, can be broken in a moment, and have no refuge.

That was a great tease and promised a wonderful book, but *The Black Prince* wasn't about that at all; it was about a whole lot of unimportant people running around and falling in love with the most improbable and inappropriate characters Murdoch could invent. It bore no more resemblance to life or reality than . . . he was stumped; he could think of no comparison.

Upstairs, Quinn and Sarah were still laughing and carrying on. They had moved into the kitchen for a while—long enough for Quinn to make himself one of those eternal drinks of his—but now they were headed upstairs. Good. They wouldn't wake Claire.

Angelo went back to his book; much as he hated it, he was determined to finish it, because he always finished any book he began.

It was quiet upstairs now, so they must be at it. Or warming up for it. What a tiresome thing sex was.

He didn't even like to think of it: his poor sick Sarah with that idiot Quinn.

• • •

Upstairs, Quinn stretched out on the bed while Sarah drew the bath and dried her hair. He tipped his head forward to have a sip of Scotch, but in his reclining position, he managed only to dribble the Scotch on his chin and on his shirt. He was wet from the rain anyway so who cared? Why care about anything?

This was the life: lying here on a white satin comforter, his shoes off, his tie loose, having a nice little sip of Chivas while his wife drew the bath.

"His wife," a pleasant thought to lie between maid's legs. She could be his wife, of course, except for the accident of birth. Hers, in Boston, of family and old money. His, no-where, of nobody and nothing. And then the lip. Still, this *could* be his life. It *could* be.

It should be.

He saw them at work in their studios—he, typing away on his second novel, then his third; she, painting privately, se-cretly, the mystery painter who never showed her work. Ex-cept to him, of course. There would be prizes, honors. But mostly, they would work, and travel, and live the good life.

He would reopen the top floor and use it as his study. That way, if he wanted to work late or early, he could do so with-out disturbing Sarah. He had never been up there; he must ask her soon to show it to him.

Just then Sarah came in from the bathroom. She was wear-ing a beige chiffon dressing gown, yards of gossamer floating about her, and she brought with her the heady scent of Joy.

"The water's hot hot hot," she said.

She crawled onto the bed and lay on her side, her head propped on her fist, studying Quinn.

He was thinking of how he would outfit his study; a leather-topped desk, inlaid of course, and a mile of bookcases.

An easy chair. Or perhaps he should use both rooms, and have one a writing study and one a reading study. Didn't Updike have four or five places where he wrote?

"What are you thinking?" she said.

"Sip?" he said.

Sarah propped herself up a little higher and took a deep drink. Her eyes closed for a second with the effort of swallowing. Quinn stared at her. She took another deep drink and handed him the glass.

"My God," he said.

"What?"

"You belted that down in two gulps."

She licked her lips once, and then again, slowly, as Quinn watched her. She drew the back of her hand across her mouth. Her eyes did not quite focus.

"What," she said, not a question.

"Are you just kidding?" Quinn said, sitting up now. "Are you all right?"

"I'm drunk," she said.

"You are, aren't you. On just that one drink."

"And the wine," she said.

"But you had only one glass."

"I don't usually"—she slurred the word—"drink very much."

"It looks to me like you shouldn't drink at all."

He started to get up, but she tugged at his jacket sleeve until he fell back on the bed.

"I'll be good," she said. "I'll be so good. I won't drink any any more, ever, more."

She kissed him on the forehead, just touching him with her lips, and then she moved to his ear, nibbling, letting her tongue run along the hard ridges of flesh.

"Mmm," he said. "Torture kisses."

She touched her lips to his jaw, his cheek, the bridge of his nose, as he lay staring at the ceiling, beginning to relax into it, surrendering to her. She touched her lips to his, so lightly it was like the movement of air. She kissed his brow. She trailed her soft hair across his face, arousing him at last. He shivered.

And then she sank her teeth into the soft flesh of his neck.

Quinn moaned lightly in pleasure but, as the pain struck, he gave a short high yelp and pulled away. He shot her a glance —of anger, of outrage—and for just a second their eyes locked. The look lasted only a second, just long enough for him to see in it the rich glint of madness.

In one fierce movement, he wrenched himself from the bed and stood, his hand to his neck, staring at her. "Are you crazy?" he shouted. "Have you gone out of your mind?"

He took his hand away and looked at it. There was blood on his fingers.

"You're out of your mind," he said. "You're crazy. Do you know that? Do you? You're crazy."

Sarah lay on the bed, her knees pulled to her chest, her hands covering her face. She was silent, motionless.

Quinn stopped shouting and looked at her. She was absolutely still. Lifeless. Was she actually dead? "You *bit* me," he said.

He went to the bathroom and examined his neck in the makeup mirror. She had broken the skin a little, and there were some red marks in the shape of teeth. It was probably nothing, really. He was embarrassed at making such a thing about it. He wet a facecloth with cold water and held it to his neck, and when he took the cloth away, the skin was red but there was no sign of blood. He squeezed the broken skin until a drop or two of red showed. He returned to the bedroom.

"Look," he said, his voice reasonable now. "You drew blood. You did."

But Sarah remained in her fetal position, her hands over her face.

"Look," he said, "look at this." He sat on the edge of the bed. "I'm not mad anymore, I just want you to see this." He touched the broken skin. "Feel it," he said. "You can actually feel the teethmark...the toothmarks. Oh, come on. I'm sorry I yelled. You scared me, that's all. You had that glassy look you get sometimes, only it was different this time; it was scary."

He thought of her face as she leaned over him, her lips parted, and that look in her gray eyes. He stood up again.

"I'm going to put some iodine on this, and I'll come back, okay?, and we'll just have a calm talk. Okay? I'll be right back."

He washed the cut again and put iodine on it. Then he went downstairs to make himself another drink.

In the kitchen, he sat for a moment with his head in his hands. He had to concentrate. He had to decide what to do. But his mind seemed to be made of cement. He could not think without a drink in his hand.

He got up and put a lot of ice in a glass and then just filled it with Scotch; never dilute the really good stuff. He stood with his legs crossed, leaning back against the kitchen sink, trying to sort out exactly how he felt about all this.

He loved her, and she was perfect for him in bed, she had helped him discover himself as a man and as a writer, as a sexual being, and God knows the marriage with Claire was doomed—that had been a mistake; he could see that now—but what did it *mean* that Sarah had scared him so? It wasn't the bite, it was the look; her eyes.

He wished he hadn't made such a thing about being scared. He felt like a fool. After all, during the past few weeks she had bitten him on every part of his body, gently though, and he had loved it. It was the booze, he decided; alcohol just wasn't good for some people. Funny; it made her crazy but it calmed her down. He took another sip of his drink and held the cold glass against his neck. He smiled to himself. Christ, this was really an *adventure*.

Sarah appeared at the kitchen door. One hand rested lightly on the doorframe, the other toyed nervously with her gown, tugging the gauzy fabric tight across her small perfect breasts. She stood there, her eyes down, as if she were afraid to come in.

"I'm sorry," she said, her voice a whisper. She continued to stand in the doorway, waiting. Finally she looked up at him, imploring.

"What?" he said.

"Can I touch you? Will you let me, ever?"

Quinn put down his glass and, still leaning back against the sink, his legs still crossed, he opened his arms to her.

She stepped into his loose embrace and lay her head on his shoulder. After a moment he pulled her close.

He tensed noticeably, but only for a second, as very gently and carefully she kissed him on the neck.

Downstairs, Angelo had finished *The Black Prince* and was just sitting, looking at Claire, when the phone rang. He lunged at it, and got there before the second ring.

He covered the mouthpiece and waited, his eyes fixed on Claire, but she did not wake up. She moaned a little, shifting on the couch, and then she cleared her throat and continued to sleep.

"Hello," he said finally, an angry whisper.

"Angie? Angelo?"

It was Porter.

"I can't talk, Porter."

"What's the matter? Is something the matter? Is it Sarah?"

"No. It's . . . no . . . it's not that."

Porter's voice fell. "You've got someone there."

"It's not what you think."

"Oh, Angelo. Oh, God. Angelo? I haven't seen you in twelve days. I've got to see you, Angie. Please."

"I can't. Not tonight."

Claire shifted on the couch once more, her hand fluttered in her lap, and she blinked herself awake.

"Please," Porter said. "Get rid of him, whoever he is. We don't have to do anything, I just want to talk with you. Angie? I want to be with you."

"I can't. I'm sorry."

Claire sat up straight and looked around, confused.

"I'm coming," Porter said. "I've got to see you."

"Don't," Angelo said, but Porter had already hung up.

For a moment there was complete silence, as Claire stared at him wide-eyed, remembering, and Angelo held the receiver suspended above its cradle, waiting, as if something definitive and terrible might happen if he hung up.

Claire closed her eyes again, and shook her head. "Oh, God," she said.

Angelo put down the receiver and smiled at her.

"You're all right," he said. "You're fine." Claire put her hand to her forehead. "What time is it?" Her eyes were still closed.

"Ten fifteen."

"And when did I get here? Oh, God, my head."

"About eight."

"Two hours. Can you get a hangover in only two hours?"

"Do you want some aspirins?"

"I want a gun. I want to shoot myself." She opened her eyes. "Sorry," she said, "that's just metaphor. I'm just regrouping my forces." She gave him a grim smile. "Killing myself seems the only polite thing to do after what I must've put you through. I *am* sorry." She tried to get up, but fell back at once, her hand to her head. "I've died," she said. "I'm in hell."

"I'll get you some water and a couple aspirins."

"I think a drink would be more to the point, frankly."

He grinned and went to get her the aspirins. An amazing woman, really. She had been hysterical and maybe even suicidal only two hours earlier and now here she was, upright and fighting, pulling herself around to face it all. And with a show of strength, too. Of humor, even. She wasn't pretty and she wasn't chic, but she had something. And, clearly, she was wasted on Quinn.

Upstairs, in the bathtub, Sarah ran some more hot water and then lay back on Quinn's chest, her head cradled between his shoulder and the white bath pillow supporting him. His hand rested lightly on her hip, not moving, not making any gesture toward sex.

This was sheer bliss, Sarah thought. Pure heaven. The air was thick with steam, and the perfumed water had lulled them halfway to sleep, and they were just together, loving, without having to do all those things she hated, without having to engage in sex. This is how it would always be.

She kissed him on the ear, not a sexual kiss, just an at-home-in-the-bathtub kiss.

"What?" he said.

"Just a little nuzzle," she said. "Because I'm so happy."

"That wasn't a nuzzle. That was a smack."

"A little kiss."

"A smack. The kind that Claire gives."

"Let's not talk," she said, bringing her leg up over his thigh. He pulled her closer. The water sloshed around them as they got more comfortable. Then they lay quietly.

Usually she loved to hear him talk about Claire. She was fascinated that Claire had put herself through college while taking care of her dying mother, that she had earned a Ph.D. in Latin and Greek, and that she had written a book about the women in Euripides. What incredible strength and independence she must have. Sarah wanted to know everything: what Claire wore, the perfume she used, how she walked and talked. She did not want to know what Claire did in bed. The thought had crossed her mind that she wanted to become Claire, but she realized that that was not true; she just wanted to replace her.

What fascinated Sarah most was that Claire admitted she'd been very fat as a girl. Sarah couldn't imagine Quinn with a fat wife. Quinn liked his women perfect; he always noticed how Sarah dressed, how she looked. When they walked together, when they entered a restaurant, she knew that Quinn was not thinking about her or about himself; he was thinking about what kind of impression they made.

Raoul had never cared about impressions. He had never cared about her at all; he had merely been trying to prove — he had actually said this on their last night together — that if he could just get her into bed, he could turn her, or any Boston Brahmin, into a whore. And he had. He taught her all those things she did in bed with Quinn. And Quinn loved it. She supposed that every man did. "You can possess a man's soul," Raoul had once said, "if you truly possess his cock." He always talked about his thing as if it were some sacred object.

But that was before. That was over. She would not think of that. She would think only of Quinn and her new, safe, mature relationship with a man.

Quinn groaned suddenly and pushed her leg off of his.

"More hot water?"

"I just remembered I haven't called Claire yet."

"Then you should do it right away." But she ran her hand slowly across his chest and began a slow descent toward his belly.

"I'll give you about twenty minutes to cut that out."

"Yummies."

Quinn sat up suddenly and said, "No, I've got to get it over with. I have to keep up appearances."

Fat Claire, she thought, fat, fat, fat.

"For the time being," he said.

He threw on the white terry robe she had bought him, floor-length, with a hood. He did not bother to dry himself.

A minute later she could hear his voice, with its edge of impatience. "I'm her husband. It's me; Quinn." A pause. "Will you tell her I called? Tell her I'm taking the phone off the hook?" And then, in exasperation, "Aunt Lily, it's me, Quinn. Her husband. Oh, this is impossible. Never mind. Just tell her I called."

Sarah was still drying herself when she looked up and saw Quinn standing at the door. She wrapped the towel around herself and hitched it tight at her breast in a kind of sarong that left one leg bare to the hip; Raoul had taught her that, too.

"Old Lily is going around the bend," Quinn said. "She's got some shoot-'em-up blasting away on the television and she doesn't listen to a word you say. She just keeps repeating "'Claire's in the bath. I'll tell her to call.' And then she says, 'Who did you say you are?' She's losing it, Claire says, and I think she's right."

Sarah took off the headband holding back her hair and moved slowly toward Quinn. She stood in front of him, her eyes down, waiting, just as Raoul had taught her. Quinn ran his hands over her shoulders, pulled her toward him, breathed into her hair—like Raoul, like any man, she thought, as she did the necessary things—and after a while she felt him begin to grow hard.

"I'm going to memorize your body," she said, "inch by inch."

Downstairs, Angelo and Claire had been talking excitedly for over an hour. At first he made anxious efforts to say anything that would prevent another lapse into hysteria, but very soon he caught her up in a discussion of Kierkegaard's three categories of men, and they had been talking easily ever since.

"But I fail to see how he differs from conventional Christianity," Claire said. "He's just proposing another version of the purgative, illuminative, and unitive way."

"No, it's different," Angelo said. "Let me try to explain it again."

"Wait. In both Kierkegaard and Christianity, when you get close enough to God you end up *united* with him in some kind of mystical embrace. Am I right?"

"No. It's just the opposite. You end up united with him, all right, but not in an embrace. You end up as his antagonist. It's you, pitted *against* God. Alone."

"No, really?"

"That's what he says it means to be a religious man. He says it. Can I read you a passage?"

"Yes, of course," she said. *"Legendo, discimus."* Angelo looked at her, a question. " 'It's by reading that we learn.' Sorry."

Angelo went and got his books. "I keep them next to my bed," he said. "I'll only read for a minute, I promise. I know how people hate to be read at."

"But I love to be read at. It's one of my favorite things."

And so Angelo read sections of *Fear and Trembling* while

Claire stretched out on the couch, listening. Since she didn't get restless the way Porter did, Angelo went on for quite a long time.

"Well, it seems you're right," she said. "Who'd ever want to be chosen as a religious man."

"What do you mean, chosen?"

"Well, you can't just choose it for yourself, can you? I haven't read Kierkegaard in years, but it sounds to me like being a religious man in Kierkegaard is like being a saint in Catholicism. You don't choose God. God chooses you."

"I see what you mean. I'd been thinking the other way around. That you choose to take God on as an adversary and then he sets up the terms of the struggle."

"No, that can't be," she said. "That sounds like those people who go around saying 'I've accepted Jesus as my personal savior' which always makes me want to ask, 'And has he accepted you?'"

Angelo laughed and then Claire laughed, for the first time. He thought of saying, You've got a very pretty laugh, but instead he said, "I don't think you're right about God choosing. Kierkegaard insists that it's man who chooses. 'Man is condemned to freedom of choice,' he says. Isn't that a great line? And that's when we experience our unique selfhood most completely, in the act of choice. Like the Abraham–Isaac thing I just read you."

"Yes, I see your point."

"But what bothers me is that most of us just schlep through life and never have to make that kind of choice at all. Let's face it, if there is a God, he's not going to bother quarreling with the likes of us. Of me."

"Then you've just got to reject Kierkegaard outright."

"No, I couldn't."

"Why not? It's just philosophy. It's not as if it *means* anything."

Angelo studied her for a moment. She had a completely straight face, without the trace of a smile. What a funny, funny woman. He burst into loud laughter. After a while he sat back, exhausted, but in a moment he leaned forward, eager again.

"Do you believe in God?"

"I used to," she said, "before I married Quinn." She considered this. "Giving up Catholicism was the single most difficult thing I've ever done in my life. It was like giving up my identity. It was like—I don't know—denying my existence."

"Then why did you do it?"

"You *do* things for love."

"But you can't stop believing just by an act of the will."

"Oh, I still believe," she said. "But now I believe in sin."

"Sin, but not God."

"Well, it's easy. If there is a God, he's out there somewhere, being irrelevant. But sin is personal. I thought this through for a book I wrote once about women in Greek drama, and I think I'm right. The conclusion I came to is that the only mortal sin—in the primitive sense of mortal—is the refusal to live your own life. What do you think?"

"It certainly simplifies things," Angelo said, smiling, but again she was serious. "Where'd you get that?"

"From experience mostly, but I found the idea in the Greeks, too, and that's when I came to understand it. When I was younger, I used to be very religious but then my mother died and I found I couldn't pray, I couldn't do anything, I didn't want to go on. I actually thought of killing myself. Anyway, a priest friend told me to just throw myself into study, that study could be a kind of salvation. And he was right, but not the way he thought. What happened is that I discovered there's only one sin: the refusal to live your own life."

Angelo thought about that and then he repeated it, speculatively. "The refusal to live your own life," he said.

"One's own life."

"So you left the church and married Quinn."

"Right."

"And now you're living your own life."

Claire looked at him sharply.

"Aren't you?"

"I wasn't sure what you meant," she said.

He could see she was drawing into herself again, so he said quickly, "Tell me about the Greeks."

"What about them?"

"You said you wrote a book about the Greeks."

"Oh, about the women in Euripides. They were very modern in their way. Very independent. Very neurotic. But the thing about every one of them is that they took charge of their lives, they weren't passive, they did things. Think of Medea, for instance. Even killing seemed better to them than not living your own life. Using it. Or even ending it, if you wanted. But taking full responsibility for it, whatever the consequences."

"When the chips are down, it's what you *do* that counts."

"Exactly," she said.

"That's what Porter says about love."

"Love? What's love got to do with it? I'm talking about an individual, unique, irreplaceable life."

"But it's only one life. A life isn't such a big thing when you think of history, the millions and billions of people. What's one life?"

Claire thought a moment. "If it's ours, it's all we've got."

"It's all we've got, but it's not that much."

"It's everything," she said.

Angelo sat forward, on the edge of his chair. Claire sat back and waited for his response.

"God, this is wonderful," he said. "I'm sort of exhausted, aren't you?"

Claire laughed, then after a moment she said, "Quinn would be bored to death."

"So would Porter."

She was frowning, in thought, when Angelo said, "I like talking to you." Claire said nothing and so he added, quickly, "Kierkegaard says somewhere that there are only three kinds of people he likes to talk to: 'old persons of the female sex who peddle family gossip'—that's a quote; people who are insane; and thirdly, people who are very sensible. We're the third."

"I'm sort of all three, don't you think?"

"I think," Angelo said, ". . . I think you're wonderful."

Upstairs, Sarah and Quinn were recovering from their first bout of sex, and Quinn was just getting to the point where he felt talky. He rolled over on his side to face her. He traced the line of her nose with his index finger.

"Lovely," he said.

She kissed his finger, and then flicked her tongue about the tip, but he took his hand away and let it rest between her breasts.

"Did I ever tell you about the conversation I overheard that time in Brighams? I was sort of looking for you, and you were sitting right next to me, and I didn't know it?"

"You told me."

"No. Did I? There were two girls, about fourteen or fifteen, and one was telling the other . . ."

"Her name was Rinnie."

"That's right. So I must have told you. But I don't remember. How come you remember?"

"Because they were using those words. That's why you like to tell the story, and I hate those words."

"Dick and cock." Quinn laughed. "You *are* something. They're only words. Words are just neutral. Cock or apple or automobile; it's all the same. At least in private. When you write, of course, it's different. Cock and cunt and tits and ass—even ass, imagine!—you just can't use them in fiction unless the context allows, and it almost never does. It's an interesting problem."

"Don't," she said. "You don't know." She sounded near tears.

"But what about the things we *do*? Fucking, it seems to me, is simply fucking, regardless of what you call it. Do you make some kind of distinction between the act of fucking and the word that describes it?"

Sarah said nothing.

"I mean, is the act good and the word bad?"

"Yes," she said, and she was crying now. "The act is all right because it's *not* really me, it's the other me. But the word *is* me."

"Oh, sweet," he said, "don't cry. Please don't cry." He drew her close to him and smoothed her hair and kissed her wet cheek. "All right? I'll stop," he said, "I will. All right? No more dirty words and no more tears. Okay? All right."

He held her for a while, surprised for the second time this evening. What did she mean? What *could* she mean? "The act is all right because it's the other me, but the word *is* me." She stopped crying finally.

"Listen," he said. "I've got a great idea. I've never seen the rooms upstairs. If I ever need to write about a house like this,

I should see the rooms upstairs, so why don't we do a tour right now?"

"Now? At midnight, almost?"

"Now."

"You're so good to me," she said.

Quinn found himself about to say "I love you" but he called the words back just in time.

Porter parked the car but left the ignition running. He sat there watching the windshield wipers flip back and forth, back and forth, should he or shouldn't he, would he or wouldn't he. But he knew he would.

He had not seen Angelo in twelve days; for a brief while he had hoped he might return to being an ordinary married man, and never see Angelo again. But that hope didn't last long. Angelo phoned to tell him that Sarah was seeing somebody named Quinn, and this Quinn was very sexy indeed, and immediately Porter was enslaved again. Two days had passed since the phone call and—good intentions be damned—he wanted to see Angelo; he had to; now.

The whole thing was a mystery to him. He was a man in his forties, a very public man—Porter Winthrop Slade—in love with his wife, devoted to his three children, and by some awful but wonderful stroke of luck, he found himself in love with another man.

Nobody was to blame. After Raoul's murder, when it became clear that Sarah must never again be left totally on her own, Porter had been sent by Grandmother Slade to convince Angelo to live at Number 17 and be Sarah's guardian. The meeting determined the rest of Porter's life. Angelo had done nothing, only looked and listened, while Porter—explaining, justifying, and explaining again—gave himself over irrevocably to this strange new love.

Porter himself had never understood it. He was not interested in men. He was not even very interested in sex. But in Angelo he found something else. He had no idea what it was, but he knew this: when he was with Angelo he didn't want anything else; he didn't need anything else; he was—and the word sounded foolish even to him—complete. If only, if *only* Angelo were not a man. But Porter had accepted that limitation from the start.

"Oh, Angelo," he said aloud, "please," and he added, silently, please let me love you. He was short of breath and he had a dull anxiety pain in his chest.

He turned off the ignition and got out of the car. He stood in the rain trying to put his umbrella up, but the button that was supposed to make the damned thing fly open just wouldn't work. He gave up and made a run for it.

He hitched his umbrella on the railing and searched his pockets for the key. He always entered through Sarah's door, publicly preserving the fiction that he came only to see his sister. He let himself in quietly, pressing his hand to the door as he closed it so the lock wouldn't click. In the foyer he ran a comb quickly through his hair.

At once he realized that Sarah was still awake; there was a light in the kitchen and he could hear the radio playing. He listened for the sound of voices but heard only soft music from the radio.

Sarah was standing at the stove waiting for the water to boil. She had on her beige peignoir and she cradled a small blue teapot against her breast. She looked up as if she had been expecting him.

"Your hair's wet," she said. "It looks darker."

"It's almost stopped, though. The rain. Nearly."

They stood facing each other, awkward as always.

"How've you been?" Porter said.

"All right. Good." An odd look crossed her face as if she

were going to say something difficult, painful, but she turned back to the stove and said nothing.

"Well," Porter said, and edged toward the door to the apartment below.

"Good night," Sarah said. "Porter? I should tell you, I guess." She had that look again. "Quinn is here."

"Oh?"

The kettle whistled as Sarah nodded and said that Quinn would probably be spending the night. At once she busied herself pouring water from the kettle into the teapot, so Porter spared her the embarrassment of asking anything more. They both knew how dangerous it was for her to be— that way—with a man. They both knew it was forbidden.

"Well," he said. "I'm glad you told me."

Sarah looked up and smiled nervously. Porter blew her a kiss as he disappeared down the stairs to Angelo's apartment.

Poor Sarah; she was sick, it was true, but he couldn't bring himself to begrudge her a few moments of love, or what passed for love, even with a married man like Quinn.

He wished he hadn't run into her; he was feeling embarrassed, even guilty, about forcing himself on Angelo and he had hoped to slip downstairs unnoticed.

He stood on the tiny landing outside Angelo's door, tapping softly. After a moment, he pushed the door open and stepped inside the kitchen. He waited there, afraid to go on but unwilling to go back. He began to hyperventilate.

He cleared his throat, and then once more, loudly this time. "Angelo?" he said, but his voice came out high and cracked. He tried again. "Angie?"

At once Angelo was there, looking angry.

"Don't be mad," Porter said, whispering. "Please don't be mad."

"I'm not mad. I'm just...I *told* you I couldn't see you tonight."

"I know, but . . ."

"Shhh."

Porter whispered, "I know, but I had to see you. I haven't seen you in almost two weeks. I couldn't bear it, Angie. I was mad at you at first because of what you said about Sarah, and then I was mad because you didn't call, and so I was going to punish you by not calling until you did, but I couldn't wait any longer, I had to see you."

"Oh, Porter." Angelo sighed, as if he were forgiving a bad child. "Look. It's all right. I'll phone you tomorrow. I promise. But you've got to go now. Right now."

"No."

"Shhh, I told you."

"No. Please."

Angelo lowered his head and said nothing.

"Send him away, Angie. Why can't you send him away?"

"I've told you, it's not what you think."

"Then send him away."

"It's not even a man, Porter. Now you know. All right?"

"Then who is it?"

"I can't tell you."

"Sophia Loren? Who? Cybill Shepherd?"

"Porter, please." And then, worried. "Are you all right?"

"It's not a woman at all, is it," Porter said. He stared at Angelo in disbelief as he remembered Sarah's words and realized now what she must have been telling him: Quinn was here, in the house, yes, but not upstairs with her; he was downstairs with Angelo and would probably spend the night.

Porter's mind staggered for a moment and a pain began in his chest. Were they lovers, Angelo and Quinn? Did Sarah know? She must. No, it wasn't possible. Angelo had sex with anybody, but he loved only . . .

"Porter, are you all right? You look like you're going to faint."

"It's Quinn, isn't it. You've got Quinn here."

Angelo smiled, or perhaps it was a grimace.

"So I'm right. It *is* Quinn."

"Porter, this is impossible, you've got to go. I'll phone you tomorrow."

"Angelo?"

"It's *not* Quinn."

Porter stared at him. He would not ask again who it was. He would preserve some last shred of dignity even if it killed him. He waited.

Angelo lowered his voice to a whisper. "It's Quinn's wife."

At that, Porter turned and left; he went up the back stairs, his head ringing, half-blind with shame and fury. He let himself out through Sarah's front door.

The rain had stopped and Porter gasped in the wet air. For a moment he could not get his breath at all, he could barely see. There was a hard knot where his heart should be and the pain from it radiated out to his shoulder and down his arm. He stood, trembling, on the stair.

After a while his mind cleared and his vision came back. The pain was killing. The words "heart attack" passed through his mind, but he was too caught up in Angelo's betrayal to think about what was happening. Angelo had lied to him, mocked him: "It's Quinn's wife." He couldn't bear it. There was another terrible surge of pain, but Porter was losing the thing he valued most in life, and he had no time to think about heart attacks.

He tried to unhitch his umbrella from the railing, but he could not pull it loose. He left it there swinging back and forth. He struggled down the stairs and, still gasping, he got into his car. He sat for a while, hunched over, trying to outwit the pain.

Porter was a reasonable man, a sensible man. He would like to say that he would never forgive this betrayal . . . he would kill himself . . . or kill Angelo. But he knew that it was not so.

Life would go on, and he would make whatever adjustments had to be made, and he would not complain. He would beg, he would grovel if he had to, for Angelo's love.

After a while the pain subsided a little and Porter drove off, his car weaving only slightly.

Downstairs, Claire was frantic. "You didn't tell him I was here," she said. "I couldn't bear it."

"That was just Porter," Angelo said. "He never comes in if there's somebody here."

"But you didn't tell him *who*. If he knew, he'd tell *her*—Sarah—and then Quinn would know, and then I'd never get him back."

"But why do you want him back?"

"Did you tell him? Or didn't you?"

Angelo paused a moment and then said, with a grin, "He thought Quinn was here."

"Quinn! My God, how sick does he think you are!"

"Oh, he knows I'm pretty sick."

But Claire didn't find that funny. She was insistent. "Did you tell him, or not?" Her voice was getting that hysterical edge once again.

"I didn't tell him you were here, all right?" He lied, and he never lied.

"Sorry," she said. "I'm just..."

They sat in silence for a while. Only moments ago Claire's hysteria seemed never to have happened, and now it was back in the room with them, hovering. Their wonderful conversation was going to end in disaster. Desperate, Angelo said, "Tell me about your book."

"Oh, it's just a book," she said. "Oh, God, I don't know what to do. I should leave. I should...I don't know."

"*I* know. Just do what I say. Tell me about your book."

"It's about Greek drama. You wouldn't care."

"It's about sin, you said. Nothing interests me more than sin."

"No. What it's about, really, is women." She laughed, a choking sound.

"Tell me."

"It's about women and the strategies by which they keep on living. Funny, isn't it. You write the book first and you become an expert afterward."

"Just keep telling me. In Euripides, you said?"

"In Euripides."

"So tell me."

Claire began, in a perfunctory way, to tell him about the enterprising women in Euripides, but before long she became interested in making a point, in proving it, and after a little while longer the hysteria was behind her once again.

They moved on to women in Greek literature and in other literature and toward early morning they fell asleep. Or rather, Angelo fell asleep.

When he seemed completely unconscious Claire moved soundlessly from the living room to the bedroom and to the nightstand where, beneath a box of tissues and a jar of Vaseline, she found the gun and an ammunition clip, just as Quinn's notebook had said. She picked up the gun, surprised by its weight, and turned it over in her hands experimentally. She examined the trigger and the safety catch. In a second she figured out how to insert the clip. So, after all, loading and firing would be easy; just like the movies. She slipped the gun back into the drawer, covered it with tissues and Vaseline, and, with the clip concealed in the flat of her hand, she returned to the living room. Angelo was still asleep.

She tucked the clip into her handbag and stretched out on the couch, fully composed. She fell asleep at once and she did not dream.

• • •

Upstairs, Sarah had finished preparing tea and had ascended
the stairs slowly, holding the tray with the tea things as if it
were an offering and she were at the head of a procession.
Hearing the rattle of cups, Quinn broke off his exploration of
Grandmother Slade's rooms and hurried down to the bedroom. Sarah held out the tray to him and said, "Tea."

"Mmm," he said, and then, "What did *he* want?"

"That was just Porter," she said. "He's here to see Angelo.
He looked upset."

She moved to the sitting area by the front window and
placed the tray on the little table there. Quinn followed, hovering.

"Did you talk with him? Did he ask if I was here?"

"Yes," she said. "No." She arranged the things on the table,
placed the tray on the floor, and poured tea into the cups. She
sat down and smiled at him. "But I told him you were here."

"Oh, God. Why did you do that?"

"It doesn't matter," she said. "Porter doesn't care. He lets
me lead my own life, so long as I'm . . . careful. And I try to
be. I always tell the truth."

"Of course. Well, so do I." He finally sat down. "This is
good tea."

"Earl Grey."

"What does he think of me? Does he know I'm married?"

"I suppose he does."

"Who told him? Angelo?"

She nodded.

"Do you tell Angelo everything? Do you have to?"

"It helps to keep me honest."

Quinn was silent for a while. He had reached that dangerous area of her life that was somehow connected with
her shoplifting. It was an area she kept closed to him,

one that he knew intuitively he must not enter. Was she only a rich kleptomaniac or was there a major scandal involved?

"I'll pour you more tea," she said.

In his book he would have to invent a scandal. As he looked at her now, though, it was hard to imagine a scandal. Here they were, at midnight, having made love and about to make love again, sitting down to a cup of tea in the bedroom of a townhouse in Louisburg Square. Even the sound of it was wonderful: tea in a townhouse in Louisburg Square. He looked around, musing. The white comforter, the white wallpaper sprigged with yellow, the Chinese carpet in white and yellow and that pale, pale green. The matching chairs in yellow velvet.

"What are you thinking?" she said.

"My book," he said, pleasantly guilty. "When you're really on to something you're writing, it stays with you all the time. It makes me impossible to live with, I suppose, always making up things in my head, always being distracted. Could you live with that?"

Sarah smiled. "You're very easy to live with."

Was she making an offer? Quinn thought of the rooms upstairs. What a spectacular study they'd make for him.

"What did you think of the rooms upstairs?" she asked.

"They're perfect. The ceiling isn't as high as the ceiling here, and the windows aren't as long, but the rooms are huge —they seem bigger, somehow, than down here—and the view from the back is...well...spectacular. You ought to make a study for yourself up there, a studio."

"The light is better down here, with the bigger windows," Sarah said. "It would make a perfect writer's study, though, upstairs."

"I love exploring old houses like this."

Sarah stretched her legs out before her and slid lower into the chair, her head at an angle. With the toe of one foot, she tipped her slipper off and then she teased his bare ankle lightly with her toe. She fixed him with her stare and he returned it. They played with each other like this for a time, until at last she said, "Ready?" They got up, shedding their robes where they stood, and returned to her huge bed for their second bout of sex, this one with Quinn in control.

Later, when Sarah had dropped into her deep sleep, Quinn got up and went to the bathroom. He ran the water loudly. He flushed the toilet. He waited to see if she might wake, but as usual after sex, Sarah was deeply asleep.

He went upstairs and explored Grandmother Slade's rooms slowly, methodically. He would have his reading study in the front, his writing study in the back. Those three small windows facing the river would have to go; he'd have them torn out and replaced by one long expanse of glass stretching clear across the back wall, with his desk beneath it. That way, whenever he looked up from his work he would see the whole world of Boston and Cambridge spread out below. A perfect study.

He returned to the grandmother's room and wandered around, snooping in the closets, the bureau drawers, the blanket chest. They were all empty. He went back and searched the other room; nothing there either.

Between the rooms was a landing and the bathroom. In the bathroom was a clothes hamper. In the clothes hamper was a pile of towels, sweet-smelling, unused. Certain now that he had found her hiding place, he dug deep beneath the towels and, yes, there they were: the three stolen handbags.

Quinn smiled to himself, satisfied, and closing the hamper and then the bathroom door, he went quietly down the stairs to bed where he lay awake for a long while, planning.

The sun had been up for some time when Claire said goodbye to Angelo and let herself out his front door. She walked to her car and stood there in the soft morning light, waiting.

I'll win by the sheer powers of my mind, she said to herself, and translated aloud, to the pigeons flocking in the Square, *"Cogitando, eos susperabo."* She smiled at how classical it sounded. Perhaps Cicero himself had said that. Or, more likely, Cicero's wife. She worked out several variant translations while she waited. She had plenty of time.

It was more than an hour before the door of Number 17 opened and Quinn stepped out into the bright sunlight. He closed the door behind him and stood on the step surveying the Square, as if he owned it, Claire thought. He spotted Porter's umbrella where it hung on the railing, tried it for fit, and the next minute he descended the stairs, swinging the umbrella like a swagger stick. Despite how she felt, Claire couldn't help laughing. He looked so funny and lovable and absurd.

Quinn was only a few feet away when he noticed her standing beside the car. Claire watched as a series of emotions, most of them in the range of guilt, washed over his face; finally he just stood there, speechless.

"Good morning," she said evenly; no anger, no sarcasm. "Get in. I'll give you a ride home."

"Oh, my God," he said.

"We're adults, Quinn. We can handle this." She walked to the passenger side of the car and held the door open for him. Sheepishly he followed her around and got in. She closed the door a little harder than necessary.

She turned on the ignition, smiled at him, and backed the car—too fast—out into Mount Vernon Street. She hit the brake and the car rocked to a stop.

"No harm done," she said.

They drove in silence up Mount Vernon and over Joy and down Beacon Street by the Common.

Quinn regained his speech, finally. "Claire," he said, "there's something..."

"Not to worry, Quinn," she said. *"Nil desperandum.* It's a summer fling. I understand." A moment later she added, "It'll be good for your writing."

He shot her a suspicious look. "What do you mean?"

"It'll give you something new to write about, a new subject matter. Marriage, adultery. It'll broaden your range as a writer."

"Oh."

"I was hurt at first, Quinn, I admit it, but then I realized that writers are different. You've *got* to have experience to draw on. So I understand."

"But Sarah . . . her name is Sarah Slade . . ."

"I remember."

"Sarah fills needs in me that you don't, Claire. It's hard to talk about. It's just that I have different needs."

"I know you do. And I'm not going to interfere. You have this fling, all right? With my permission. With my blessing."

She pulled the car to a smart stop in front of 65 Marlborough. "Here you are," she said. "I won't go upstairs, Quinn. I'll head straight back to Hanover. I'll phone you in a week or two, okay?" She kissed him on the cheek. "You're a free man, sweetheart."

"Oh, Claire," he said, beginning to melt.

"Not on your life," she said, and leaning across him, she flipped open his door. "Out." He got out. "Love you," she called, very upbeat.

He leaned in the window and looked at her sadly.

"Give my best to little Leopold," she said, and threw the car in gear. She pulled out into traffic, waving gaily back at Quinn, goodbye, goodbye.

16

It was Sunday night and Sarah was sitting in her living room listening to music like any normal person—Beethoven's Sixth, the "Pastoral." Angelo was lying with his head in her lap, his eyes closed, his long lashes making a shadow on his cheek. He had not left her side since yesterday morning and the terrible phone call about Porter.

A myocardial infarction, the doctor had said; serious, but probably not fatal, at least not this time. If he pulled through, he'd need a good two weeks of bed rest and a lifetime of caution. But to Sarah, Porter's heart attack was God's judgment on her. She was to blame. If she were not having this affair with Quinn, Porter would be all right.

She looked down at Angelo. He was perfectly calm, perfectly at peace, even though he was in love with Porter and Porter might die at any minute. He loved her, too, she supposed, in his way.

But *she* was not allowed to love anyone.

She tried to concentrate on Beethoven: the final movement had begun—the shepherd giving thanks for the passing of the storm—played allegretto. Simple pleasures. Joy in nature. Peace.

She could not allow herself to be in love.

Nonetheless, she was.

She had been in love once before, with Raoul, and he had

left her. That was when the other Sarah did things, the Sarah who was not really her. *That* Sarah had gotten him drunk, and then lay in bed beside him, waiting, the revolver held to his brow. He woke and looked at her and she killed him.

And now her period was due, with that black blood, the stink of it. She had wiped it on Raoul's face.

She shook her head, no, she would not look at what she saw. That was the other Sarah, the crazy one.

Why, then, did she feel that Porter's heart attack was God's judgment on her?

Angelo lay with his head in Sarah's lap, pretending to listen to the music, but really thinking of Claire; wonderful Claire, witty and brilliant and acid-tongued Claire. Had they been characters in Murdoch, they would be in love by now, he realized. But he was not in love; he was just fascinated by her.

It was late Sunday night, thirty-six hours since he had seen her, and—he reminded himself—thirty-five hours since the phone call with the news about Porter.

It was still touch and go with Porter and only Maria was allowed to see him. Which was probably just as well, Angelo thought. He couldn't leave Sarah by herself, after all, and he wouldn't dare take her to the hospital with him. She might go bats. She looked haggard, spacey; as if at any minute she might lose it altogether. For some reason, she felt responsible for Porter's heart attack. It made no sense. But then again madness never did. Tomorrow, thank God, he would take her to see the shrink. In the meanwhile it was his job to keep her calm, to let her think that life was under control.

His mind drifted once again to Claire. How smart she was and how quick. Talking with her was like talking to O'Brien, in the old days before O'Brien left the Jesuits, except it was better with her. She didn't try to teach you, she just said things and then listened to what you said back. And she had opinions about everything. She was really an exciting person. If he were straight, he could imagine falling in love with her. In fact, if he were straight, she was exactly the kind of woman he would want to marry. She wasn't beautiful, in fact she was even a little plump, but she had intelligence and life and—despite her spying on Quinn—she was absolutely truthful. Of that, he was certain.

He felt Sarah take a deep breath and hold it; then she breathed out slowly between her lips. She was trying to remain calm.

She smoothed his hair and then lightly traced the line of his mouth, lingering for just a second at the small mark on his upper lip.

"You all right?" he said, not opening his eyes.

He thought of Quinn. He thought of Porter. Poor Porter, he thought. He thought of Claire.

The terrible pain in his chest had turned into a deep dull ache, with a slight edge of fire to it. Porter felt as if they had scooped out his insides and filled the hollow with ice.

He had just been given another shot of morphine and he was going under again. He rather liked this. He was beginning to understand why people took drugs.

He was supposed to be thinking of something, but he couldn't remember what it was. Maria? The children? Maria stood at the foot of his bed, tan and beautiful and worried, a rosary clutched in her hand. She was praying for him; what a nice thought.

And then it came back to him. Quinn. With his awful lip. He was having an affair with Angelo. Or had he dreamt that after the heart attack?

He could hear music. Was it music? He opened his eyes and

saw two Marias and then three; the drug was taking effect. He resisted it for one last moment. He wanted to say, Tell Angelo I understand; say goodbye from me; tell him he has always made me very happy. His lips moved and Maria came closer, but the only words she could catch were "made me very happy."

Maria clutched her rosary to her breast. A single tear slipped from the corner of her eye.

Quinn sat at his typewriter, absorbed in the task of turning his sex life into fiction. It had taken at least ten drafts, but he finally got it right: a sex scene that was pure art. The amazing thing was that he managed to write it amid all the emotional hoopla. Only yesterday Claire had dropped him off, saying you're a free man and have a nice fling, and he had come upstairs and sat at the typewriter and just *did* it, finally, despite or maybe because of those nine earlier drafts. Sarah had called with the news about Porter, but that hadn't put him off at all; he had continued straight through the chapter without one false move. He had gone for a walk then, his head aching and his throat sore—he wrote out loud—and when he got home, he read over what he'd written and, with only a few more changes, it was going to be great.

Today he had knocked off a quick narrative chapter, set— for economy—two weeks after the bouncy sex scene. Q wakes up in S's bed and realizes that he's in love with her. A gentle, human chapter; very short, only four pages.

He made a note to go back later and do something about Q's wife. Obviously, she was going to get in the way of his narrative drive and he would have to dispose of her somehow. Divorce? Death? ??? Something economical. Perhaps, in the rewrite, make Q an unmarried man?

He wasn't going to worry about that now. Because tonight

he was beginning the big chapter, the revelation from which the whole novel would unfold. In this chapter Q discovers that S, though she is in love with him, has had a long, incestuous affair with her brother, A, harelip and all. Porter's heart attack, and Sarah's bizarre reaction to it, had given him the idea for that; let's hear it for Porter. Quinn knew he would have to handle it very carefully; there was a great danger of being merely sensational, even schlocky. But he could do it; he could make it work.

He couldn't be with Sarah until Porter either kicked off or decided to live, but so long as the fiction kept coming, who cared? This was wonderful, this was as good as sex any day—making these things up. Perhaps he was a writer after all.

Claire was eating pretzels as she sat beside Aunt Lily watching television. On the screen there was a lot of action. A car took a corner at an impossible angle; a crash, a shout. A black man leaped from the burning car. Police began shooting. More cars. More screams. Aunt Lily nodded and, with her joy stick, turned up the volume.

Claire ate pretzels and looked straight ahead, seeing nothing. She was not here; she was in a far place, at a bad time. She had made her decision and she was steeling herself to carry it through.

She would have the abortion. Whatever the cost, she would get Quinn back.

17

"But you are not responsible," the shrink said, "and besides, your brother-in-law is not dead."

"My brother," Sarah said. "Porter's my brother, not my brother-in-law."

"He is not dead, your brother."

Sarah's face tightened against the tears she could feel coming. She was going to break down. Once again, she was going to surrender to this ridiculous woman.

The shrink waited.

The tears came, and then heavy sobs, and finally the admission. "It's my fault. I did it."

"Do not say this. Do not keep saying this. You cannot have the blame for everything."

"But it would never have happened if I weren't seeing Quinn."

"Yes?"

"Porter was worried. He's got so many worries: Angelo, and his family, and now me again."

"You again. Why does he worry about you again?"

"Quinn was with me. It's my fault."

"Ah."

"I bit him." More tears.

"You bit him. Yes. Tell me about this."

Sarah confessed that she had been seeing Quinn. That she

was in love with him. That she had had a drink, two drinks in fact. That afterward, making love, she had bit him.

"It was a small bite? It was a love bite?"

Sarah thought about that.

"You say that you made love afterward. This sounds to me like a love bite."

Sarah agreed that perhaps it was a love bite.

"But you connect this with Porter's heart attack. There is no connection, no. You are not responsible for the world's good health, no. You are only one person."

Sarah had stopped crying. This absurd woman—with her fake accent and her bulky figure—was, after all, her friend.

"I've tried so hard," she said.

"Yes, well. There is trying and trying. You know that drink is fatal for you. Yes?"

"Yes."

"And why is it fatal for you? You know why."

"Because I become that other person."

Suddenly the shrink was furious. "No, no, no!" she said. "This is not it at all!" She leaned into Sarah, speaking rapidly. "Why are you saying this? This is not the case. You are not some schizophrenic who can blame the other person. There is no other person—a bad you and a good you. There is only you. You, sitting right there. It is you who were sick. It is you who killed Raoul. It is you who have spent nine years in therapy with me. And it is you who are no longer sick. It is just you. There is no other person. There is no other you."

Sarah covered her face with her hands.

"Yes?"

"Yes," Sarah said.

The shrink rearranged her bulk in the chair. She took a deep breath. In a moment she leaned back, calm again.

"So. You have had a drink, two drinks, and you made love

and bit this Quinn. But you have learned from this. And what have you learned?"

"That it was me and not some other person."

"That it was you and not some other person. And you have learned that you do not have to do this. You do not have to do these things. You were sick before, but you are not sick now."

"I think I'm about to have my period."

The shrink paused.

"And how do you feel about this?"

Sarah lowered her eyes. She saw the black gobs of blood on the white sheet. The stink. She saw Raoul's head between her legs, twisting, thrusting as he ate the bloody mess.

"Yes?"

"It's normal. It's..."

"Normal? What is this normal? Is there any such thing as normal?"

"Ordinary. It's nothing but the ordinary menstrual cycle of an ordinary woman."

"Ah, good. This is good."

In a single motion Sarah slipped from her chair to the floor and knelt, sobbing, with her head in the shrink's lap.

The shrink said nothing, did nothing. No hand on Sarah's head, no word of consolation, no interference with the workings of a mind in search of itself.

"Oh, help me, please help me," Sarah said finally.

The shrink sat in silence while Sarah pulled herself together, got up from her kneeling position, and returned to her chair.

"What is it you want?" the shrink said. "Tell me what you want."

"I want Quinn. I want to be normal. Ordinary."

"Yes."

"I want to be just ordinary and good."

"Yes. Tell me how you would like to see yourself in a year from now. In five years. Let us fantasize together."

Sarah ran a handkerchief beneath her eyes and thought. It seemed all over suddenly—the craziness, the other Sarah, the worry—and she could see a future that was real. She would have it. She would be like other women, like Claire.

"Tell me."

"I want to be a professor's wife. I want to make him breakfast before he goes to lecture, and I want to have the faculty for dinner and listen to them talk about books and things, and I want to invite his students for tea in the afternoon and . . ."

"And for yourself you want?"

"That *is* for myself. That *is* what I want."

"So. Well, there is much to do. But first I think it better you do not see this Quinn until we decide, together, it is right. Yes?"

"After my period? When Porter is better?"

"We will talk of this. But no Quinn now. Not at all. No telephone calls. No letters. Nothing."

"Nothing."

"It is better this way. It is safer. You know this."

"Yes. Nothing."

"And I will see you tomorrow. The same time. And every day after that. You are no longer sick. We must work now, together, to keep you well."

Again Sarah saw the blood on the sheet and her legs spread wide and Raoul's head moving, thrusting between them. With enormous effort, she turned from the sight and gazed instead into the broad bland face of the shrink.

"Yes?"

"Yes," Sarah said.

18

On Thursday afternoon Claire explained to the director of the summer school that she would miss Friday classes because of a woman's thing, a medical procedure, letting him think it was a D and C. An hour later she checked into the clinic for an abortion.

Twice it threatened to be a hideous experience; once, for no reason at all, when they laid her on the table and swabbed her with a warm fluid, disinfectant no doubt; again, when she came out of anaesthesia and realized the baby was gone, dead, it would never be. She had wanted to scream, to run, to do anything that would stop what she had set in motion. But both were moments of irrationality—mere panic—Claire realized, and she reminded herself, firmly, that her own right to life came first. And so she got through it all without a whimper or a tear.

That was Thursday night. On Friday, with the help of a couple Nembutal, she had surrendered to a full twenty-four hours of drugged and dreamless sleep. And now it was Saturday, exactly a week since she had last seen Quinn, and she was in Boston to assess the progress of his summer fling and to decide what to do next.

She parked her car in the garage beneath the Common and walked across the Public Gardens to Baileys. It was ten o'clock in the morning, too early for lunch, but she was still pale and shaky from her medical procedure and she intended to fortify herself before continuing her investigation. She ordered a hot fudge sundae with coffee ice cream—hold the nuts—and sat back to contemplate her future, or rather their future.

But as she bent to the task of applying cold reason to the consideration of hard facts, something happened in her brain. She had a momentary vision of the future stretching out before her: where the city of Boston had stood, there was only a barren plain littered with the bodies of the dead and the near dead, there was thick smoke and the smell of blood, and somewhere a baby was crying. She thought she was going to faint. She pushed back from the table and bent her head to her knees. Everything went black and then red, and finally her vision cleared and she could see, and think, again.

Tricks of the body, Claire said to herself, tricks of the mind. She was still exhausted from the abortion. So for the moment she refused to give any further consideration to her future or to Quinn's.

She sipped from her glass of water and tried to make her mind a blank. She succeeded so well that when the waiter brought her order, she tucked into the hot fudge sundae as if the future did not exist—not for the baby certainly, but not for Quinn either, nor for her. The only reality was the present, the ice cream, her infinite hunger.

She finished the sundae and ordered coffee, black, no sugar. She sat quietly, drinking it. With her mind clear and her appetite at rest for the moment, she could now ponder her immediate line of attack.

First, call Quinn. His voice would tell her plenty. Then, find out what Angelo knew and what he would be willing to tell. But how would she reach Angelo? She disliked the idea of just showing up at his place; no telling who might be there or what they might be doing. Well, that would work itself out. She'd think of something once she talked to Quinn.

She had all the time in the world—indeed, the longer she delayed the easier it would be to get him back—and so she was going to play this by ear.

How would you translate that? You'd have to invent a Latin idiom. *Agere de talis?* Or without the preposition? *Talis,* alone? Or would you say *ex sortibus? Agere ex sortibus* was more likely. It was impossible, of course, to translate idioms from one language into another, but it was irresistible to try to find the equivalent. Quinn was trying, but she would get him back, because there was no translating him into the idiom of Beacon Hill. Not with that lip. Not with those years of inferiority. She thought of her own years of inferiority: the fat girl. But she had outlived that fat girl, thanks to the wonderful powers of her intellect. The fat girl had become a scholar, respected, *tenured* moreover. She smiled, pleased at the way her unconscious had made the connection between language and love. She would get him back.

She passed the candy display on her way to the phone, and paused for a second, but only for a second. Her eating binge was just a summer fling, like Quinn's, except that she was giving herself only one week of folly—not a day more. How much damage, after all, could she do in a single week?

Quinn answered the phone on the second ring, his voice eager, if a little raspy, but when he heard it was Claire, he turned shy.

"How are your classes, Claire?" he said. "How is your aunt?"

"I just wanted to say hello," Claire said. "I just thought I'd ask how the work is going."

"That's nice," he said.

"How are you, Quinn?" A loving voice, a forgiving voice.

"Are you in Boston? Or in Hanover. Claire?"

"Hanover."

"Oh," he said, disappointed. A rather long silence, and then: "This is difficult, isn't it. I can't think of what to say."

"I just wanted to hear how your work is going."

"Claire?" That tone of his.

"Don't worry about it, Quinn. It'll be fine."

"I haven't seen her once, Claire. Not since last week. Not since Saturday."

"We won't talk about it. It's just a summer fling, as I said." There was silence, and she added, *"sicut dixi."*

"I miss the Latin."

"Bene," she said. *"An scribas,* Quinn? *Libellum scribas?"*

"Certissime," he said. "Oh, Claire, the book's going great, really. I'm doing five pages a day, sometimes six. Well, they're rough pages, of course, because I'm going too fast. I mean, nobody can write this much every day and keep it under control. But it's just pouring out; it's almost easy, you know? I wish I could read you some parts, just a couple lines even. I've got a section—two pages or so—that are the best thing anybody's ever written on sex. I mean physical sex. People in bed. Doing it."

"Quinn? Hold on a minute."

"Oh, I'm sorry," he said. "I shouldn't have said that. Oh, my god! It's just that it's *fiction,* Claire. Really."

"Quinn?" Her three minutes were nearly up, and if the operator suddenly broke in to ask for more change, he'd know she was in Boston. "Quinn, Aunt Lily's calling me," Claire said. "I'll phone you back in a few minutes." Before he could say anything more, she hung up. So. Aunt Lily was proving useful. She must remember that.

At once she rang the operator, explained that she had no coins, and charged this new call to her Hanover number. Claire congratulated herself; she was getting very good at this sleuth business.

Quinn answered immediately. "Do you think you'd like to drive down?" he said. "For the weekend? I could read you my stuff? It's awfully good."

"I don't want to be in the way," she said.

"No," he said. "No. I'm not seeing her. She's not like... Sarah isn't..." And, after a long pause, "It's just a summer fling, Claire."

"I'll wait another week at least," she said. "You can save up your writing for me."

"I think you'd really be impressed by this new stuff I'm doing."

"I think we should wait."

"I could use a break. Really."

"If it's what you *want,* Quinn."

"I want you to come down," he said. "It's what I *want.* More than anything in the whole world. Okay?" And he added, perhaps sincerely, "I want to see you."

And so she let him persuade her to drive to Boston for the weekend. She would be there in just a few hours. "And Quinn? We won't talk about the fling, all right? Not a word."

She hung up and smiled to herself. That had gone very well indeed. Now, should she risk stopping by Angelo's? Perhaps just loiter in Louisburg Square? She was too tired for that, she was exhausted, and hungry. She would think about Angelo later.

With three hours or so to kill, and with everything going so smoothly, the first order of business was celebration. A muffin and coffee? Pastry? No, she'd go the whole hog. *Porcus absolutus. Porcus ultimus.* She'd have a cinnamon bun, with that sugary spicy perfectly magic cinnamon concoction separating whorls and whorls of soft sweet dough. Why not! It's a poor heart indeed that never rejoices.

She left Baileys and walked to the corner to hail a cab. She cast an eye in Brighams as she passed, but their cinnamon rolls would never do. She wanted the real thing. She would go to Quincy Market on the other side of Beacon Hill.

At the crosswalk she stepped out into the street and took a long look up Boylston. Not a sign of a cab. She turned to look at Arlington. There were cabs in front of the Ritz, less than a block away. But she didn't want to walk even that far; she was so tired, so hungry.

She stepped back into the shade of Shreve's awning to think for a minute. She closed her eyes and concentrated, willing a cab to appear or, if not a cab, at least Angelo. She opened her eyes. There was no cab. But standing at the curb only five feet away was Angelo, glorious in a cream-colored suit. She had summoned him and now she willed him to turn and look at her. He did. Actually, his eyes were following a middle-aged hunk in T-shirt and running shorts, and as he jogged past Claire, Angelo's look crossed hers and she smiled at him, a little distant. Angelo continued following the hunk with his eyes, but he did a double take as he recognized Claire. He made a series of ridiculous gestures, quick, urgent, meaning what?

The light changed and people all around him began to cross the street. He turned away and took the arm of the woman waiting at his side. She was blond and insultingly slim in her smart cotton shirtdress, but she was clearly an older woman, well past her prime. She looked haggard, dazed. She stared straight ahead, oblivious to the traffic, oblivious to everything, and it was only when Angelo took her by the arm that she came out of her trance and walked with him dutifully— like an invalid with her keeper—across the street and into the Public Gardens.

Claire watched them go, realizing with a pleasant shock that the woman was Sarah Slade. For a second she thought she recognized that face—haggard, empty—from somewhere else. But from where?

She waited in the shade of the awning until once again the light turned green. She felt a great deal better after her little rest. She felt good.

Ad proximum, she said to herself, *ad astra.*

Claire crossed the street with a light step on her way to the Ritz for a cab. She was young and in control and she had her whole life ahead of her. She was an enterprising woman.

To Claire, Quincy Market at noon on Saturday seemed the still point of the turning world. Large stalls for fruit and fish and meat and bread contended for attention with jiffy stands selling absolutely everything she could desire: ice cream, oysters, chocolate, popcorn, pizza, hot dogs, baklava, tacos, corn on the cob, carrot cake, peanuts, pickles, homemade pastry, grape leaves stuffed with cheese and rice, push-up pineapple on a stick, and more, and more. It was God's plenty, with lots of little tables to eat things at.

Claire had eaten half her cinnamon bun—it was enormous, delicious—and she was taking a break before attacking the rest of it, when she spotted little Leopold. He was walking solemnly in the midst of a small bunch of children, all of whom were out of control. They were hopping around and pushing one another and generally demonstrating a need for discipline, but the woman who was conducting them didn't seem to notice or to care. She had teacher written all over her, Claire thought, watching the woman shuffle along, moony and fat, holding the string of a silver balloon with PINE HILL SCHOOL on it in large black letters. What a crowd: the kids looked manic and the teacher looked depressive. It was pitiful. Only Leopold seemed to know what he was doing and why he was there.

Leopold had almost passed by her table before Claire finally caught his eye. He started, surprised.

"I saw you," Claire said, her voice high and thin.

Leopold giggled and put his fists to his mouth.

"Are you having a nice time, Leopold? Do you enjoy Quincy Market?"

Leopold stood at her table staring at her cinnamon bun.

"Would you like a bite of this?" she said.

"I saw Mister."

"Did you? Isn't that nice! And was Mister alone or was he with somebody?"

Leopold nodded.

What was that supposed to mean? "You always are the first to see, aren't you. You're a clever little boy, aren't you. Well, *I* think you're a very clever little boy."

Leopold shrugged, and then brought his shoulders back up to his ears and left them there. He looked like a gargoyle.

"And was Mister alone or was he with somebody else?"

Leopold shook his head.

"Can you tell me?"

Leopold tried to hide his face with his fat little hands.

Claire looked around to see if anyone was watching this. She was beginning to feel like a perfect fool.

"Do you know what?" Leopold said.

"Tell me."

"My grandma made peepee in her bed." At once he turned from her and disappeared into the crowd. Claire could see the Pine Hill School balloon bobbing in the distance.

Well, that had been a failure, but it cut both ways; if Leopold wouldn't tell her about seeing Quinn, he wouldn't tell Quinn about seeing her. And, who knows, with the way things were going, she might yet be able to use Leopold as her informer. Everybody, she was discovering, had a use.

She sat back to enjoy her cinnamon bun and contemplate human nature. The whole world was here today. There were sightseers checking out Faneuil Hall. There were preppies buying quiche for Sunday brunch. There were panhandlers and police and political types, crazy teenagers with cigarettes and tight pants; bag ladies, jugglers, muggers, mimes, and—armed with cameras, and spending, and smiling—there were Japanese tourists by the score. What a wonderful place. What wonderful food. Claire raised her face to the hot noon sun. It was good just to be alive.

Angelo was standing in front of Number 17, shifting anxiously from foot to foot, when Claire's cab pulled into Louisburg Square. He sprinted over and opened the door for her, waiting nervously while she fished several bills from her purse. It was as if he were expecting her.

Claire tipped the driver a great deal more than necessary—she did it consciously, to bribe the gods for a successful day—and then she turned her full attention to Angelo.

"I was afraid you wouldn't come," he said softly. "It took you so long."

"Well, I didn't realize I was expected," she said. "I didn't realize those frenzied gestures constituted an invitation."

He looked at her as if she were being deliberately obtuse.

"Come in, come in," he said in a whisper, and as she followed him down the stairs, he added, over his shoulder, "I'm glad you came. I was afraid you wouldn't want to."

"Not at all," she said. "Of course."

Angelo closed the door and gestured toward the couch, Claire's place. "Come in," he said, still whispering. "Well, you *are* in, aren't you. I mean, please sit down. You look so smart. That's a beautiful dress, very becoming."

Claire looked at her dress, which she knew was too tight, and looked at Angelo and said, "Why are we whispering?"

"Oh, sorry." He pointed upstairs. "Porter had a heart attack and Sarah is . . ."

"He had a heart attack and he's upstairs? Shouldn't he be in the hospital?"

"He *is* in the hospital. He almost died. It's Sarah who... well, you saw her an hour ago. I just gave her a tranquilizer."

"Is she all right? Is *he* all right?"

"Porter's going to be okay. It happened last week, actually, right after he left here; he lost control of the car and he was lucky because it veered right instead of left, so he only hit a parked car. If he'd veered left, he'd have had a head-on collision."

"I'm sorry."

He smiled at her.

"But he wasn't hurt," she said. "That's good."

"Not from the accident. Just the heart attack, which was a bad one. It was touch and go for a couple days, but he came around on Monday, and they say he's going to be all right now. Poor Porter."

He seemed unconcerned to Claire. If Quinn had had a heart attack and then a car crash, she'd be frantic. Perhaps gays didn't love the way other people did.

"It's Sarah I'm worried about," he said.

"Is she very attached to her brother?"

"She thinks she caused it. She blames herself. She blames herself for everything."

"But nobody causes heart attacks. Heart attacks just happen."

"But it wouldn't have happened, she says, if she..."

Claire took a guess. "If she hadn't been with Quinn."

"I'm sorry," Angelo said, and nodded.

So. She had the upper hand; she could play the woman wronged. "And you wanted to see me about something, I presume. You *did* ask me if I would come by and see you."

He looked confused or perhaps guilty.

"The hand signals. The frenzied waving in front of Shreve's. You *did* want me to come."

"Oh. Yes."

"You wanted to tell me something about Quinn and... your sister-in-law?"

"I just wanted to see you." He spread his hands, palms up. He was actually blushing. "I just wanted to talk with you, Claire."

He looked at her then so ingenuously, with such childish affection, that for a second she was disoriented. He could have been Quinn in the old days, when Quinn still needed her, when they were still Claire and Quinn, Quinn and Claire. She was tempted to reach out and touch him. She wanted to.

"What did you want to talk about?"

He gave her a half-smile, started to say something, and then stopped.

"Why don't you tell me about Quinn."

"Please, no," he said. "Claire."

"Or about your sister-in-law. Sarah."

"They haven't seen each other since Porter's heart attack. Honest to God."

"Are you sure? Quinn's a very busy little boy."

"I've been with her every second. Sarah's too sick to see anybody."

So. Quinn had been telling the truth after all. Did that mean he would come back without putting up a fight?

"Poor Sarah. I don't like to talk about her; she's had things very... hard."

"What is she sick with? Do you mean she's physically sick? Or is it mental?"

"No! No, she's not sick that way. She was for a while, a long time ago, but she's fine now. She's just weak. Delicate. She's not very strong."

"Not very strong."

"She sees a doctor, a good one. In fact, we were on our way back from her appointment when I saw you at the corner of Shreve's and, just on the spur of the moment, asked you to come." They sat, silent, for a moment. "I didn't think you would. I *hoped* you would." More silence. "I'm glad you did."

"Why does her name sound familiar to me? Sarah Slade. That sounds familiar. And when I saw her today, she even *looked* familiar, just for a second. I thought: I know that face. But I can't place it."

"It's a famous name, Slade is. And Sarah has a Beacon Hill face. Brahmin. It's a type, don't you think so?"

"Yes, but that isn't it. There's something..."

"Can I get you some coffee, Claire? Or tea? Would you prefer tea?"

"Nothing," she said. "I'm on a diet. And I should be going."

"Do you have to? What I hoped we could talk about—I mean, if you wanted to—is Kierkegaard. Like the other night."

"Oh, honestly!"

"What?"

She saw he was serious, so she modified her tone. Ridicule was fine and satisfying, but it never really got you anywhere.

"I was hardly at my best the other night," she said. "You were nice to take me in and let me talk. Or rave, should I say."

"But it was wonderful. It was the best conversation I've had in years. I've been thinking, too, about what you said: that the only sin is the refusal to live your own life. But I still can't see how you..."

"Did I say that?"

184

"*Yes*. You were telling me about your book on Greek women and you said . . ."

"Oh, that. Yes."

"Have you changed your mind or something?"

"No. It's just that I wasn't really talking about Kierkegaard or about the Greeks or about sin, for that matter; I was talking about me. About abortion."

"I don't get it."

"I was in the process of deciding on an abortion."

"You're pregnant?"

"I was."

"Oh, geez. I should never have given you so much to drink. I'm terribly sorry. I hope nothing . . ."

"There's nothing to worry about," Claire said, a little too cheerfully. "I had the abortion—on Thursday, as a matter of fact—so no harm's done."

Angelo sat back, appalled.

"Well, I did," she said.

"Oh, Claire." He sounded heartbroken. "Was it because of Quinn? And . . . ?"

"I want him back, Angelo," she said softly. "I'll do anything to get him back."

"But abortion! That's killing! That's taking a life!"

"You were the one, as I recall, who kept saying that an individual life didn't count for all that much. You were the one who . . ." She was very angry.

"But I was thinking of *my* life, not a baby's."

Claire leaned forward suddenly, her arms around her belly, her head bent to her knees. "No!" she said, and her body shook as she began to cry soundlessly. Angelo moved to the couch and sat down next to her, his hand on her shoulder.

"Oh, Claire," he said. "Oh, Claire."

After a while the crying stopped and she leaned back into his arms, her head on his chest. They sat that way for a long time.

"Angelo?" It was Sarah calling down the stairs to him.

"Oh, God," he said. "She must need another pill. I've got to go to her. Wait for me. Will you please wait?"

"Angelo?" Even from here Sarah's voice sounded thick with sleep, or with drugs.

Angelo disappeared from the room and in a moment Claire heard him going up the stairs to Sarah.

This was the perfect opportunity to take the gun. She had only to get up from the couch, go into the bedroom, and slip it into her pocketbook. The easiest thing in the world.

Claire wasn't at all clear about why she wanted the gun or why she had taken the ammunition clip. She had not planned it ahead of time. But her brain worked this way, quickly, making vital connections of terrific importance before she understood what those connections were or why she was making them.

Waiting in Angelo's living room, she turned this phenomenon over in her excellent mind. Having the gun and the clip in her possession was a kind of insurance. Like frozen food in the refrigerator. A candy bar in the handkerchief drawer. Something Quinn owed her, in justice, that she could call upon later when she needed it. A life insurance policy, of sorts.

But she let the opportunity pass. Taking the gun would argue a lack of faith in herself, in Quinn, and in her determination to get him back and keep him.

She went to the bathroom and washed her face. She touched up her lipstick and eyeliner. She combed her hair. She was ready now for battle.

•   •   •

As Claire paused on the second landing, she could hear Birdie shouting at Jim.

"Put in your hearing aid. You're deaf."

Claire leaned toward the door, but she couldn't catch what Jim said in return.

"What? What are you saying?" Birdie shouted.

"I said I'm not the only deaf one around this place."

"You're getting senile. I'm going to put you in a home."

Claire trudged up the next flight of stairs, leaving Jim and Birdie to their quarrel. It was recreation for them, she figured. It didn't mean anything at all. They were just walking their wits, or what was left of them. What a deprived way of living. She'd rather be dead.

She rested outside her door, looking around for Leopold, who of course was crouching on the stairs that led to the floor above. He peered through the rails at her, his fat little face pressed against them, his tiny eyes fixed on her every movement.

"I saw you," she said.

Leopold nodded his head, yes.

"Did you have a good time at Quincy Market? Did you have something to eat?"

Leopold nodded again.

"What did you have? Can you tell me?" But then she thought of a way to use this ghastly child. "Was that your teacher with you? On a Saturday?"

Leopold stopped.

"Was that Miss Slade?"

Leopold shook his head emphatically. No.

"Do you like Miss Slade?"

Leopold nodded just as emphatically. Yes. And then suddenly he came alive. "I luh-uh-uh-uh-ve Miss Slade," he wailed. "She's my favorite in the whole world."

"She's mine, too," Claire said. "Does she ever come here to visit Mister?"

Leopold shook his head, no.

"Never at all? No?"

Leopold shook his head harder and kept on shaking it.

"Do you know what? Leopold?"

He stopped.

"You're *my* favorite. You *are*. You're my favorite in the whole world."

Leopold, ecstatic, plunged his hands between his legs. His tiny eyes goggled.

Claire was getting ready to ask a good deal more about Miss Slade when the door opened and Quinn said, "What's going on?"

"I saw you," Leopold said, full of joy, grinning like the little gargoyle he was.

Quinn had been reading to Claire for nearly an hour and was still going strong. What an astonishing man he was.

At first he'd been a little uncomfortable with her, awkward, maybe even guilty, but after she'd made them a cup of tea and some sandwiches—she really was putting on the old weight, he noticed—he settled easily into the routine they always followed when he was writing something. He read her a couple good lines he'd just finished writing, and then a paragraph that came earlier, and after she insisted that she'd love to hear the whole thing, he began at the beginning and read straight through.

Claire marveled once again at the economy of writers. It was all there—the stuff from his notebooks, the anger from his tenure try, their own recent separation—but it was so artfully distorted that you couldn't prove a thing. It was just a piece of fiction about a second-rate store detective, a rich and languorous blonde from Beacon Hill, and her simultaneous affairs with lover and brother. The detective was charmingly naive, a sexual novice, but under the careful guidance of the blonde, he had begun to assume a personality and a character of some strength and independence. The novel was about this detective's growth as a man solely through the power of sex.

The sex scenes, to be sure, were graphic. Claire was not really embarrassed by them, and not really shocked; as fiction, she found them altogether credible and perhaps even necessary, given the novel's assumptions.

What surprised and intrigued her was relating these sex scenes to real life. Quinn as the adventurous lover? A sexual athlete? Good old in-and-out, wham-bam-thank-you-ma'am Quinn? She found it hard to imagine him writing these things, let alone doing them. All that mounting and dismounting, his penis slick with lipstick, the endless exploration of each other's bodies. It sounded like fun, actually, but she just couldn't relate it to Quinn.

Claire listened and watched as he read page after page, shamelessly. He seemed to think that if he called it fiction, then everything he'd done was justified. That Claire could not possibly think she had been misused, let alone betrayed. That Sarah would be happy to have her kinky sex life on display. And that Angelo and Porter would be delighted to find themselves conflated into a single harelipped, effeminate, incestuous lover. *O quam gloriosum!* He truly was an *interesting* man and once again, silently, grimly, as she nodded and smiled and listened to him read, she resolved that she would never, ever, let him go.

"Well, it's a marvel, Quinn. It's your best thing so far."

"Oh, Claire, do you think so? Do you think it's good?"

"It's wonderful."

"Do you think the stuff in Bonwit's is convincing? Does he really seem to you to be a detective?"

"Is it really so important that we believe he's a detective? Or should we just be convinced that as a man he's insecure? Sexually insecure, I mean."

"Oh. Do you think I should make him something else? A civil rights activist? Or an ecologist? How about a high school counselor; they're *all* sexually insecure."

"Why don't you wait and see what happens? Just sort of keep the question open? Perhaps as you go on, you'll find you want to give him some other occupation." Claire smiled at him; they both knew she was his ideal critic. "In the interest of economy," she said.

"And what about the sex stuff? Does it work? Is it functional, do you think, or does it stick out?"

"It sticks out," she said, "but I like it."

"But does it *work*? It has to be purely functional."

"It works, Quinn," she said. "It functions."

They sat in silence for a moment, thinking.

"It's hot in here," Quinn said.

Claire said nothing.

"About the sex stuff, Claire, you know...a novel these days...well, I never really wanted to..."

"We're not going to talk about it, Quinn."

Quinn cradled the manuscript lovingly against his chest for a moment, and then he put it down on the desk. He patted it twice, and Claire smiled at him.

"So how are you feeling, Claire?" he said. "Are you feeling okay? I see you've put on a bit more weight." Her eyes filled and he added, "Just a tiny bit."

A single tear rolled down her cheek.

"Well, I'm sorry," he said, the beginnings of annoyance in his voice. "But people *do* put on weight when they get pregnant, you know."

"I lost the baby, Quinn," she said. "I miscarried."

"Oh, no!" he said, genuinely shocked. "Oh, Claire. Oh, my poor Claire. I'm sorry. I am sorry." He moved next to her on the couch and put his arms around her as she let herself slide, gratefully, into tears. He rubbed her shoulders and her back.

"How did it happen?" he said finally. "When?"

"I can't talk about it," Claire said. "It was too awful." She felt his arms close firmly around her, comforting. "It happened Thursday night."

"Thursday night! My God, that's only twenty-four hours, or thirty-six, or something. You should be in bed. You should be in the *hospital.*"

"I'm fine," she said. "I'm just tired."

"Well, we should get you in bed right away. Come on," he said, "I'll put you to bed and I'll make you some tea and toast and I'll take care of you like the best doctor in the world."

She could hear the relief in his voice, the new energy, the first rumblings of high spirits, not because she was okay but because the baby was gone. She wondered if he were aware of it himself.

Well, she thought, if he'd been planning to tell her the marriage was all over, *that* plan was certainly on hold.

Quinn brought her the tea and toast, and then sat at the foot of the bed, a hand on her knee. "I'm sorry about the baby," he said. "Are you okay? Psychologically?"

Claire nodded.

"In the long run, you know, it's probably just as well. We weren't really ready for one. I wasn't. I guess you know that."

"It's us that matters, Quinn, not the baby."

"But I know you must have taken it hard. And I'm sorry that I . . . you know . . . with Sarah."

"A writer has to have freedom," she said.

He moved up on the bed and kissed her softly, sweetly, on the forehead and then on the lips. She waited for him to say I love you, but he only gazed into her eyes.

"I'll tell you about it, Quinn," she said, and as she began the story, she turned her head sharply on the pillow and brushed away tears. After a moment, she went on anyway.

She told him how she had been standing in the center of her circle of students, firing Latin questions at them, moving quickly from one to the other, encouraging them, beckoning with her hands for more and more response, when suddenly, with no warning, a pain ran from her heart down to the depths of her womb, and everything began to go black before her eyes. She felt herself falling, she felt somebody catching er, but she was aware only of the terrible convulsion inside her, as if the baby, too, was feeling these pains, and the pains were killing it. She wanted to cry, or at least scream—and maybe she did scream, she couldn't remember—because the pain went on and on until she wanted to die and just have it over with, just have it end, and then they were lifting her, and a car was speeding through the streets of Hanover...

She went on for some time while Quinn listened, fascinated and clearly in pain for her, with her, and then she fell silent. "I've got to rest a little," she said, thinking how easy it was to write fiction. With a hard fact and a gift for lying, anybody could do it.

"I'll hold you," Quinn said. He lay down on the bed beside her and very carefully placed an arm beneath her back, a hand gently on her breast.

Claire left for Hanover after Sunday brunch, enormously satisfied with her trip to Boston. She had not let Quinn apologize for his affair with Sarah. She had not let him assume any blame whatsoever, not even for all that filthy stuff he cleverly disguised as fiction.

Moreover she had refused to discuss the future with him. She was not going to let him off the hook that easily and she was not going to let him feel that now he was trapped all over again.

He was free, and he had to feel free and to feel guilty about what he was doing with his freedom.

Summer school would last for two more weeks and she was determined not to tighten the net before then. Why give him time and space to struggle?

She had taken care of the baby. She was taking care of Sarah at this very moment, passively, letting her self-destruct. Poor Sarah, as Angelo called her. Porter's heart attack seemed to have broken her and a good final dose of Quinn should finish her off. Wait till she got a gander at his idea of fiction.

Sarah Slade. Sarah Slade. Claire pondered the name for the hundredth time, certain she knew it from somewhere, remembered it in a way that convinced her Sarah Slade would be no match for her, despite the rich looks and the rich life and the infuriatingly skinny body.

The name and whatever it meant was just about to come to her—she almost had it—when some damned fool who was gawking at the scenery drifted from his lane into hers and practically locked fenders. She swerved onto the shoulder of the highway and at the same time gave him a blast from her horn so loud and prolonged that it woke him from his trance and blew him back into his own lane where he belonged. But he had completely destroyed her concentration. She cursed him in English and then, from habit, in Latin.

She went back to consoling thoughts about Quinn. She drifted into prayer. *"O dea Venus,"* she said aloud to the car and the scenery and the teeming heavens above her, *"juva ignes amoris quos dedisti.*" She translated her prayer in several ways, none of them satisfactory because they all involved terrible English repetitions—inflame the fires of love, and so forth—but it didn't matter, because the goddess Venus knew what she had in mind.

19

It was midnight, Sunday, and Sarah turned from side to side in her bed before she woke up, staring, terrified. Her breast was slick with sweat and there was a strong smell of acid—sharp, scalding. Slowly she became aware that it was the smell of her own body. She put her hand between her legs and brought it back to her face; she was dry; the stench was not there, it was everywhere inside her and it was coming out.

She turned from side to side, trying to go unconscious once again. But something was keeping her awake, alive. Not the smell but something else, something she had to do.

She pulled herself to the edge of the bed and sat there for a moment, her head lolling to one side. She spread her legs and touched herself again. No, she was dry. She had done that already.

She forced her foot into a slipper and sat looking at the floor. After a while she fished the other slipper close to her, and pushed with her foot, but the slipper wouldn't go on. She tried again, pushing harder, but the slipper turned on its side, and her foot followed it somehow, and then she knew that her body crashed to the floor, but she felt nothing. She lay there, resting, until she was able to get up on her hands and knees. After a while, supporting herself on the bed, she stood up and looked around the room, confused. She had something to do.

A light showed from the bathroom and Sarah walked shak-

ily to the door and looked in. Nothing. She caught a glimpse
of herself in the mirror and turned sharply away; her hair was
matted and filthy, thick with sweat, and all her flesh seemed
to sag—her face, her breasts, her belly even. She was the
crazy woman again. Her whole body stank: urine, feces, menstrual flow. "Piss," she said, slurring the word. "Shit." "Your
fucking baby blood." She glanced back and caught sight of
Raoul in the mirror, making her say these things; she saw him
kneel between her legs, with his head pushing into her, as she
said the words over and over, "My piss, my shit, my fucking
baby blood," and she saw his face covered with that black
blood, and she was holding the gun against his forehead, and
then at last came the sound of the gunshot that ended it all.
She leaned against the doorframe and slid once again to the
floor and for a while, grateful, she went unconscious.

Later, when Angelo appeared at the landing of the stairs,
Sarah was in her studio dragging out the canvases that had
been stacked against the wall. The most recent stood on the
easel, half complete, and others were spread around the room,
propped against the wall, the windowsills, the doors, leaning
against one another, facing out into the room. There were so
many, in different sizes and colors, but all of them represented
the same thing: a landscape of barren earth against an empty
sky. In some, a feeling of heat rose from the earth, the intense
yellows and tans taking on the color of fire, but in others the
heat was muted by the dull hue and the low intensity, though
the colors themselves remained the same. In all but the most
recent, the sky was a flat silver blue; the canvas on the easel,
though, and two recent canvases propped against it, had skies
stained with some other color—not black or midnight blue or
purple, but a dead shade that had no name.

Sarah stood in the center of the room beneath the blinding
light looking from picture to picture.

"Sarah," Angelo said softly. "Come on."

She turned and stared at him as if he were a stranger or someone she knew but could not recognize.

Angelo put his arms around her and pressed her head against his chest. Her hair needed combing and she was wearing only her nightgown and a single slipper, but she was beautiful still, and pathetic. He could smell the Joy she had used in her bath. "It's all right," he said. "It's going to be all right, Sarah, I promise."

She let him hold her, but then suddenly she pulled away from him and shook her head, and said, "No." She shook her head again, and touched her hand to her thigh, moving it slowly toward her crotch, and then she lifted it to her face, palm out, waving him away. "No," she said once more.

"There is no smell," he said firmly. "You do not smell of anything. Not . . . anything."

She looked at him, her eyes focusing for the first time, a question.

"You're very lovely and you're very much loved and it's all going to be all right."

The corner of her mouth pulled to the side in a sneer as, for a long time, they stood looking at each other. At last she let herself be led back to her bedroom where he gave her another tranquilizer, kissed her once on the fingertips, and sat on her bed until she fell asleep.

It was midnight, Sunday, and Quinn sat before the television with his notebook in his lap, a drink in his hand. On the screen a thirty-year-old man who looked like a bad child was doing a skit in which a newscaster delivered sardonic reports about the President and the Mideast and the Pope, while the live audience roared and applauded and carried on as if he were terrifically funny. Everything he said was utterly predictable or off-color or just vulgar.

197

Quinn checked the *TV Guide* to find out what he was watching; it was some cable thing, described as witty wacky satire. *Wacky* satire?

Quinn watched television, he told himself, because this stuff was Americana and because he was a writer who had to know his place and his time, but he was lying and he knew it; the truth was that he used television as a kind of hypnotic device to keep his conscious mind distracted while his unconscious mind thought up new ways to render experience, to tell lies about it, to turn it into fiction.

He sipped his drink and smiled at the screen; transforming Angelo and Porter into a single character and making him Sarah's half-brother and incestuous lover was a stroke of genius, one of those creative accidents that keep writers writing. He was sure of it. You got that kind of thing only when you'd paid your dues, worked for years at your craft, confronted the empty page at a set time every day, no matter how you felt, no matter how much you wanted not to. It depended on a flash of—what?—insight, maybe, that struck for one millisecond as you sat at the typewriter without the least idea of what should come next. Real people didn't believe in those accidents, and they didn't believe that the seven types of ambiguity resulting from such accidents were actually intended by the writer, but real people were wrong and that was all there was to it.

Quinn lifted his glass in a toast to the real people on the screen, even as his unconscious mind turned over the problem of what could happen next, what should happen next, what had to happen next in order to exploit the material to its full potential. He needed to break for a while from this barrage of writing, he needed to see Sarah again.

He thought of phoning her, but it was now well past midnight. He'd phone her tomorrow, after coffee and a little writ-

ing, even though he didn't *have* to write tomorrow, since he
had given himself Sunday as a break day. Maybe they could
have a late brunch, take a long walk by the river, maybe—if
she felt up to it and Porter weren't still banging on death's
door—maybe they'd go back to her place and make love. It
was odd, though, how he didn't think about making love
these days now that the book was going so well. It was as if
he channeled all his sex drive into the writing. As if he'd never
had any sexual doubts whatsoever. He was becoming his own
character, in a way: a man who achieves maturity through the
miracle of sex.

Well, writing was wonderful; there was nothing so wonderful as writing. *Mirabile est,* as Claire would say. *O quam
gloriosum.*

Claire. That had all gone very well. She had really liked
what he'd written so far; she had laughed at the right places,
she had wanted to know—the true test of how well he was
working—what happened next. And she wasn't faking it;
that was one thing about Claire. She'd never lie about his
writing. She'd never lie about anything. There was nobody as
lousy with integrity as Claire.

He smiled to himself as he thought of his own daring: he
had read Claire things about sex—about people doing things
that he and Claire would never even *talk* about in a million
years, let alone *do*—and she had never blinked an eye. It
worked as fiction, all of it.

Good old Claire. He was being a bit of a shit, in a way,
getting it on with Sarah while Claire was up there in Dartmouth teaching her ass off all summer. And then there was
the baby, the miscarriage. Well, at least Claire hadn't had an
abortion. The Church still regarded abortion as murder. Not
that he cared what the Church said; the fact was that he just
didn't like the idea of abortion. Maybe it was one of those

vestigial Catholic feelings, those live nerves that somehow still quivered in him even though his Catholic body was dead. He wanted none of it.

Writers who had once been Catholics were always talking about how their Catholicism had left them with permanent scars and those scars were visible in their work, but that was nonsense. Worse than nonsense, really, because they were using their cast-off religion to claim for their work a moral dimension that the work didn't actually have; as if by making a character remember the Hail Mary as he faced torture in Equador, you somehow sanctified an otherwise shitty life. Not for him. Not for Quinn. He didn't want any live Catholic nerves twitching in him and he would make sure that none was twitching in his fiction either. He'd face eternity with the only Catholic scars he cared about: his torn lip and his torn psyche.

For the first time in weeks, Quinn lifted his hand to his mouth and felt the hard line in his upper lip. Bunny Quinn. Rabbit. This lip made him who he was. He accepted it. And he'd make something out of it, thank you. His writing would be the sole justification for his life. Not God. And not Catholicism.

Of course for Claire it was different. She'd left the Church for him, and she had really wanted the baby. Maybe he *was* being a bit of a shit.

On the other hand, Claire was sensible, practical. She knew she couldn't handle a baby now. And she was handling the miscarriage very well. And the Sarah business, too, for that matter. Good God, she had given him *permission*. Imagine having your wife's permission. He was proud of her, really.

Moreover, to be fair, it wasn't *just* a summer fling; it was research. It was growth as a person. As a man. And, besides, maybe this was a time for major changes in his life. He and Claire were growing in different ways; it may be that they had just outgrown each other. She was an academic. He was a novelist. He had other needs now. In fact, if that damned Porter hadn't had his heart attack, Sarah might have already asked him to leave Claire. That's what he was waiting for. In fact, if Sarah would just say she loved him, then he'd ask her if she wanted him to leave Claire; no problem. But she had to make the first move. That was the proper thing, really.

Still, Claire was being awfully nice about everything, he had to admit that. And she was awfully good in her reaction to his writing. She was the perfect reader, the perfect critic. Would Sarah react as well? He thought of the sex scenes, he thought of Sarah reading them.

On the television, nearly naked women were dancing on the news desk. Their backs were to the camera and you could tell that the anchorman's face was right at their crotch level. What was the point of *this*? That the evening news is some kind of substitute porn? It was disgusting.

Maybe he'd better change Sarah's physical description. Make her black-haired instead of blond, fat instead of thin... but he got only that far. He laughed aloud. Of course, he could just turn her into Claire, physically anyhow, and throw everybody off the track. It was wicked. It was awful.

At once he got up and made a little entry in his notebook. If you didn't write these things down at once, they slipped away. He made the note—change S to C, physically—and, having begun, he kept on writing, amplifying physical detail, giving S a tendency to fat, little rolls of flesh at her waist, hips slightly too plump, and a marked tendency to get fatter as her psychological conflicts grew worse: her need to choose between Q and A, between the nightmare of incest and etc. etc. etc.

He sat back, guilty for just a moment, thinking of how Claire would react when the book appeared, how betrayed she would feel. But that was silly, of course, because by then Claire would be married to some other harmless academic and he himself would be married to Sarah, and the book would be just another novel by somebody Claire used to know. It would be all right. That's what writers did.

He went back to his notebook and began a list of her Latin phrases. Was he taking too much from her? Not really, when you considered the terrific sex life he was giving her in return. It was a fair exchange. And what did it matter anyhow? It was only fiction.

It was midnight, Sunday, and Claire woke from her first deep sleep and from that same dream again.

She was in a deep wood, in a grove of trees lit only by a pale moon. Dark figures moved at the edges of the grove, waiting. There were whispers, soft laughter, the sounds of lovemaking. They were waiting for her.

She was a priestess, her long black hair hanging loose about her bare shoulders, and as she moved across the dark ground her thin white chiton clung to her breasts, which were huge, and to her hips and to her belly. The sounds ceased. They were waiting for the sacrifice.

She approached the altar, a slab of stone, where the attendant priest would assist her. He wore the mask of a goat and blood trickled from his eyes. From the waist down, he wore nothing at all. He was massively erect. He held out to her a silken pillow on which lay a long curved knife. She took the knife in both hands and turned to face the altar and the grove beyond.

But something was wrong. The goat was to have been the

sacrifice. The goat should be stretched out upon the altar. But there was nothing on the altar. A flat stone, not even marked with blood.

And then she realized what she must do. She had no choice. She must offer the sacrifice.

She lifted the knife high above her head and plunged the curved blade deep into her belly. There was a loud cry, an animal scream. And it was done.

She woke, drenched in sweat, sick in her head and stomach. She threw off the sheet and sat on the edge of the bed. She must not think of this. This way lies madness. *Noli meminiscere, Clara.* Forget. Forget.

She clutched her head, pressing hard, as if she could crush the memory from her brain.

There was a funny noise somewhere. She got up and went down the little hall to the living room. Pictures of men shooting at one another flickered on the television—apparently it was a news program because none of the actors was wearing nice clothes—but the sound was off and Claire realized that the noise she had heard was Aunt Lily's snoring. Claire turned off the television and Aunt Lily woke up.

"Have a nice bath?" she said.

"It's very late," Claire said. "Time for bed."

She bent down to help Aunt Lily from her chair, but as the old woman shifted her bulk forward, she paused and lifted her hand to Claire's cheek, looking into her eyes as if she had lost something there and hoped to find it. After a moment, Aunt Lily's gaze flickered and went out.

"What a good girl you are," she said. "You're too good."

It was long after midnight, and Angelo was tossing back and forth, unable to sleep. He'd gotten Sarah back to bed, and he'd sat beside her until she fell asleep, or went unconscious rather, and now it was practically morning. No chance of getting down to the river for a little sucking and fucking; it was too late. And he didn't dare leave Sarah alone. He couldn't. But it seemed to him about twenty years since he'd had any sex, and his balls felt as if they might explode.

He thought of Porter, and how he liked to be teased into sex, the little tortures by which he held Porter off until, when he came, it was like Vesuvius... well, maybe not Vesuvius, but it was good, it was plenty good. Porter was going to be all right. And maybe Sarah would be all right once she absorbed the fact that Porter was going to be all right. *He* was the only one who wasn't going to be all right.

He tried to think of Claire. But right away he thought of her having an abortion, and he couldn't bear it, so he tried not to think of Claire.

How could anybody kill a baby? He was used to the idea of killing; he was a modern man, after all; he lived in the city of Boston; he was Family, like it or not. But to kill her own baby Claire must have been desperate, crazy.

Crazy made him think of Sarah. She mustn't find out. She'd take the blame for that, too.

He tried to think of Kierkegaard.

Nothing worked.

He flicked on the light and reached beneath the bed for *Fear and Trembling*. He couldn't concentrate; he could barely follow the words across the page. Was it all just delusion? He closed the book and forced himself to think of the three classes of men, of man condemned to freedom of choice, of choice determining a man's struggle with God.

How preposterous it seemed. A struggle with God? Him? The only struggle he wanted was a struggle in bed, one that would go on and on and on. To hell with love. When the chips were down, all he wanted was sex.

But right now he had to stay where he was because Sarah needed him more than he needed sex.

He saw no contradiction in this.

20

Porter lay in bed looking more fit and less worried than he had in years. He was now on the safe side of the heart attack. It was Monday morning, the beginning of a new week, the beginning of a new life. He seemed to glow from inside.

"You look good, Porter," Angelo said. "You look all pink and yellow."

"I feel good," Porter said. "It's amazing how the fear of dying becomes just another fear—like losing at squash or taking a bath on the Dow or just making a fool of yourself. It's still scary, but it's just there, it's just part of you. You accept it."

"Well, if this is what dying does for you, we could all use a little. You look great."

"I won't be the same as before," Porter said. "After a heart attack, you have to think differently and you have to live differently."

"Hmmm," Angelo said.

"What it comes down to is this: you have to accept the way you are, and go on from there."

"Very Existential, Porter. Have you been reading Sartre?"

"No. Michener."

Angelo laughed, thinking it was a joke, but then he saw it wasn't. They had not been alone since the night of Porter's heart attack—Sarah was always with them—and so there were many things that had not yet been said. But right now neither of them said anything.

"The way you are," Sarah said. "You accept the way you are and you go on from there."

They both looked at her.

"What are you looking at?" she said.

"You accept it and you go on," Porter said.

"She's just tired," Angelo said. "Aren't you, Sarah."

"I'm just tired," Sarah said in a dead voice, funny, as if she were satirizing the shrink. They laughed nervously, and after a minute she went on. "If you repeat whatever they say, and make it sound as if you mean it, then they let you out and you're not crazy anymore."

"Are you seeing her today? The doctor?" Porter said.

"I see her every day now. Until Friday."

"She leaves on Friday for the Vineyard," Angelo said, lifting one eyebrow significantly. "For the month of August."

"*All* of August?" Porter said.

"*All* of August," Angelo said.

"I'm just tired," Sarah said. Her voice turned hard, sharp. "And...I...smell. And...I'm...sick"—she touched her head—"here."

There was silence in the room. From the corridor came the rattle and squeak of the juice cart, a woman's laughter, and then more silence.

Angelo said to himself, I can't go on with this; I'm not meant to be anybody's caretaker; I'm going to ditch her in the street and head for the baths and go fuck my brains out.

The silence continued until Sarah picked up where she left off, her voice unnaturally loud. "But if I tell her I accept the way I am and I just want to go on from there, then I won't be tired anymore, and I won't..." Her words trailed off into a mutter and then to a low moan of disgust, an animal sound.

After a while Porter spoke to her, and she answered him,

and Porter said something else. He was talking about leaving
the past in the past and then about everybody having limita-
tions and then about other things, but Angelo's mind had
long since left the room in pursuit of a body. *Any body,* any
age, so long as it had a cock attached. After a while the talking
stopped again.

"What?" Angelo said.

"I said maybe that's how you are or maybe it isn't, but if it
is, maybe you should just accept it and go on from there." He
was looking at Sarah. He was unaware of Angelo. "Maybe
just try it. For real."

"Yes," Sarah said.

"Michener again?" Angelo said.

Porter smiled and ignored him. "You just accept the whole
mess," he said to Sarah, as if he too were crazy and had come
to terms with it.

"Yes," Sarah said, "I see."

"Do you?" Porter said. "Do you see?"

Sarah frowned a little in concentration. The two men
looked at her and then looked at each other, but at once Porter
turned away, back to Sarah. They waited for what seemed a
long time.

"I should wash my hair," Sarah said finally. "I should have
it done."

"Yes, exactly. Begin with something you *can* do something
about."

"I'll wash my hair," Sarah said.

Porter beamed at her.

"We've got to see you-know-who in another hour," Angelo
said. "Freud's mother awaits." He was getting very annoyed
at Porter. His simplemindedness. His self-congratulation.
"Accept the way things are." "Wash your hair." Good God!
The heart attack must have affected his brain. "I think we
ought to keep that appointment," he told Sarah.

"She can wait," Sarah said.

Porter continued to beam at her, as if she were his child, his first patient.

"I'm not so sure," Angelo said.

"I've got to wash my hair and do my nails. And maybe I'll buy a new dress, something different."

Angelo and Porter exchanged a quick glance.

"*Buy*, I said." And for the first time since Porter's heart attack, Sarah laughed, a harsh sound, half-crazy.

Porter laughed with her.

Angelo tried but could not laugh because he saw suddenly that Porter was done with him, had set him free. He did not feel free.

The nurse bustled in. "What a fun family," she said. "There's nothing that makes a patient feel better than a good laugh, that's what I always say."

"Michener again," Angelo said, not free but lost.

Quinn phoned shortly after lunch, but Sarah was not able to meet him, she said. There were little problems, there were women things. He concluded, as she meant him to, that she was having her period. But in fact all signs of her period had miraculously disappeared: the slow ache of the gathering blood, the smell, the madness.

What had happened, Sarah reflected, was like a dream sequence in a foreign film, where you couldn't understand the meaning but you couldn't deny what you had seen either.

It was like this: she was herself, Sarah, standing at the foot of Porter's bed, frowning in concentration, and they were watching her. But at the same time she was the other Sarah, no longer standing there, but down on her knees, desperate, clawing at the tile floor with splintered bleeding fingers. Spurs of bone shot out, pointy and white. But she went on.

Ignoring the blood and the bone and the terrible pain, that other Sarah scrabbled and scratched at the resistant floor until she dislodged the thing they had always told her was there: a new mind—clean, beautiful, with no memories. She dug it out, and stood up, holding it before her like some ritual offering, and then she crushed it through the holes of her eyes until it lodged, safe at last, inside her skull. And then it was over. She was standing at the foot of Porter's bed and they were waiting for her to say something. "I should wash my hair," she said. "I should have it done." And with that, she was one thing again, whole, and not mad.

It had happened at the very second she decided to accept everything the way it was—the whole mess—and just go on. Or maybe it had been decided for her; maybe it had just happened to her, like Raoul, like Quinn.

You did things and things happened to you: what was the difference?

But that was a question she no longer had to consider. Not now. Because she had done it. She had unearthed herself.

And so an hour later with her ridiculous shrink, and later still on the phone with Quinn, Sarah kept before her eyes the fading, fractured picture of her own redemption. It might fade altogether, simply flicker and go out, but that would not matter, because right now—for this instant—she was sane. She was no longer mad. She was sane, sane, sane.

As sane as sunlight. As sane as Claire.

"Let's meet for tea at the Ritz," she said to Quinn, her voice rich with promise. "At four. Tomorrow."

21

Sarah spent the larger part of Tuesday at Elizabeth Arden, getting the full "Maine Chance" treatment: steam room, body massage, facial, manicure, pedicure, makeup, and a hair styling that she immediately combed out so that it looked careless, accidental. The entire treatment took five hours, with an hour off before lunch so she could visit the shrink, and then back to Elizabeth Arden for deeper, cleaner, more lasting beauty. All that was over now and, with Angelo trailing discreetly behind, Sarah hurried the few short blocks to the Ritz to meet Quinn for high tea.

She arrived just after four, only a little late, and Quinn noticed at once that she was wearing a new dress—in the wrong color, deep blue, a Claire color—and she seemed a little breathless, as if she had run to meet him. Quinn ignored the drss and concentrated on the excitement of being wanted, which was especially nice in this atmosphere of careless money. Sarah led the way to the upstairs lounge.

"Very nice," Quinn said, looking around the plush sofas, the armchairs, the low tables with their heavy silver trays and teapots and clinky tea things. They sat down. "It's like old times."

"You used to come here a lot?" Sarah leaned forward to make her hair swing free. She gave him her full attention. "With Claire?"

"No, I've never been here at all. I meant 'old times' like the turn of the century; having afternoon tea in the drawing room, the silver stuff, the sofas." He added, "I'm not Beacon Hill."

"Beacon Hill is just a state of mind," she said.

"It is, isn't it!" Quinn made a mental note to use that. What interesting things this woman could do for his fiction. "Tell me about Beacon Hill as a state of mind."

"I haven't seen you in over a week," Sarah said.

"Ten days," he said, "or nine, depending on how you figure it."

Sarah paused for only a second, but Quinn could tell what she was thinking and knew they would have to talk about Porter's heart attack after all. The forms had to be observed.

"I guess it was a close call for Porter," he said.

"It was," she said, perfectly composed, "and I was very upset, but he's much better now. He's going to be all right."

"Good. That's good," Quinn said, closing the topic.

"I had nothing to do with it. I wasn't responsible."

"Of course not."

"Not everything that happens is my fault."

"No. No, of course."

"I can't assume the blame for everything."

What on earth was this woman talking about?

"A heart attack can happen to anybody. It didn't happen because I was with you. We didn't make it happen."

Ah, so that was it. "Us," he said. "Oh, of course not. I'm sure Porter had the heart attack all on his own. Nothing to do with us. We're two mature adults, just having a summer..."

But she was not listening to him. "I've come to the conclusion," she said, "that in this life you have to accept the way things are and simply go on from there."

The waiter brought their tea and Quinn used the interruption to sit back and take it all in. Not the tea, but Sarah. She was amazing, really. He had spent the morning at his novel—changing Sarah into Claire, as a matter of fact—so he hadn't given a minute's thought to himself, but he realized now, listening to this thin elegant rich sexy blonde, that their minds were perfectly attuned to each other since, even apart, they had reached the exact same conclusion. "You have to accept the way things are and simply go on from there." The power of the concept lay in the immaculate simplicity of its formulation. For a second he considered whether it really was brilliant or merely a cliché, but just then Sarah leaned toward him in that way of hers, and her hair swung loose, and he realized that he was right and she was right and it was time they accepted things as they were and just went on from there.

"You were saying . . . ?" he said.

But she said nothing. She merely fixed him with those glittering gray eyes, as if she were hypnotizing him or accusing him or inviting him to another plane of existence.

If only she would say something. If only she would make the first move. If only.

Sarah ontinued to stare.

Quinn's hand involuntarily moved toward his lip, but he stopped in mid-gesture and—still staring into her eyes—extended the hand, palm flat, toward Sarah. She placed her palm against his. They let their fingers twine in a knot.

'Palm to palm is holy Palmers' kiss,' Quinn thought, but he said nothing.

The waiter veered toward their table, took one look, and veered away.

And so it was done without a word spoken. He would leave Claire, he would move in with Sarah. They would marry and he would get on—no, *they* would get on—with their new exciting lives. This marriage would be different. He would work harder at it. He would not lean on Sarah for support as he had on Claire. He was holding Claire back,

really; she needed to grow as an independent scholar the way
he had grown as an independent artist. Not the same way, of
course; that was the problem; they had grown in different
ways. They were no longer the same people. They had nothing, or almost nothing, left to share.

He would be a better husband this time. He would make
sure that he and Sarah grew together, as artists, as individuals.
They would just accept and go on. Accept the accidental pain
this was going to cause Claire, cut away that dead relationship
as quickly and cleanly as possible, and go on with this new
vital living one.

If only Claire would die, he thought, or disappear, or eva-
nesce, but he suppressed the thought at once.

He would phone Claire tonight and break the news. But
meanwhile there was the immediate, the now: tea at the Ritz
and then—he was feeling horny as hell for the first time in ten
days—dessert. *Ta-daaa!*

Life was good, life was full, life was rich.

"To us," he said, and they clinked their teacups together—
Royal Doulton, he guessed.

Angelo had accompanied Sarah to Elizabeth Arden's and then,
with a six-hour reprieve, he went home and showered, put on
his Miss Piggy T-shirt and his cruising jeans, and took himself off for a day at the baths. But the place was deserted, and
after he'd made three or four tours of the sauna and the
weight room and the Jacuzzi, he holed up in his cubicle—
with the door at a friendly angle—and waited for somebody
interesting. Nobody came.

Angelo closed his eyes and tried to snooze for a while, but
his mind kept wandering to Porter, and he couldn't stand it.
Did Porter actually think he was having sex with Quinn? Had

Porter been telling him that their affair—his and Porter's—was now over? He decided to distract himself by flipping through some porno magazines. They were the standard stuff, silly. Who could care. What he needed was the real thing, not pictures. He considered propositioning the kid who was vacuuming the Romper Room, but he really didn't like kids all that much, and this one looked underage and sickly besides, and who needed disease? Who needed any of this shit? He decided to leave.

He got dressed and turned in his key and was checking his hair in the mirror before leaving, when the reflection of a big blond guy in a raw silk jacket appeared and then disappeared behind him. Angelo turned and saw him enter a cubicle down near the weight room. He stared for a minute at the closing door, and before he had time to consider the facts rationally, they all clicked into place.

It was Jim—or whatever his name really was—the guy from Lexington or Winchester who'd picked him up at the river and then beat him to a pulp. Common sense said it couldn't be. The law of averages said it couldn't be. But Angelo was sure it was, and he was right.

He walked to the door of the cubicle, prepared to wait. But at once the door opened and there he stood, blond and huge and naked except for the towel at his waist. Jim.

He looked at Angelo and gave him a big smile.

"Jim," Angelo said, warm, extending his hand.

"Name's not Jim."

Angelo's hand hung in the air, empty, until he placed it lightly on Jim's shoulder and tugged at a single blond hair.

"Jim," he said, "we had such a good time together, there's something you might want to know." He watched as Jim searched his face for who he was, for how they'd met. "On the first of July, remember? We met down by the river?" Angelo said. "We went back to my place?" He waited. And then he leaned into Jim and said, "I've got AIDS, sweetheart. AIDS. Have a nice day." And he left.

So Angelo was in the Ritz bar now, snappy in his gray suit, but in every other way depressed. He'd been stupid. He'd been cruel. I've got AIDS. God. He felt like a complete shit. And he hadn't even got his rocks off either.

He looked at his watch. How long could they spend over tea? Poor Sarah. You had to admire the courage it took: pulling herself together, buying that terrible blue dress so she'd look like Claire. She was nutty as a fruitcake again, but she was trying. That was something at least. And all on the strength of Porter's sappy philosophy: you've got to accept the way things are and go on from there. Where did he get such ideas? It couldn't really be from Michener.

A big blond guy stood at the door of the bar taking a look around, and for a second Angelo thought it was Jim. But of course it wasn't. Jim was probably in a state of collapse back at the baths, or at Mass General getting a blood test, or phoning his wife in tears. Jim would make a jump for morality, not murder.

Though, if Jim did want to find him, he could. And who knows, he might get crazy some night and drive down from Winchester and hide in the stairwell at Number 17-A, waiting. With a tire iron or a knife or a gun.

"Something else, sir?" the waiter asked, with something else in his voice. But Angelo, preoccupied, merely nodded and ticked the glass with a fingernail.

He would have to take the Walther from its hiding place and put it back in the nightstand. After Claire's first visit, he'd hidden the damned thing in his closet, in the back, inside a boot, where nobody would ever think of looking. But he'd move it back now, just for peace of mind.

He smiled to himself. The gun was empty of course, since

he'd never be willing even to risk shooting anybody, but the principle reason it was empty was that—for the life of him—he could not remember where he'd hidden the ammunition clip. Some killer. Some Family member.

The waiter hovered for a second until he had Angelo's attention, and then he slid the drink across the table and paused for just a beat, his hip forward. Angelo caught his gaze immediately and the waiter did not look away. He was fifty if he was a day, smokey hair, used eyes.

"Anything else, sir?" the waiter said.

Sarah appeared in the doorway, Quinn on her arm. They were ready to leave.

Angelo stood up and prepared to follow them. "I could suck you dry," he whispered to the waiter.

The waiter nodded, solemn, and said, "Very good, too, sir."

Porter lay in bed and smiled lovingly at Maria and the kids. How lucky he was to be alive, to be in love, to have people who loved him. All his life he had been privileged: birth, education, money, and love. And not just love, simply, but every kind of love. His wife, his three beautiful children, his poor trusting loving crazy sister, and then the dark mystery and the inexplicable fulfillment of his life: Angelo.

He had it all, everything. And as usual with life, he'd never appreciated what he had until he'd nearly lost it. That heart attack had been his salvation.

These were terminal thoughts, Porter knew, and he was enjoying them. He liked the melodramatic ring in the words: that heart attack was my salvation.

Because now he could love Angelo without expecting to be loved back. And love Sarah without expecting or even hoping to control her fate . . . and her fate was clear to him . . . she'd end up hopelessly mad. And love Maria and the kids, and let them love him back. He had learned all this from Angelo.

Man is condemned to the freedom of choice, Angelo always said. At the moment of choice he is totally alone. The right choice means a struggle to the death, with God.

And it was true, all of it. At the moment of his heart attack, when that terrible hand seized him by the throat and for a single telling second choked off all life, Porter had seen it as the hand of God. Had fought against it. And had won.

Nothing that followed could ever live up to that. He'd lose from here on in. He'd lose the people he loved. Or maybe the love would go first, who could say.

But there would be some kind of a stripping away, he was sure of that. In the end there'd be total loss. And he accepted it. He was prepared. Because Angelo's words were burned into his brain: you accept things as they are and you go on from there.

Claire had thrown a cookout this evening for her class, all twenty-three of them, and though they seemed rooted to the ground around Aunt Lily's Gen-Air Cooker, Claire had somehow managed to root them up and send them off, grateful and happy, well before time for her midnight devotions.

The cookout had been necessary to turn a bad moment to her advantage. Murmurs had begun about her early departure on Thursday last; her missed class on Friday; where would this end? It certainly didn't take much to make a bunch of bastards turn on you.

She had sent around a whisper about her miscarriage and followed it up with this brave invitation to a cookout; the combination of suffering and generosity seemed to have done the trick. Everybody showed up, and they had eaten and drunk and sung bits of the *Carmina Burana* while they could still sing, and afterward they attempted several scholiast drinking songs in Latin and destroyed them of course. Aunt Lily had forsaken her television for the evening and sat on a funny stool off to one side of the party, like some hand-thrown ornamental pot with a hairline crack in it, meant to be seen but not handled. The students brought her beers and burgers and she seemed perfectly content. Claire herself was indefatigable. She moved from group to group, providing more to eat, more to drink, gifting each of them with that enduring smile that finally won them all back. She was once again the model of the selfless teacher. *Magister et domina.*

She had managed them all.

So would it be with Quinn.

So would it be with Sarah.

And now the cookout was over and she was alone with her devotions. She stood in a grove of tall firs that she had discovered in the mile of woods that stretched out behind Aunt Lily's house. There was a picnic table and benches, long deserted and falling apart, but if you closed your eyes to them, you could believe you were in Greece, in a sacred grove, and that the gods were watching you, and cared.

"*O dea Venus,*" she prayed, "*inflamma me. O dea Athena, sapientia infunde ut hostes meas confunderem.*"

She had been born in the wrong century, Claire was sure of that. She would have flourished in classical Greece. Or even Rome, if she hadn't been able to make Greece. Because it was the glory of the ancients that they could look hard at a future that offered no eternal life, no punishment, no joy, and could say of the present: this, this is enough. *Hoc sufficit.*

Christianity had simply confused things with its promise of eternal life, of redressing the balance, of justice levied in the end to all men, to every woman. It was not so. If the balance were to be righted, she would have to do it herself. And she would, too, because at moments like this, communing with the gods, she felt invincible and she knew she could do anything.

She looked up and saw the white moon streaked with rain clouds. A shadow passed above the grove.

"Umbrae transitus est tempus nostrum," she said. "As transitory as a shadow is our allotted time."

At that moment she came back to herself and looked around the little grove and saw the picnic table, the fireplace, the can for trash. This was not after all a pagan temple in the woods, the haunt of goddesses, the place of human sacrifice.

And yet she had done that: she had sacrificed her unborn child, she had killed it, she had done it for love.

Love. What a mockery.

Suddenly it all collapsed—the night, the triumph, the feeling of invincibility—and Claire knelt on the hard ground and thrust her elbows deep into her empty belly, until a howl came out of her, an animal wail she drew up from the ache in her hollow womb. After that she was silent.

Rain began to fall like knives.

22

It was a rainy Wednesday and Angelo was able to sleep late because, so far as he could tell, things were back to normal. Sarah seemed to have miraculously recovered, the idiot Quinn had spent the entire night upstairs, Porter would be leaving the hospital in a day or two, and he himself was free once more to fuck his brains out if he wanted. It was too good to be true.

He went with Sarah for her morning shrinkage and waited in the outer office until the shrink herself actually called him in. She did that only when Sarah was very bad or very good.

She was concerned, she said, about this Quinn. Was he a serious person? Was he a safe person? Had he really separated from his wife?

Angelo looked at Sarah and then back at the shrink, and the hope was so clear in Sarah's face that Angelo stretched the truth and said yes, Quinn seemed for the most part to be a serious person, and he probably was safe, too, but he didn't think that Quinn had separated from his wife. But Sarah assured them both that it was so, that he had done it, that Quinn was going to marry her and they would live—she laughed a little, a smart self-mockery—happily ever after. The shrink said she would like to talk to Quinn. Tomorrow.

It would be their last meeting for a month, she said; she was concerned, she said; so much depended on this Quinn, she said. She had to be concerned, yes? Correct me if I am wrong. She smiled, open to correction.

She was concerned, she was not wrong, Angelo could see that. He could see too that she was more eager than Sarah herself to be done with it at last. And so was he. And so was Quinn, he supposed.

And Claire? How would she feel about all this? She was well rid of Quinn, Angelo knew that, but did *she* know that?

Angelo sat in the office listening to the shrink wind up the hour, and the thought crossed his mind that here was Kierkegaard's fear and trembling, here was the sickness unto death —was Claire the sacrificial lamb?—but the room was hot and his crotch was sticky and he could not grasp what these ideas meant, and he consoled himself that within an hour he would turn Sarah over to Quinn and he would be free for an afternoon and a night and an entire life of . . . what?

It was a rainy Wednesday, even at Dartmouth, and Claire was teaching her way deep into their hearts. They would never forget this summer. They would never forget her.

"Optime," she said, *"clarissime,"* congratulating the fat redhead on another perfect answer. He was ugly, but he had learned his Latin. Who was he, really? Just another person, another man she would never know, somebody she could teach or fall in love with or kill; it was all the same.

"Clarissime," she said again, a delaying tactic—because for just a second she saw him sitting there naked, with wispy red hair around his fat hard thing, and it was arching up and out toward her, raw and brutal and disgusting. She could smell it even. She was going to be sick.

She turned her back to the class and covered her eyes for a moment, until her vision cleared and she was able to turn and face the class and the fat redhead and say, as if nothing had happened, *"Nunc ad colloquium de amore Ovidiana. Incipiamus."*

She could get through anything.

Magister et domina.

It was a rainy Wednesday in Boston and there was no school outing, so Leopold spent the entire day at his watchpost on the stairs.

He had his books and his pillows and his "whatchaknow," as he still called his favorite pink blanket, but they were his only entertainment, for though he gripped the rails with his fat little hands and pushed his face up close to see, he saw nobody because nobody came.

Mister didn't come home on Tuesday night and he didn't come home on Wednesday either.

Mrs. didn't visit, even once, in her red car.

Birdie screamed at Jim and then didn't say anything.

Jim screamed at Birdie and then didn't say anything.

The mailman came but he didn't come in.

Nobody came in and nobody went out until late in the afternoon when the singing delivery boy brought the groceries from the Star Market. He ignored Leopold as he ignored everybody, until on his last trip up the stairs, he focused on Leopold's fat little face scrunched up against the railing and said in an exaggerated voice, "Lawdamercy, Mistah Percy, you an ugly little muh-fuh." And then he laughed like a fool and went on singing one of his songs.

Leopold, who saw and heard everything, pretended not to see or hear. He went on waiting.

23

Claire took a long hot bath, the air and water redolent of Huile Parfum by Lancôme, and then she patted herself dry. She applied a good dose of Lotion Douce pour le Corps and topped that off with La Poudre Magique, Lancôme also. Everything she did, she did slowly, consciously, because she had come to herself at last. She knew what to do. She knew how to do it.

She had remembered Sarah Slade.

It had been nine years ago, perhaps ten, that she first saw the name Sarah Slade.

Claire was still a graduate student, fat, unpromising, living in a slum in D.C., when there had been this flurry of scandal among her fellow graduate students that promised excitement even in their ranks. Some Boston debutante had murdered her boyfriend—a graduate student from Argentina—and fled the country, and then returned. There was a brief hope that the debutante herself might be a graduate student, perhaps even at Harvard, but that hope was disappointed. Her name was Sarah Slade, one of *the* Slades, and the whole distinguished family was a mess. That was all. Just that.

But now, a decade later, thanks to her amazing mind—how keen it was, how utterly lucid—Claire remembered each detail: the lunch counter where she had read about it, the jelly donut she was eating, the *Post* open on her lap to catch the crumbs. She had glanced down at the photo of Sarah's horsey face and thought, bemused: if I were that thin, I'd never kill anybody. And at once, and nearly forever, she dismissed Sarah Slade as an irrelevance. Claire had no time except for Enterprising Women.

It is true that rumors continued to circulate about the Slade murder—a severed head, a mutilated corpse, a Fanny Farmer box containing a human hand—but the rumors came to nothing more than the graduate school passion for a sexual frisson. The story soon disappeared from the front page of the *Post* and life went on, both Sarah's and Claire's.

Looking back over her long life alone and her short life with Quinn, Claire could see there the finger of the gods: the kind of classical pattern she most approved. For events had come full circle; Claire herself was thin, or almost. She had become the Enterprising Woman of her learned book. And she would destroy the irrelevant Sarah Slade, but civilly, with a word.

Claire dressed slowly and with care. Restraint was every-thing—in dress, in action, in possession. *Ne quid nimis; in ultima tendimus.*

She was ready.

It was six o'clock on Thursday night.

She could drive to Boston, reclaim Quinn once and for good, and be back by midnight for a little walk to her sacred grove and then a bang-up class on Friday morning.

She got her keys and went to say goodbye to Aunt Lily, who was getting daily more unpredictable. Claire wondered, speculatively, if the old lady's brain was simply setting out to sea, leaving her body behind in its wake, or if she had suffered a minor stroke while Claire wasn't looking.

Aunt Lily was watching the financial news without a great deal of interest.

"Back so soon?" Aunt Lily said.

"I haven't been anywhere," Claire said. "I've been in the bath."

"You had a call," Aunt Lily said. "I told them you were with that Quinn. In Boston."

"Aunt Lily, I was in the *bath.*"

"But you can't be always in the bath. Sometimes you have to be somewhere else. It stands to reason."

"But I *was* in the bath."

The financial news gave way to a shoot-out—drugs again, of course—and Aunt Lily leaned forward, all eyes for the action.

Claire wanted to tell her to snap out of it and act her age, that this passion for real-life carnage was an absurd affectation, but she followed her own principle of *ne quid nimis.* Say nothing. She might yet need old Lily, who was in a way the perfect alibi, since you could neither prove nor disprove a word she said. She was simply the dotty aunt, harmless, uninvolved.

"I'm going to the library," Claire said, "I'll be back in a little while."

"Give that Quinn my best," Aunt Lily said, caught up once again in the larger life of television.

Quinn had phoned just before six, from Sarah's bedroom in fact, and was told by Aunt Lily that Claire was in Boston. That was just like Claire, to show up with no warning, to try to catch him out. Still, it might be better this way; he'd be plunged into the showdown without wasting time and energy worrying about what to say, how to act.

Quinn hotfooted it home—his courage screwed to the sticking place, wherever that might be—and paced around the apartment for an hour rehearsing his speech.

The marriage was over. They had grown in different directions. They had grown apart. Claire could have everything: the stereo, the car, the furniture. He wanted nothing for himself except his books. He and Claire had shared some good years, and it was nobody's fault really—though, if it came to that, he was willing to take the blame—it was just the way things were, and he honestly hoped they could remain good friends. But, and this was final, he was leaving her for Sarah Slade.

He poured himself a stiff drink. He would never buy cheap Scotch again.

In another hour he had simplified his speech even further, but still there was no sign of Claire. Of course, now that he thought of it, he should never have believed Aunt Lily anyhow. She was bats. For all he knew, Claire was at the library researching the feminine caesura pause in Lucretius and here he was, like a fool, preparing his breakup speech.

He had another drink.

He phoned Sarah to say Claire had not arrived yet. Sarah's voice sounded metallic, as if a spring in her throat had been wound too tight, and after a second she went silent. That depressed him, and suddenly he didn't want to talk to Sarah or to her psychiatrist or to anybody. He should have told the truth this morning—that it was his intention to break up with Claire, though he'd not yet done it—but the damned psychiatrist seemed determined to make him say he *had* already done it, and so he said it, and now he had to do it. He wanted it over. He wanted out. He shook the telephone cord like a whip, and then he twisted it around his neck like a noose, and then he sighed into the silence at the other end of the phone. It was all too much. He promised Sarah he would be there in an hour. Maybe two. He told her to go talk to Angelo.

After a while he phoned Aunt Lily again.

"She's at the library," Aunt Lily said.

"She can't be at the library," Quinn said. "I'm her husband.

Quinn. You told me two hours ago that she was in Boston. With me."

"She was in Boston, and she was in the bath, and now she's in the library."

"Oh, God," Quinn said.

"She can't be always in the bath," Aunt Lily said. "It stands to reason."

"Do you know *where* she is?" Quinn said. "Do you have any idea *where*?"

"She's too good, that girl. She works too hard."

He was getting angry and wondering how to end this when suddenly, an answered prayer, Claire let herself into the apartment. Quinn thanked Aunt Lily and hung up.

Claire had put on more weight, exaggerated maybe by the billowy shift she was wearing, but he was relieved to see her, and glad all the waiting was over and, without thinking, Quinn gave her a big smile. He took it back at once; no point in misleading her.

"Claire," he said, "we've got to have a talk."

"Have a seat, Quinn," she said. "She's a murderer, and you'll be able to take the news better if you're sitting down."

"We've grown in different directions," he said. "We've grown apart. You can have everything . . ."

Claire let him have his say.

"But," he concluded, "and this is final, I'm leaving you for Sarah Slade."

Claire said nothing for a while, and Quinn watched with horror as her face went white and hard. He hadn't expected this. She looked like she might keel over with a heart attack, like Porter. *Then* what would he do?

She looked so defenseless and hurt. Everything came rushing back to him: the shy way she made love, her pride in his writing, her fierce defense of him at Williams. Mr. and Mrs. Indignant. She had really been selfless and good. He should go to her and put his arms around her and say it was all right, it would be all right. But he held back. Better to end it now —do the hard thing once and for all—and get on with the business of living.

And still she said nothing. But how could it be such a surprise to her? She was a modern woman, for God's sake. She knew he was having this affair. She had given permission. And now she was carrying on this way, as if the shock were going to kill her. He was beginning to get annoyed with her. It really was unfair.

"I'll get us a drink," he said. "But my decision is final."

When he came back, Claire seemed to have got hold of herself. He put her drink down next to her, and went to stand over near the windows. Claire didn't touch her drink. Quinn sipped at his and then, frantic, bit at the rim of the glass.

"Nothing's final, Quinn," she said. "Not yet."

But he was ready for her. "This is final," he said. "This is it." He really had become a new man.

"Facts are facts," Claire said, and slowly, with the measured pacing and the calculated emphasis of the master teacher she was, she laid out for him the facts about Sarah Slade: the murder, the scandal, the newspapers. She added the bloody rumors as well, discounting them but letting them make their point, and then she sat back and gave him a long look.

"Suppose it were true," he said.

"It is true."

"Suppose it were. We all have a past."

"As a *murderer*?"

"There are all kinds of murders, Claire. There are psychological murders too, you know."

"That's not fair. That's not worthy of you."

He smiled. He was winning.

"We're talking about murder, Quinn, not the flu. We're talking about blood and mess. Killing someone. A bullet through your head. Forget about fiction for a while; this isn't fiction; this is real life, with a person who was alive—like us—and who is now dead. She *killed* somebody."

Quinn was impressed, but he showed nothing.

"She'll kill *you,* you fool."

Quinn shook his head slowly, tolerant even now.

Claire raced ahead, breathless, losing. "This is *doing* something, Quinn, not just *writing* about it." She choked back what sounded like a sob. "You're talking about leaving me for a fucking murderer. You've been fucking her and fucking her, that fucking bitch, all summer long. You've been sticking that fucking cock into her day and night while I . . ."

So. She had lost. Language goes, and then it all goes. He was home free.

She stopped, but in a dizzying second she pulled herself around. "Well, there's no point in this behavior, is there. This is completely inappropriate."

She rose and walked to the door. "Just check the facts, Quinn. You used to be honest and you used to be a scholar. Just go to the library and have them dig out the *Globe* for you. Summer. Ten years ago. Nine or ten."

Quinn stood across the room from her, looking at this stranger, waiting for this awful scene to end.

"I'll give you till Saturday to pull yourself together, Quinn. I'll take you back."

She opened the door and stepped onto the landing. Saturday? So it wasn't over? But he couldn't go through this again. Not Saturday. Not ever.

In a second he crossed the room and closed the door—hard —behind her. And then he opened it. She was still there.

"This is final," he said. "No matter what she is, no matter what she's done, I'm leaving you."

They stared at each other and then, at the same instant, Claire flung herself at the door and Quinn slammed it shut.

They stood there, pressing wildly against one another, the heavy door between them.

And no one saw this madness except, of course, Leopold.

Claire drove the car around the block and then parked a little way up the street to keep an eye on Number 65 Marlborough. The light stayed on in the living room and once, for a moment, she caught sight of Quinn in the window, holding a glass, just looking out and up, as if he were any normal human being and not the lying cheating fucking son of a bitch he was, and then he moved back into the room and she lost sight of him.

Claire was badly shaken. This was not how she had planned things. She had imagined the scene as hard, cold, logical. Two tough minds engaging the hard facts of an emotional subject. But precisely because they *were* two tough minds, and because they loved each other, Claire and Quinn, Quinn and Claire, they would work through the problem together. And he would break off with Sarah. And they would go back to being who they were. That was how she had seen it.

She had not planned on Quinn's having the courage to leave her. She had underestimated him or else he had changed. It struck her for the first time that perhaps his silly book was right; perhaps all that sexual nonsense had made him another man.

She got out of the car and walked down the street to Number 65. Slowly, almost in a trance, she opened the door and began to ascend the stairs. She rested on the second landing; not a sound from Birdie and Jim. She continued up the stairs until she stood outside her own door. She could hear music inside. Music! After what they had been through, he was playing music. She took out her key and looked at it.

231

She would beg him to come back. She would let him have Sarah. She would let him have anyone he wanted, so long as he didn't leave her, so long as . . .

She turned and saw Leopold crouched on the stairs. His fat face and his piggy eyes startled her only a little, but enough to bring her to her senses. Saved by the piglet. Saved by the troll.

She put her fingers to her lips, a secret, and Leopold did the same. They remained looking at each other for a long minute.

She'd given Quinn her religion and her baby and, almost incidentally, she'd given him her soul to use in his fucking fiction. But she'd be damned before she'd give him Sarah Slade. She'd kill the woman first.

She blew Leopold a little kiss, gave him a smile and a wave, and went quickly down the stairs, herself again, possessed.

Leopold watched her go, and he blew kisses after her in a transport of joy and love.

By the time Claire reached Angelo's, light rain had begun to fall. Angelo must have just seen somebody off because he was still wearing a little shorty robe with—she could tell—nothing on underneath, and so he had to go get dressed before they could talk.

He seemed surprised and happy to see her, but she was not interested in any of that; she just wanted to get the gun and get out.

She was in control again, however, and she knew that her power lay in waiting for the right moment. You could never let yourself be distracted by irrelevant emotions; the thing was to know what you wanted and to get it. So she was prepared to wait.

Angelo returned to the living room, dressed, and with a towel for her to dry her hair. She fluffed the towel around her head to satisfy him and then handed it back. She tried not to look grim. He disappeared again and came back with drinks.

"Here's to you," he said, and they clinked glasses. "Well, this is nice," he said. "This is a surprise. You're looking very good, Claire. Like an enterprising woman." He laughed too loud.

She frowned at him, and smiled.

"Are you all right?" he said. "I've thought of you so often. I've felt so bad. Are you all right?"

"Of course I'm all right," she said. "Why shouldn't I be all right?"

"Well, the baby," he said, embarrassed.

She sipped from her drink and paused. She must not allow herself to be distracted by the irrelevant, by the baby, but suddenly she was very angry. She took a long swallow and—deliberately, to mask her anger—she choked a little. "Cold," she said, adding like an afterthought, "I did it for Quinn. I want him back."

"Do you? Do you really want him back?"

"You wouldn't understand," she said. "It's about men and women."

He bit his lip as if he were trying not to say it, but then he said it: "Gays don't understand men and women? Love is different for them?"

"I didn't mean gays. I meant you."

"Ka-chung," Angelo said, and sat back in his chair.

"I'm sorry. I *am* sorry."

"I'm getting a new line on Quinn. You really know how to bust them, don't you. Jesus."

"I'm sorry."

"And what is that supposed to mean, exactly? 'I didn't mean gays; I meant you.'"

"Well, look at you, the way you live." It was his own fault; he shouldn't have mentioned the baby; he'd asked for it. She rushed ahead: "I mean, you talk about Kierkegaard and his three categories of men, and freedom of choice, and all that nineteen-sixties rubbish, as if you were caught in some kind of time warp, and yet you live as if you had only one moving part."

"My penis?"

"Yes, as a matter of fact."

"My cock?"

"Your cock." She had never said the word in her life before today and now she had said it twice in the last hour. But really, it was too much; men thought that grotesque thing was so special, when actually it was just a lightning rod to attract disaster. Look where it had gotten Quinn. "Call it what you want," she said. "Words don't affect me in the least."

They were silent then and sipped at their drinks, defensively.

"What do you mean, sixties rubbish?" he said finally.

Oh, *why* couldn't she just get up, take the gun, and go? Must everything be paid for with patience and reason and good sense?

"In the sixties, maybe even the fifties," she began, as if she were lecturing, "even intelligent people commonly said things like 'the only true philosophic question is whether or not to commit suicide,' And they meant it. But that question doesn't make any sense today. Nor does any of that Kierkegaard stuff: choice and struggle and how you live your life. We've gotten beyond all that."

"To where?"

"Oh, God. Let me try again." She took a deep breath. What she wanted was the gun; she would put up with anything to get it. She glared at him, and then leaned forward, summoning his concentration with her own fierce intensity. She began again, not explaining now, but pronouncing: "Existentialism," she said, "if it's about anything, is about disorientation. About not belonging. That is its essence. That is its reason for existence. Am I right? Am I not right?"

"I guess."

"And do we need any proof of *that*? That we don't belong? Or that we might just as well kill ourselves?" She paused for a single long beat. "Kill yourself. Go ahead. No one cares. That is not philosophy. That is fact." She sat back, and said softly, the prophet who has prophesied and will not be heard: "The problem today is not whether to live or die; the problem today is . . . getting through it. Dealing with it. Coping."

"Coping? That's a philosophical problem? Coping?"

"Getting what you want."

"No."

"Knowing what you want and getting it."

"But that leaves out everything that matters," Angelo said. "It leaves out human suffering, human values, human meaning. It leaves out the primacy of man's relation to . . ."

"Wait a sec," Claire said, tired now, almost disinterested. "Is this Kierkegaard coming up again?"

"Well, as a matter of fact . . ."

"Can you hold the thought? And may I . . ." She pointed in the direction of the bathroom.

"Sorry," he said, "of course," and turned on the stereo to give her privacy. "And you haven't told me what brings you here. Or about how your work is going." He smiled as he had when she first came in. "I'm so pleased," he said.

"It's my pleasure." She could see he was looking forward to another hour of jabber about Kierkegaard. "Could you turn the music up, just a bit?"

She slung her bag over her shoulder and went down the hall, not to the bathroom, but to the bedroom. She knew what she wanted and how to get it.

She flipped on the light and walked straight to the night-stand. In the top drawer there was only a copy of *Playgirl* and a *TV Guide*. In the next drawer a box of tissues. Junk in the bottom drawer, the usual stuff: nail clippers, shoe polish, pencils. She went back to the tissues and turned them out of the box; underneath was the gun and a bottle of pills, 30 Valium, for S. Slade.

Men were so wonderfully imaginative. They hid things in three places: their nightstand, their underwear drawer, or at the back of the closet in a boot. Pitiful.

She shook out a few Valium and dropped them in her change purse. The gun she pushed deep into her bag. She stuffed the bottle of pills beneath the tissues, and put the tissues back into the drawer, and she was done.

Suddenly the scent from the bed struck her; a man scent, filthy, semen and sweat, mixed. Angelo's short green robe lay at the foot of the bed. She touched it with her fingertips and then raised her hand to her face. The stench. She was going to be sick. She closed her eyes and took a deep slow breath; she felt lye in her throat and for a second she gagged. But by a final effort of will, she got hold of herself and left the room.

From the hall she could see Angelo pacing in the living room, concentrating on giving her privacy. She stepped into the bathroom and flushed the toilet. That should keep him waiting just long enough.

She walked through the kitchen and up the back stairs to the first floor. There was a light in the living room. Sarah sat there on the watered silk sofa, her elbows on her knees, her face in her hands.

Sarah's hands caught the light and Claire noticed what extraordinary hands they were: long, attentuated, with a look of power that you find in precision instruments. Scalpels. Calibrators. Quinn had described them very well indeed. Now he'd have to learn to forget them.

Claire made no effort to conceal herself. She moved slowly through the room, pausing less than a foot from Sarah, thinking—I could do it now if I had the bullets—and then she opened the front door and left.

She imagined Sarah lifting her head at the sound of the closing door, going to the window to find out if she had really seen Claire or if the game was over and she was now definitely mad.

She imagined Angelo hearing the door above, listening to her heels on the stairs, and then looking back and forth between the bathroom and the front door. And then running to the stairwell as she drove away. Running back to check for the gun. Frenzied? Desperate? Or just annoyed?

But it didn't matter, of course. They were nothing to her. They were figures in the landscape merely. Insufficient, inadequate, unintelligent people. Scarcely alive.

"Leave the dead to bury the dead." What was that from? *"Mortui mortibus sepultiendi sunt."* Rather nice. Rather elegant.

Claire began the long drive north with a light heart and a positive mind. The trip had been good. She would get what she wanted.

He would be hers by Saturday.

He would be hers forever.

He would never belong to Sarah Slade.

In the middle of her life Claire had wandered in a dark wood and, except for the bad parts, she was enjoying it quite a lot. She was enjoying the sense of being somebody special.

She told herself this, aloud, as she stood in the grove of tall firs behind Aunt Lily's house. It was well after midnight and Claire was exhausted from her long drive, but she had come out among the owls and the fieldmice and the creepy night things in order to commune with the goddess.

"I am enjoying it quite a lot," Claire said. *"Multum mihi placet."*

The rain had stopped and the white moon glowed in the dark sky. Claire fixed the moon with a knowing eye, and raised her arms in worship. *"O Athena beatissima,"* and she was off, improvising a prayer of thanksgiving to the goddess of wisdom who had brought her to this dark wood, on a dark night, and filled her once again with awareness of the thrilling power of her own mind.

She was a prodigy of strength and energy and resourcefulness; she had learned that much and more from this difficult summer. There was nothing she could not cope with. There was nothing she could not do. She was a woman of the twentieth century, a neo-pagan, in full possession of her marvelous powers. A woman of mind and will. *Mens et voluntas. Clara. Clarissima Quinn.*

24

"I'll tell you then," Sarah said, "I'll tell you everything," and she leaned forward on the bed. Her gray eyes glittered with the drink and the Valium, and she spoke in a voice that was a whisper.

"His name was Raoul and he was from Argentina."

Quinn sat on the blanket chest at the foot of the bed and listened, though he knew the facts—he thought—for Claire had been right, and besides he had done research.

"He was a graduate student at MIT, an engineer in something I couldn't understand. He liked it that I couldn't understand. He liked to teach me. He taught me everything."

Sarah's voice went on and on, softly, soothing, as if she were reciting to a child a Grimm fairy tale of love and murder that nonetheless would turn out all right. The story got worse as she went on.

"He liked to hear me say those words. They excited him. They made him hard. I couldn't do it. I couldn't say them. For the longest time I couldn't say them, and then he left me, and came back, and still I couldn't say them. And then he left me and he didn't come back. I wrote him letters and I telephoned and I stood outside his apartment building one whole night and in the morning when he came out, I said to him all the things he wanted me to say. I said give it to me, I want it, and he said no, he said not yet. He said what do you want, you have to say it, and I said, cock, I want your cock, and he said where, and I said in my cunt, and he laughed and said, in time, in time, but first you want it in your hand, and then in your mouth and down your throat, and then you want it in your cunt, when I am ready for your cunt and not until. I said yes, whatever you say. And he said buy a lipstick and I'll teach you things you've never known before. I'll teach you who you are, you whore, you fucking whore, you'll love it. Here, he said, and he pulled his cock out as we stood there on the steps, and he said kneel down, and I knelt down and took it in my mouth with people going by, and I did it, and I didn't care, and then he pulled it out and walked away and said now you know who you are and they all know who you are. And I was kneeling there."

Quinn looked at her and she looked somewhere beyond him.

"And I was kneeling there," she said in her soft voice.

Quinn was silent. Then he said, anguished, "Why?"

Sarah's eyelids flickered but she gave no other sign that she heard him.

"Why did you do it? Why did you let him?"

"He wanted me."

Quinn lowered his eyes. He could not look at her.

"He ate the blood. He liked the smell of it. He liked to put his mouth there, and take the blood in his mouth and chew and let it drip and drip and drip until his sex, his cock, he'd make me say his cock, was red with blood and then he'd say now suck it, suck it hard, it's baby blood, it's yours, and I'm sticking it back inside you, you cocksucking whore, and I did it, and I said I liked it, and I said I wanted more and more and more, and I did, I think I did, because I couldn't stop, I couldn't not, and that was who I had become . . . until he left me and he left me and he left me, and then I killed him."

"Yes."

"But that was later. That was after I became the other Sarah." For the first time, she looked at him.

"The other Sarah?"

"This Sarah. The murderer."

"You killed him."

"Sarah did. He was leaving her, he said, but he always said that, and so she did more things to him, and said those words, but he said, no, he was going back to Argentina, he was really leaving her, he was going to get married, he said, to a nice girl, he said, not to some whore. I said no, he had to marry me and I would do the things he wanted, all of them, and all the time, and he said, no, that a whore was just a piece of meat and that a man could cut a whore or kill a whore or fuck a whore but no real man could marry a whore and bring her in his mother's house. And I said no. And he said but you see, it's done, *finita la commedia,* and I said please, just once more, just one more time, tonight, just once, and he said no, and I said it's my period, and he said blood, and I said come to me one last time, and he thought awhile but he said no."

"But he did come."

"But he did come and then she killed him. I bought champagne. He drank it all, and after all the sex he fell asleep, with my blood still on his lips, and then I took the gun from the nightstand where I had it ready and I lay beside him in the bed, with the gun resting on the pillow, pointed at his temple. And for most of the night, he slept. But when he woke, I was still awake, and waiting. And I waited till he saw the gun, and saw that it was me, and then I fired. I lay beside him for a long, long while. My blood had crusted on his lips and teeth, his blood was soaking through the pillow. I took the blood from between my legs and closed his eyes with it, I sealed them shut. The smell of it."

She looked beyond him once again.

"I got a knife and cut it off. I cut it off. I held it with one hand, and took the knife and I cut it off. I ran out in the street with it, the knife, the bloody stump of cock still running blood. I ran into the street, into the rain, I ran from him, and the rain came down and I was running and the blood was running in the rain, and I said let it come down, let it rain blood, let it all come down."

She looked at him for the second time.

"Sarah did that," she said in her soft voice, "it was Sarah who did that."

She looked at him and he did not turn away. So she told him the rest: the bloody thing in the stolen handbag; the flight to Argentina; the jail, the hospital, the years, and the years.

For a very long time they sat in silence.

Quinn knew it was not too late to save himself, but he sat there, unable to go, unwilling to stay.

"Go," she said, very softly.

He only looked at her.

She shook her head no. She raised her hand before her face and with a tiny gesture waved him away.

But still he stayed.

She eased herself from the bed then, and took him by the hand, but not before he saw the smear of blood on the sheet, the fresh dark stain on her nightgown. She led him from the bedroom across to her studio and threw on the lights. There was his picture, everywhere: barren earth against an empty sky.

She dropped his hand and walked to the easel. She looked at him. "Go," she said. Silence. She wavered slightly as if she might fall, but then she stood straight, lifted her gown, and plunged her hand between her legs. She touched it to her face, a crimson blotch across her lips, and then with the flat of her hand and her long fingers, she dragged the mess across the canvas. She leered at him.

"Now go," she said.

25

It was midnight, Friday, and Claire was once again in her little red Ford, pelting down the highway to see Quinn. She felt she had spent her entire life in this car, on this highway, in pursuit of her slippery husband, but now he was hers for good. Quinn and Claire, Claire and Quinn, that's how it would be again. Like old times. She would forgive him and take him back. He wouldn't be expecting her until Saturday, though of course technically it was Saturday, though just barely; and who knows, perhaps a little surprise was just what he needed.

She had a bag of Oreos by her side—her last treat, this was it, the diet would begin tomorrow—and in her handbag on the floor was the Walther, loaded, and the three Valium she had taken from Angelo's nightstand. Insurance, merely. Talismans.

Everything was in order. Everything was ready. She drove straight ahead, her face set, her mind clear. She was at once love's hostage and deliverer.

"*Festinat supremum, Clarissima,*" she said. "This is the final hour."

It was midnight and Angelo pitched *Fear and Trembling* into a Hefty Bag and tossed *The Sickness unto Death* in after it. They were going out with tomorrow's trash, every last Existentialist, as a first gesture toward coming to terms with his life. What those terms might be, Angelo had no idea, but he was certain from his talk with Claire last night that, whatever they were, they weren't that sixties rubbish, or the fifties either.

Claire had appeared like an avenging angel—no, like a prophet come to announce doom—and she had disappeared as soon as she had executed her commission. As he interpreted her message, it was this: Angelo, you're all fucked up . . . literally and metaphysically.

Claire had gone to the bathroom and then up the back stairs and then out the front door. And away, forever, probably. But Angelo had heard her message and he knew she was right. You had to know what you wanted in this life and then you had to get it. Now, if only he knew what he wanted.

He flipped through a pile of things by Sartre and then, reluctant but determined, he tossed them into the Hefty Bag with Kierkegaard and Husserl and Bucky Fuller.

When Claire left last night, refusing to hear another word about Kierkegaard—and who could blame her—he had dashed to the stairs just in time to see her pull away in her little red car. He'd felt abandoned, and then furious, and then he felt an overwhelming desire to strike her, to beat her unconscious. He was astonished by that because he had never wanted to kill anyone before, not even during his beating by "Jim." But he had truly wanted to kill her. He had wanted to take her out of existence. Because of what she had said.

That's when it struck him that Claire was—for him, at least—a kind of prophet, and that her message to him was true. The true prophet was always a sign of contradiction. "Forget that sixties rubbish," she had said. "Know what you want, and get it."

He had gone out at once, of course, and got laid, conscious that that wasn't what he wanted, that was just what he did. Whatever it was that he wanted, it had nothing to do with sex. It occurred to him that perhaps sex was a metaphor for what he wanted, but that struck him as too literary, too philosophical again, and he knew Claire wouldn't like it either.

In the morning, after a lot of casual sex and a little sleep, he had gone to the hospital with Maria and the three kids to help bring Porter home. Sarah was still asleep upstairs with the idiot, he presumed, since there wasn't a sound from there, and as close as Sarah was to Porter, it was never a good idea to mix Sarah and Maria. So he went alone.

Porter had lost weight; he looked pale, exhausted, not at all the way he'd looked in the hospital right after the heart attack. But he was different in some other, more profound way, too. He seemed resigned, as if his life were over and his fate had been pronounced. As if all hope had disappeared from his future. Whatever happened would happen, and it could neither be changed or postponed or altered; it could only be mourned. That's how he seemed, anyway, and that made him unapproachable. He might as well have said to Angelo, "It's done. It's finished. Go away." But Angelo had stayed on, hoping for a minute alone with him to set things right, to say—because for the first time he could say it honestly—I love you, Porter, but people kept dropping by and the home nurse kept interrupting and finally it was time for Porter to sleep, and the minute alone had never come, and so he had not yet told Porter he loved him. But he would, soon.

The day had been—at very best—gloomy, and the evening had been gloomy, and when Angelo got back to Louisburg Square, he was disappointed to see that it was gloomy there too. All the lights were out upstairs—the lovebugs were at it again; well, why not—and so he was left to his own resources, which now no longer included that sixties rubbish. Nor Porter. Nor Sarah. Nor Claire. Nor that idiot Quinn. And he loved them all, in his way, or at least he wanted to.

And so at midnight, unable to sleep and not up to any more

sex at the moment, he made a start on the new life by pitching out the Existentialists. He hated to part with the Camus books; they had nice print and good margins.

He flipped open *The Plague* to where the binding had broken, at the scene where Tarrou explains that the only thing that interests him is becoming a saint. "But you don't believe in God," Rieux says. And Tarrou says something about being a saint without God—that's the real problem of the twentieth century. What rot. Claire was right.

Angelo pitched *The Plague* in with the other rubbish and twisted the plastic tie around the top. He lugged the Hefty Bag out to the curb for pickup.

As Angelo turned to go back down the stairs, a red car drove by on the far side of the square. He stopped to take a look, and the car speeded up and then was gone, but for just a second he was sure it was Claire's. Then he realized that was just wishful thinking, and foolish. Like Existentialism.

It was going to rain again. He stood at the stairwell and took a deep breath of the heavy air.

What, *what* did he want? More sex? He could check out the traffic at the river, he supposed, and see what was up. Or hit a bar. Or the baths.

Suddenly he was exhausted. All those bodies, all those cocks, all those spent emotions.

What he wanted, really, was a little peace, and perhaps a job, and somebody to care for. Love was too much to ask for; forget about love.

He wanted to want something. He wanted.

Angelo went inside and locked the door and lay down on his bed, sleepless, despairing. And then lightly, lightly, the rain began to fall.

• • •

It was midnight and, though Quinn had drunk a very great deal, his mind remained clear enough for him to make an important decision. He suspected—rightly—that it might be the most important decision of his life, and so he wrote it down. "I want to help," he wrote, saying the words aloud to make them more real. He closed his notebook, put it away safely with the box of manuscripts by the door, and then went out for a walk in the rain to think about Sarah and Claire and again about Sarah.

It had been a day of surprises, to say the least. At the library he had discovered Claire was right; there had been a scandal; Sarah had committed murder. And so he had gone to Sarah— he owed it to her, he owed it to himself—to break it off forever and go back to Claire. But Sarah had known since yesterday that he would end their affair and in those few hours she had retreated into herself.

He was not prepared for the Sarah he encountered: lost, and very likely mad. Nor was he prepared for the love—or was it pity, was it fear?—that took him by the throat and would not let him leave her. Nor for the slowly growing conviction that for once he did not want out, he did not want it over. He must be mad himself.

"I must be mad," Quinn said aloud, walking in the light rain, through the Gardens, through the Common, up Beacon Hill, across on Joy Street and down to Louisburg Square. "I must be mad," he said, standing on the far side of the Square, staring at the black windows, promising "I will help," promising "I will be there tomorrow."

Then home again for this one last night to Marlborough Street, where Leopold crouched on the stairs, asleep, and where Quinn found, waiting for him at the door, the smiling, patient, long-suffering Claire.

"You've been out in the rain," Claire said. "You're wet."

She kissed him shyly. "And you've been drinking quite a lot."

"Oh, Claire," he said. "I'm so *so* sorry."

"But you're home," she said, "and so am I, and from now on it's Quinn and Claire and Claire and Quinn, I promise."

"No," he said.

They were still standing at the door, and they stood there for quite some time, in silence, before Claire fully understood him. And then she said come in, and he went in, and she shut the door for good.

It was nearly three hours before Leopold awoke—still squatting on the stairs—and heard the single shot reverberate from room to room and echo in the stairwell. He covered his ears and squinted his tiny eyes and hunkered farther down to wait for what would happen next.

It had taken Claire an hour to talk Quinn into sense. To have a Scotch, to get some sleep, to think about it in the morning. The Valium she put in his drink took effect almost at once. He slept.

But then she couldn't find the notebook... to see what had happened, to see where she stood. It was not on his desk—all his writing stuff was gone—and it was not in his nightstand, nor with his underwear, nor in a boot in the back of the closet. It was only when she'd given up, and poured herself some gin, and paced around the rooms that she saw the box of manuscripts, all set for the big move to Beacon Hill. Sly Quinn. Sly old sleazy Quinn, his notebook at the ready.

Claire stood by the door, the notebook in her hand, and read—transfixed—what Quinn had written. He had got it down in Sarah's words, flat, without elaboration, and he had not tampered with the names. It was there just as Sarah had told it: the hideous sex, the murder, the madness, and Raoul's bloody cock. She'd wrapped it in tissue in a stolen handbag, and she'd flown to Argentina. A gift for his parents.

Claire read the scribbled pages once again. It was beyond belief, it was beyond the laws of possibility, except in mythology, of course. The Greeks.

She laughed aloud at that fool, that Quinn, who had gone so far past all reason that he could think of tying his pitiful talent to that diseased mind, sodden with sex, obsessed with it. What did *he* know about sex? They weren't sexual people, Claire and Quinn, Quinn and Claire, they were people of the intellect, the only aristocracy that counted. And here he was slavering over a woman whose intellect was so confused that she could do those things and think she wanted them. A bloody cock? *Any* cock? She was beyond pity, Sarah Slade. And so was Quinn. With his torn lip and his feeble soul. Bunny Quinn indeed.

She could taste contempt in her mouth, like a rusty knife. But she would be merciful—as the gods were merciful—and just: she would leave them each to the other.

She poured a farewell drink. To *Clara. Clarissima.* She took a sip and, standing at the sink, she read again Quinn's story of the murder. "The bloody cock," she said aloud, savoring the sound of the words.

She took his notebook to the living room and curled up with it in a corner of the couch. She adjusted the lamp. She flipped the pages backward to the days before the murder. She would read it all. What she read proved fatal.

"Change S to C, physically
—a tendency to fat
—as tension grows, C grows fatter and fatter
—little rolls of flesh at her waist, above her panty-line, beneath her bra"

• • •

249

The writing continued as Quinn, in his rapid scrawl, meticulously noted her big teeth, the grossness of her body, her fear of nudity. He speculated: clothing as compensation? as disguise? an index to frigidity? He listed her little tics of speech and added a compendium of her favorite Latin phrases.

He had stripped her clean and there was no further hurt he could inflict, she thought, until she turned the page and read: "Am I taking too much from her? Not really. Not when you think of the terrific sex life I'm giving her."

At this, she closed her mind and she closed her heart, though she read on doggedly until she reached the final entry with its pitiful, self-indulgent "I want to help." Then she closed the notebook and did what she had to do.

She took the gun, and lay down beside Quinn until he woke up and saw that it was she and that she had a gun and then, just as he was raising a finger to his lip, self-conscious, she pulled the trigger.

She worked with a cold mind and a steady hand, eager to finish up the messy business quickly. She got a knife. She placed a plastic bag beneath his crotch to catch the blood. She cut and hacked and twisted, and then she dropped the bloody cock inside. Barnes and Noble, Books, the bag said. A nice touch for Quinn. It was all done in no time.

She put the bag in the bathroom sink while she tidied up in the kitchen. She washed her glass, dried it, put it away. She washed the knife, with special attention to the handle, and then let it lie in the sink until the bloody swirl of water ran clear. She wiped down the counter with a sponge, wrung it out, put it away.

She went to the living room then and curled up on the couch, the vigilant scholar with her text, and scrutinized the novel manuscript itself. It might be helpful as corroborating evidence—to prove it was Sarah up to her old tricks. Reading

it, she marveled at the priorities of the writer, because however shaken Quinn was by what he'd heard, however eager he
was to help—oh, helpful, treacherous, lecherous Quinn—he
had found time to transcribe Sarah's story from the notebook
to the novel intact. Never let material go to waste. It was all
there, only slightly altered for economy. And—what luck for
the police—Sarah was still Sarah; he had not bothered changing her to Claire. Nor would he ever.

She would leave the novel here. It could not incriminate; it
could only help. She, after all, was its one real victim.

She put the guilty notebook in her handbag and the gun in
beside it. She got Quinn's key to Sarah's place. She was ready
to leave.

But on the landing outside the door, Claire remembered the
Barnes and Noble bag lying in the bathroom sink. She left the
door standing open, and went back to get it.

Leopold crouched on the stairs, a finger at his lips, a secret.
He stood up, he peered over the top of the bannister, he
waved at her with his free hand, but he never took his finger
from his lips.

Claire was otherwise engaged. She locked the door and
pocketed the key and, holding the Barnes and Noble bag
away from her dress, she went quietly down the stairs and out
into the rain on Marlborough Street.

From above, Leopold blew her kisses.

The rain was much heavier now and of course there were no
parking places, so Claire just pulled up on the curb in front of
Number 17. This wouldn't, after all, take long.

It was Claire's intention to shoot Sarah; indeed, she had
wanted to shoot Sarah from the first time she saw her. She
intended, once she'd done it, to put the gun in Sarah's hand

and the bloody Barnes and Noble bag at her feet, making her in fact what she was in the eyes of the gods: a murderer and a suicide. The plan was simple but refined.

As she parked the car in Louisburg Square, however, Claire sensed for the first time a problem of logistics. What if Angelo were at home, as he usually was, and heard the gunshot, as he certainly would. And bolted up the stairs in time to see her . . . on the instant, she abandoned that plan.

But such was the speed of her marvelous mind that, before she was even out of the car, she had formulated a new plan— foolproof, a marvel, with the grace and economy of a play by Euripides. *Festinat supremum*.

The rain scarcely touched her as she stepped from her car, crossed the cobblestones, descended the stairs. A soft tap. Wait. A louder tap. A light in the living room. A pause. And then the open door, and Angelo, his eyes heavy but his smile wide, and gratitude large upon his face.

"You've come back," he said. "In the middle of the night."

"Oh, yes," she said.

"Like a dream," he said. "Like an apparition."

He was wearing that disgusting robe and it was open in front. She could see his hairy chest and she could see below. She held the plastic book bag out from her side.

"I'm an answer to your prayers," she said.

"You are," he said.

Claire stepped inside, and Angelo shut the door, and went off to his bedroom to put on some clothes. Claire paused for only a second and then she followed him, stopping at his door as he threw off his robe—admiring, in her fair-minded way, the line of his back and the thrust of his hips—and then she continued on down the hall. She crossed the kitchen. She ascended the stairs.

She was going up to Sarah, and he would come, too; that

was essential to her new plan. Claire had decided to spare Sarah after all, to punish her through Angelo, letting her use her feeble intellect to concoct her own version of hell.

Claire stood in the dark in Sarah's kitchen and listened to the silence. Nothing from below, nothing above. Where was he? Why wasn't he following? But he would. He would. She needed only patience, because the gods were with her.

She became aware of a whirring sound, a steady hum, some electrical thing. She knew. She knew. She moved to the stereo and then to the front door. From the door she moved to the stairs. She heard a sound. She paused, listening. And the lights went on.

Claire stopped where she was, one foot on the stair. Angelo stood in the kitchen doorway. No one moved.

Claire turned to face him and, in a single glance, she saw how perfectly things had worked out. Because between them —on the couch before the stereo—Sarah lay with her head thrown back. Asleep. Or unconscious.

Slowly, Claire raised the gun. She pointed it at Sarah and then at Angelo and then at Sarah.

"No, Claire," he said.

"Choose," Claire said, and pointed once again at him, then at Sarah.

He was coming toward her. "No," he was saying.

"Choose," she said.

But he was not choosing, he was not even thinking. He was only trying to get between Claire and Sarah.

"Well, you've chosen," she said, and the gun went off, and "No," Angelo said again, slumping to the floor as a great red spray burst across his chest. He made some living sounds, but she could see that he was done for.

And so it was almost finished. Only the tiring, tiresome things remained. Claire took a deep breath and began.

Sarah was still alive, though barely, with the quantity of Valium she had consumed. Claire yanked the body to a sitting position, but Sarah was so limp, so nearly dead, that Claire had all she could do to crush Sarah's fingers around the handle of the gun. She pulled and pressed, but the hand would not take the shape of the handle. The prints would be a mess; it was the best she could do. Claire gave the fingers a final squeeze and shook the gun loose from Sarah's hand.

She put the plastic bag on the floor beside the sofa. The stump of flesh looked pitifully small, but by plunging her own hand into the bag along with Sarah's, Claire was able to curl Sarah's fingers around the thing. She placed the hand, and the object, on Sarah's lap. "The bloody cock," she said. She let her own hand drip into the bag.

Claire stepped back to scrutinize the scene, as a critic might, as the police surely would. Angelo lay near Sarah's feet, his chest opened, the blood flowing freely. Sarah sprawled, Quinn's cock in her hand, the gun beside her on the floor. They'd have to search for the knife. They'd have to search for the cockless body. But something was missing. Something was not here.

She needed the handbag to tie it all together. She went upstairs to the top floor and plucked it from the hamper and came back down and dropped it at Sarah's feet. It was chocolate brown, Godiva bittersweet.

She should finish the job, she realized that; she should pull down Angelo's pants and cut it off. That filthy thing. That fucking cock. Filthy. Fucking. Cock. But she was exhausted suddenly and the words that had once driven her to action failed completely to move her now. She couldn't go on. She wouldn't go on.

She walked to the stereo and leaned against the wall, watching as the record went round and round. It made a pleasant hum, a summer sound. She could stand here watching this forever. Sometime later she came to herself and saw the black sky beginning to go gray outside the windows. It was nearly dawn.

She switched off the stereo and stared at the record for a moment. The *Winterreise*. A lovely piece.

And then, carefully, she studied her hand, crusted with Quinn's blood. A purple flake had fallen on the record. She clenched her fist and the flakes fell thick. If she clenched her fist, unclenched her fist, and kept on doing it, perhaps she could turn the whole record purple, cover it up, cover the stereo up, cover the room and the bodies up . . .

"This way lies madness," she said aloud, and stood with her eyes closed as she ritually, consciously, called to mind—to her marvelous, lucid, logical mind—just who she was, and what she wanted, and how at last she was going to get it.

At once she was all action. She had things to do. She had miles to go.

She stepped outside in the morning air. The rain had stopped and the Square was empty.

She turned to look in through the open door. This is what they would see. This is what they would find. Bodies. Blood. A sacrifice. But who would it be? Porter? The police?

To open this door. To step inside. To see up close, and recognize, the sorry face of pity and fear.

Claire was driving north and Angelo was dying, slowly, bleeding to death, drop by drop. He was unconscious for a while, and then partly conscious, and then not conscious at all but very much aware.

He was supposed to make a choice, but it was too late, and he wanted something very badly but he didn't know what it was. He was making a great struggle against dying, or perhaps it was against living, he wasn't sure. But he was supposed to be doing something else, he was supposed to be choosing one thing or another. And then everything began to pale a little, and the pain grew slower and less urgent, and he began to sink into it, this painful embrace, and to cease to struggle, and then it came to him that of course he was waiting for a lover, some new and superior kind of lover, and if he could just have this little sleep, this little moment to rest in these strong arms, he would be ready. Then, surprised, he realized this *was* the lover, no other was coming. The lover was already here.

He ceased to struggle. And it was very easy for him at the end.

Porter went into shock, but for just a few minutes. It took him only that long to accept what he could not comprehend: that everything that mattered was being stripped away. He summoned the police.

Because it was he who found the bodies and the thing in Sarah's hand. And it was he who told them about Sarah's affair with Quinn. And later about Quinn and Angelo. And still later about the stolen handbags. And it was he who explained the menstrual blood smeared on the painting upstairs, though by then they did not believe him; there were limits after all.

Sarah could explain nothing, nor would her lawyers let her try. She was guilty, she confessed it over and over and over. And she was mad, of course.

"Claire is in the bath," Aunt Lily said into the telephone, and for once she was right. But Claire had been expecting the call and she came running now, wrapped in a towel and trailing perfume.

"Quinn?" she said, "Is that you, sweetheart?" She did it very well.

It was the police, in Boston, with the usual questions: "Are you related to... Are you the wife of..." They were polite, concerned, and they offered no information.

"Something's wrong," Claire said. "Is Quinn all right? Tell me that. Please tell me that," her voice shaking only just enough. She did it very well indeed.

And so she was driving south to Boston in her little red Ford, humming "Courage" from the *Winterreise,* composing her soul.

The day was bright and her mind was clear and she was ready for them all.

In Boston, on Marlborough Street, Quinn's mutilated body had just been removed from the apartment. Police had scoured the place for evidence, for fingerprints. They hauled away Quinn's manuscripts to see what clues they might contain.

The interviews would take place later; Birdie and Jim; the old lady upstairs. The police were being very thorough. They did not want another Slade scandal fucking up their image.

They were finished with the apartment for the time being. The last policeman out the door tacked up the plastic strip that said "Police Barrier—No Admittance." He had to tack both sides himself; his partner, a woman, just stood behind him, doing nothing. She was always like that, useless.

"Let's go," he said at last, "let's haul it."

But as they turned to go, they saw the little boy, his face scrunched up against the railing. He was fat, with tiny eyes, and he was very nearly bald. They stopped and looked.

"Jesus," the policeman said. "That's enough to make you give up drink." He started down the stairs.

But his partner, the policewoman, paused and made big eyes. She sank to one knee to get a better look.

"I saw you," the little boy said.

"Hi ya," she said, "how are you today?"

"I saw you."

"Of course you did," she said. "I bet you see everything, don't you. Sure you do." The policewoman tended to fat and had three ugly children of her own, so she knew just how to deal with this one. She put her face against the railing opposite his and stared at him for a minute. Then she stuck her tongue out, quickly, and pulled it back in. She gave him a little smile. He didn't smile back, but that didn't stop her. "You hang out around here a lot?" she said. "Hmmm? You cute fat thing? You see what's going on?"

He stared for a moment and then he nodded, violently.

"Tell me what you saw right here," she said, and pointed to the door. "Anybody coming? Anybody going?"

He was shy suddenly and put his hands up to his fat cheeks, and squinched his tiny eyes.

She did the same back at him, until finally he laughed.

"Okay, now," she said, "tell me. Tell me what you saw."